DISCARDED

The Moment
of Tenderness

DISCARDED

ALSO BY MADELEINE L'ENGLE

DISCARDED

The Moment of Tenderness

DISCARDED

MADELEINE L'ENGLE

With an Introduction by
Charlotte Jones Voiklis

GRAND CENTRAL
PUBLISHING

NEW YORK   BOSTON

The events and characters in this book are fictitious. Certain real locations and public figures are mentioned, but all other characters and events described in the book are totally imaginary.

Copyright © 2020 by Crosswicks, Ltd.

Cover design by Tree Abraham. Cover illustration by Aitch. Cover copyright © 2020 by Hachette Book Group, Inc.

Hachette Book Group supports the right to free expression and the value of copyright. The purpose of copyright is to encourage writers and artists to produce the creative works that enrich our culture.

The scanning, uploading, and distribution of this book without permission is a theft of the author's intellectual property. If you would like permission to use material from the book (other than for review purposes), please contact permissions@hbgusa.com. Thank you for your support of the author's rights.

Grand Central Publishing
Hachette Book Group
1290 Avenue of the Americas, New York, NY 10104
grandcentralpublishing.com
twitter.com/grandcentralpub

First Edition: April 2020

Grand Central Publishing is a division of Hachette Book Group, Inc. The Grand Central Publishing name and logo is a trademark of Hachette Book Group, Inc.

"Madame, Or…" initially published in *The Dude* magazine, September 1957. New edition copyright © 2020 by Crosswicks, Ltd.

"The Fact of the Matter" copyright © 1991 by Crosswicks, Ltd. Originally published as "A Connecticut Eskimo" in *Marion Zimmer Bradley's Fantasy Magazine*, 1991.

The publisher is not responsible for websites (or their content) that are not owned by the publisher.

The Hachette Speakers Bureau provides a wide range of authors for speaking events. To find out more, go to www.hachettespeakersbureau.com or call (866) 376-6591.

Library of Congress Cataloging-in-Publication Data
Names: L'Engle, Madeleine, author.
Title: The moment of tenderness / Madeleine L'Engle.
Description: First edition. | New York : Grand Central Publishing, 2020. |
Identifiers: LCCN 2019041840 | ISBN 9781538717820 (hardcover) |
ISBN 9781538717813 (ebook)
Classification: LCC PS3523.E55 A6 2020 | DDC 813/.54—dc23
LC record available at https://lccn.loc.gov/2019041840

ISBNs: 978-1-5387-1782-0 (hardcover); 978-1-5387-1781-3 (ebook)

Printed in the United States of America

LSC-C

10 9 8 7 6 5 4 3 2 1

Contents

CONTENTS

Introduction

By Charlotte Jones Voiklis

I was about nine years old, curiously but quietly poking about my grandmother Madeleine L'Engle's manuscripts so as not to disturb her writing and risk losing the privilege of keeping her company in her "Ivory Tower" while she worked. The Tower was just a room over the garage in the eighteenth-century New England farmhouse where she and my grandfather had lived and raised three children during the 1950s and where they still spent weekends, holidays, and long stretches of summer. I'm not sure who christened it "the Tower," but the name was used ironically by both her and the rest of the family, an acknowledgment of the privilege of solitude and time. The manuscripts I was poking about in were housed in repurposed ream boxes with words like "Eaton" and "Corrasable Bond" on the sides, and in black three-ring binders whose leather casings were beginning to crack. There were dozens of boxes and binders, including ones with *A Wrinkle in Time*, *The Arm of the Starfish*, and *A Wind in the Door* written on them, but I wasn't interested in the manuscripts of stories that could be read as real books: I was more curious about the scraps and stories and studies in the other boxes. I came across "Gilberte Must Play Bach" in one of those. I'm not sure why I stopped to read this particular one, but I liked the French name in the title, and the imperative. The story was strange to me, and sad, and although the girl in the story was named Claudine, I understood it to be autobiographical. The sadness of the story—and its unresolvedness—shook me and gave me a glimpse at the depth of things we might discover about the people we love.

When my grandmother died in 2007, there were papers and manuscripts distributed among three different houses and an office. It's taken time to organize and inventory those materials, and it's also been a considerable emotional journey for me to read, assess, and come to the decision that these stories should be shared publicly.

When I read "Julio at the Party," an onionskin manuscript held together with a rusty paper clip and folded in half, tossed in a box of artifacts, books, and papers, I thought at first that the story must be by some other writer who had given it to her in a class, or over tea or coffee for comment. However, on a second read I recognized details—the nickname Horrors, the malapropisms of the title character—that convinced me it was indeed hers. I later found that the short story had been taken from an unpublished novel manuscript, written and rewritten several times in the 1950s, called *Rachel Benson* (or, alternatively, *Bedroom with a Skylight*).

More exploration over time into the loose-leaf binders and manuscript boxes revealed more than forty short stories, most written in the 1940s and 1950s, when she was first an aspiring playwright, then a promising novelist, and then a despairing writer who struggled to find a publisher. All but one were written before *A Wrinkle in Time*, the 1962 classic that made her career, and I date that one story post-*Wrinkle* because of the unique typeface of the typewriter she used—oversized, square, and sans serif. It was an early electric typewriter and I remember the satisfaction and mastery I felt when my fingers were strong enough to prevail over the resistance the keys provided. That story, called "That Which Is Left," shocked and shook me, too, because of the narrator's selfishness.

The earliest stories were written for college creative writing classes. The manuscript for "Gilberte Must Play Bach" has teacher's comments and a grade (A–). Some have more than one version, reworked over time, and there is one bound manuscript of collected short stories called *Stories from Greenwich Village*, which was compiled in the early 1940s when she was working as an understudy and bit player. She lived with a rotating band of roommates in the Manhattan neighborhood of Greenwich Village, which at the time was an affordable haven for artists and "bohemians."

The stories collected here are arranged in a loosely chronological order, and you can see her growth as a writer. The first five are the earliest, and in each the protagonist gets progressively older, almost a cumulative coming-of-age narrative. Many of these earliest stories were re-imagined and revised and appeared in other forms in later work. In particular, her novel *Camilla* has a scene similar to "The Birthday," *The Small Rain* incorporates much of "The Mountains Shall Stand Forever," and "One Day in Spring" is a scene that is later revised in *The Joys of Love*. Later stories, too, were incorporated into other books: "A Room in Baltimore" and "The Foreigners" were revised as episodes in *Two-Part Invention* and *A Circle of Quiet* (which also mentions Julio's party).

Several of these stories were published in Smith College's literary magazine. "Summer Camp" was published in *New Threshold*, a national journal of student opinion, and it was that story that caught the attention of an editor at the publishing house Vanguard, who wrote to Madeleine and asked her if she was working on a novel. She wasn't, but she quickly got to work on *The Small Rain.* "Please Wear Your Rubbers" was published in *Mademoiselle*, and "Madame, Or..." in *The Dude: The Magazine Devoted to Pleasure.* "Poor Little Saturday," a story that combines Southern gothic and fantasy, has been anthologized a number of times. Some stories have multiple drafts, and those collected here are from the most complete and finished versions.

A great deal in these stories is autobiographical, especially in those that carefully observe an intense emotional crisis. One doesn't have to be familiar with Madeleine's biography to enjoy them, but it does add a layer of interest and understanding to know that her childhood was marked by loneliness, that her adolescence was spent in the South, that she was an actress and a published writer before she married, and that her early years of motherhood were also years that she described as being a decade of intellectual isolation and professional rejection.

The most surprising story to me is "Prelude to the First Night Alone," which I understood only after learning more about her friendship with Marie Donnet while my sister Léna Roy and I were doing research for our middle-grade biography *Becoming Madeleine.* Marie was Madeleine's best friend in college, and together they moved to New York City to pursue theater careers. The friendship frayed as their circle enlarged and they had different opportunities and rewards. Their breakup was devastating to Madeleine, and "Prelude," written shortly after, is raw and imperfect and fascinating for this reason.

The rest of the stories are in a variety of genres: there's satire, horror, and science fiction, as well as realism and the careful observation of human interaction and moments of change or renewal. In "Summer Camp," the protagonist fails a moral test. "That Which Is Left" has an unreliable narrator. In "Madame, Or..." and "Julio at the Party" there are subtle adult sexual themes. "The Foreign Agent" has a protagonist who struggles against a controlling writer mother, and "Poor Little Saturday" and "The Fact of the Matter" have elements of fantasy and horror that highlight Madeleine's skills at pacing and suspense.

In some ways only a tiny handful are what may be considered "vintage L'Engle," or the kind of story a knowledgeable reader might expect from her: one in which challenges are overcome and growing pains are real, but so, too, is the promise of joy and laughter. Even the title story in this collection is bittersweet, as the moment of tenderness becomes a memory and something apart from the main character's daily life. The final story, "A Sign for a Sparrow," is set in a post-apocalyptic future, with Earth no longer able to sustain life after nuclear war and civil society in disarray. The only hope for human beings is to find other habitable planets. The main character is a cryptologist who must leave his wife and child in order to find a better world for them and the rest of Earth's inhabitants. His journey and what he finds at the end of it recalls what she said of her most famous book, *A Wrinkle in Time*: that it was her "psalm of praise to life," a story about a universe in which she hoped to believe.

In another way, though, all of these stories are indeed "vintage

L'Engle" in that they resist fitting easily into "young adult" or "adult" categories. She always insisted that she was simply a writer, with no qualifications or labels. When *A Wrinkle in Time* was making the rounds of publishers she would be asked by skeptical editors, "Who is it for? Adults or children?" and she would respond in frustration, "It's for people! Don't people read books?" These stories, too, are for people, and while some feature younger protagonists, they also span a range of genres and styles. Additionally, most of these stories resist a resolution and a tidy triumph for the protagonist (a feature that some would argue is the necessary hallmark of books for younger readers). Taken as a whole these stories express a yearning towards hope—hope for intimacy, understanding, and wholeness. In moments of despair or seasons of doubt, that yearning and its depiction can feel more authentic and optimistic than more neatly resolved narratives or stories with overtly happy endings.

The Moment of Tenderness

The Birthday

She couldn't sleep because tomorrow was her birthday. Tomorrow she would be a year older and it was Sunday and Mother and Father would be with her all day long and perhaps she could go skating with Father on the pond in the park if it was still frozen and there would be presents and she could stay up an hour later. She lay in bed staring up at the pattern of light on the ceiling from the rooms across the court, from the rooms of the people who hadn't gone to bed yet. Cecily slipped out of bed and stood by the window, shivering with cold and an ecstasy of anticipation. In one of the windows was the shadow of someone undressing behind a drawn shade, someone pulling a dress over her head, and then a slip, and bending down to take off shoes and stockings. What was she thinking while she got undressed? What did other people think? What did other children think when they weren't with Cecily? And that was funny. Cecily had never realized that they thought at all when they weren't with her. She felt very strange, and puzzled, and cold.

She turned away from the window, shivering, suddenly frightened, because people must think when they get undressed at
night, not only people across the court but strange people on the
street, people she passed walking to the park and the children
who played in the park. She turned on the light and stood in
front of the mirror, looking at herself, frightened because people thought while they were getting ready for bed and didn't
think about her because she wasn't the most important thing in
their lives at all. All the people she passed in the street didn't
know who she was and wouldn't remember that they had passed
her, a little girl with long fair plaits. That was frightening. That
was the most frightening thing she had ever known. She did not
know why she had thought of it. Perhaps because tomorrow was
her birthday. But if that was what happened to you because you
had grown another year older, she did not want any more birth-
days even if they meant presents and a party. She stared hard at
the thin little face in the mirror for comfort, because here she
was, and she was Cecily Carey, and this was her world. It was
her world because she had been born in it, bought from a balloon man and guaranteed absolutely, Mother had told her so, and
Mother and Father were hers and Mother and Father were the
most important people to everyone in the world but she was the
most important of all to them. She was Cecily Carey, bought
from a balloon man with white hair and red cheeks and blue
eyes, Mother had told her so—she was Cecily Carey and she was
very frightened because the world had changed all of a sudden
and it wasn't hers anymore and she didn't know who owned it.

She started to cry, and she ran and got back into bed and cried
loudly, shivering and frightened. And no one came. Someone had

always come when she cried. Mother had come and held her and comforted her and brought her drinks of water. She cried and she cried and no one came.

"Mother!" she called. "Mother! Mother! Mother!" She kept on calling, shrilly, and by and by the door opened and Mother came in and her face was very tired and drawn and she looked different. "Mother!" Cecily sobbed, "Mother!"

Mother sat down on the bed and held her close. "Hush, darling," she said, "hush, Cecily. You mustn't make so much noise." And her voice was different, too. Or was it because of the world being different? Cecily didn't know and she was frightened.

"Mother," she sobbed, but more quietly. "Mother, who does the world belong to?"

"What, baby?" Mother sat huddled on the bed, and she swallowed strangely when she spoke.

"Who owns the world, Mother?"

"God owns the world, dearest."

"Did he make it, too?"

"Yes, my sweet, God made the world, and he made you, too."

"Did God give me to you?"

"Yes, Cecily."

"But I thought you bought me from the balloon man."

"The balloon man got you from God."

"Oh. And it's God who owns the world? Not anybody else?"

"No, dear. Nobody else owns the world." Mother was stroking her head, running her fingers through the long fine hair, but she was looking at the door as though she were listening. "Are you all right, now, darling? Will you be quiet and go to sleep now if I leave you?"

"Is it very long till morning? Is it very long before it's my birthday?" Cecily asked, becoming drowsy as the thin gentle hand ran over her forehead and back through her hair.

"The sooner you sleep, the sooner it will be your birthday," Mother answered, and kissed her, and stood up. "Will you be quiet now, baby?"

"Yes." Cecily snuggled down into the pillow sleepily, and watched Mother slip out of the room, and she was frightened because Mother swayed as she walked. But she was sleepy and tomorrow would be her birthday and she would have lots of presents and Mother and Father would be with her all day because it was Sunday.

She woke up very early because she always did on her birthday, and all the fears of the night before were gone and instead she had the lovely birthday feeling of anticipation and happiness and excitement and mixed up with it a new feeling as though she was going to make a marvelous discovery. She slipped out of bed and caught a glimpse of herself in the long mirror on the closet door that she had stared into the night before. She didn't run out of the room and into bed with Father and Mother right away, as she usually did on her birthday and on Christmas, but wandered slowly over to the mirror. She stood with her feet on the cold floor just off the edge of the rug and stared into the face of a pale child with wide eyes and a nightgown like hers. And all of a sudden she wasn't thinking at all. The child in the mirror was someone and she was someone and she wasn't sure who because she didn't know either of them and they weren't the same person, and she wasn't there at all, because she wasn't thinking, because her mind was quite blank. And then something in it seemed to go "click." This is me. I am Cecily Carey. I'm me, I'm me, I'm really me, and this is what I look like standing on the floor with my feet just off the edge of the rug, staring into the mirror in my room. This is my birthday, this is the birthday of Cecily Carey, and I'm a real person just like the people across the court, like the one who got undressed with the shades drawn last night, like the people I pass on my way to the park, like Mother and Father and Binny and Cook. I am me, I am Cecily Carey and no one else, and no one else is me. The world is God's and God made the world and the balloon man got me from God and gave me to Mother and I am me because he guaranteed me absolutely.

But it was all very confusing, staring at yourself in your mirror standing with your bare feet on the cold floor just off the edge of the rug so that they ached because it was winter, staring at yourself in a mirror and getting lost someplace and then seeing yourself again and being different. It was all so confusing that she wished it hadn't happened and she was frightened and wanted to cry, only then she remembered it was her birthday and she was getting to be a big girl and it was bad to cry on your birthday or do anything naughty because then you cried or were naughty every day for the rest of the year. She was always good on her birthday. She would not cry. She would not cry. She would not cry. And she would have lots of presents and Mother and Father would be with her all day because it was her birthday and it was Sunday.

She slipped her feet into her slippers and pulled her bathrobe clumsily around her and was all ready to run into Mother and Father's room and get into bed with them and open her presents sitting up in between them, as she always did, when the door opened and Binny came in. Binny came in and it was still early and Binny didn't usually come in at all on her birthday. But she stood there in her blue serge dress and her face was solemn and she had forgotten to put on her white apron.

"Hello, Binny. It is my birthday." Cecily could tell by the sudden movement of Binny's face that she had forgotten, and that was as frightening as finding out that the world didn't belong to her, as frightening as having Mother not come when she cried. "It's my birthday," she said again, but she almost asked it, as though she weren't sure.

Binny's face twisted a little, and she said, "Happy birthday, darling. Supposing you get up now and see your birthday presents after you're dressed. You're getting to be a big girl."

"But can't I get in bed with Mother and Father and open my presents there like I always do?" Cecily asked. "I'm not too old for that, Binny."

"Don't you think it would be fun to get dressed first?" Binny pleaded, and got some clean underclothes out of the bureau.

"I want to get in bed with Mother and Father and open my presents there," Cecily said, and stamped.

"Oh, oh, and you mustn't stamp on your birthday," Binny said.

Cecily's lips began to tremble. "Please, Binny, can't I go and get in bed with Mother and Father the way I always do?"

Binny shook her head helplessly. "Well, your mother and father aren't here just now, Cecily," she said.

"But where are they? It's my birthday! Where are they?"

"Well, your mother didn't feel very well last night so they went to see someone about it to make her feel better."

"Will she come back soon?" Cecily asked anxiously.

"Oh, yes, she'll come back soon," Binny said reassuringly. "You get up and get dressed now and you can open your presents while you're having breakfast."

"Will Mother and Father be here by then?"

"Well, maybe they will," Binny said, "but maybe they'll have to wait for the doctor. That's why your mother gave me the presents to put on the breakfast table for you, in case they didn't get back on time."

"Are they going to see Dr. Wallace?" Cecily asked.

"Yes. They're going to see Dr. Wallace. Such a nice man. You like him a lot, don't you, Cecily?"

"Oh, yes. Will he come back with them and bring me a present, too?"

"Maybe he will," Binny said. "Come along, Cecily, let's get dressed. You want to see your presents, don't you?" She slipped a woolen shirt over Cecily's head.

Cecily stepped onto the floor to slip into a pair of bloomers. "Ow! The floor's so cold, Binny," she said.

"Oh, and you shouldn't be stepping on the floor." Binny picked her up and stood her on the bed, kissing her harshly.

It felt all wrong to sit at the breakfast table and look at a pile of presents beautifully tied up and not to have Mother and Father there. Cecily didn't want to open them, she didn't quite know why, so she drank her orange juice and started her oatmeal. Binny came in and stood behind her chair.

"Aren't you going to open your presents, Cecily?" she asked.

"I'd rather wait till Mother and Father get back."

"Well, maybe they won't be back till after you've finished your breakfast."

"I'd rather wait."

Binny stood behind her chair and watched her for a moment. Then she picked up the presents and put them in a neat pile on the sideboard. "You better open them after breakfast. Then we'll go to the park. We'll go to the museum and you can go in the Egyptian tombs, if you like."

"I don't want to go anywhere till Mother and Father get back," Cecily said, her face clouding angrily.

Binny spoke sharply. "Maybe your mother and father won't get back till lunch and your mother told me to take you to the park if they were late."

Cecily stood up and stamped determinedly. "I won't go till they come back," she said. "I won't go!" she screamed, "I won't go!" and the tears began to roll down her face. She ran over to the pile of presents and began to throw them on the floor, sobbing with anger and fear. Binny went over to her quickly and picked her up and carried her into the living room. She sat Cecily down on the couch and went back into the dining room. Cecily could watch her through the glass doors to the dining room, picking up the presents, smoothing their rumpled wrappings and laying them back on top of the sideboard. She came back into the living room and sat down beside Cecily, putting her arm about the child's shoulders. "Don't you want to open just one of your presents now?" she pleaded.

Cecily stood up and stamped again. "I won't! I won't! I won't!" She looked over at Binny and there she was sitting on the sofa with tears streaming down her lined cheeks. Cecily stared at her for a moment in appalled silence; then she turned and ran into her room, slammed the door, and flung herself upon the bed, gasping but tearless. Because she couldn't cry any more. She tried and the tears wouldn't come. She was so frightened that all she could do was to lie there with big choking sobs trying to tear out of her. It was her birthday and Mother and Father weren't there and Binny was crying. That was the most dreadful thing of all, because Binny didn't cry. If Binny was crying there must be something dreadful the matter. Had Mother and Father both died in the night and been taken away? She remembered a dreadful story one of the children in the park had heard from a nurse about a little girl whose mother and father had died and been taken away in the night and she never saw them again or knew what had happened. Was that why Mother had seemed so strange last night, because she was dying? Binny had said that Mother didn't feel well. Was she afraid to say that she was dead? Cecily stretched out stiff on the bed and tried to feel dead, too, to check the sobs that kept coming and that seemed to tear at her throat and hurt it. But they wouldn't stop. She got up and stood in front of the mirror again, watching herself, with her face all blurred and blotchy from crying, and screwed up into a strange shape with the effort not to sob. If Mother and Father were dead, what were they thinking now? Did they remember her or had they forgotten her? Why didn't they come? Did the people in the rooms across the court know that she was unhappy? Were they thinking about her birthday presents?

But they couldn't be. Nobody knew, nobody cared.

("Mother, who does the world belong to?"

"What, baby?"

"Who owns the world, Mother?"

"God owns the world, dearest."

"Did he make it, too?"

"Yes, my sweet, God made the world, and he made you, too.")

If God made the world and he made Cecily, perhaps he might care a little even if the people in the rooms across the court didn't. She went across the room and knelt on her bed and said, "Now I lay me" and "Our Father" and "God bless" the way she did at night to Mother and Father, and it didn't seem to do any good at all because she said it every night when everything was happy and it was just something comfortable to do, like pulling the blankets around your neck on a cold night. God who made the world was so big and if he made the people in the rooms across the court and the people she passed on the way to the park, did he really have much time to pay attention to her? Perhaps the balloon man who sold her to Mother would care, so she prayed, "Dear balloon man, please make Mother and Father not dead and taken away in the night but make them come back quickly so I can open my birthday presents." Then she lay down on the bed and stared up at the ceiling and waited. She pretended she could see the square of light with the three lines of shadow across it that lay in the center of the ceiling when she went to bed at night and she tried to count in English and French and German as far as Miss Evans, who came every morning, had taught her, and by and by her eyes grew heavy and closed.

When she opened them again, Father and Dr. Wallace were standing in the doorway.

She jumped off the bed and rushed over to her father and butted her head against him. "Father—" she whispered. "Father, why weren't you and Mother here when I woke up? Why weren't you here? I thought you were dead."

Father picked her up and swung her onto his shoulder. "Why, kitten, whatever made you think of such a dreadful thing?"

"You weren't here when I woke up and you always are on my birthday so I can open my presents in bed with you, and Binny said Mother didn't feel well and you'd gone to see Dr. Wallace. Where's Mother? Father, where's Mother? Is she dead?"

Father swung her down and stood her in front of him. "Somebody's been putting very funny ideas into your head, my darling," he said. "Mother isn't dead. She just isn't very well and so she's in bed in a place where Dr. Wallace can take care of her and make her get better."

"But I want her!" Cecily said shrilly.

"Darling," Father said, tilting her head back so he could look down into her eyes, "Dr. Wallace and I have come to take you to see Mother for a little while if you promise to be very quiet."

"I promise," Cecily whispered.

And Dr. Wallace said, "All right, baby, come along and we'll take you to see Mother, but only for a few minutes. She didn't sleep much last night, you see, so she's very tired today and wants to sleep."

"But it's my birthday."

"If you'd like to go to the movies, Binny will take you this afternoon," Father said.

"I don't want to go to the movies."

"What would you like, then, kitten? Would you like to go for a ride on the Fifth Avenue bus? Or would you like to go see the Statue of Liberty and ride in a little boat?"

"No."

"Well, what would you like to do, baby? You may do anything you like."

"I'd like to be with you."

Dr. Wallace bent down and took Cecily's hand. "Listen, chicken," he said. "This is just as tough on you as it can be. It's a rotten shame that your birthday should have to be spoiled, but you'll just have to be a brave girl and make the best of it. Mother wants Father to be with her because she doesn't feel well, just the way you would if you were sick. You see that, don't you?"

"Yes."

"But I'll tell you what we will do. My birthday comes in the middle of July, and I'll lend it to you this year if you like."

"Oh, you couldn't do that! I couldn't take your birthday!"

"Well, let me share it with you, then. That would be fun, wouldn't it? We could have a birthday together. Would you like that?"

"Oh, yes!"

"That's a girl. Now you run and put on your coat and hat and we'll go see Mother for a little while."

"All right." Cecily slipped her hand out of Dr. Wallace's and pulled her coat off the hanger. "Would you get my hat, please?" she asked. "I can't quite reach it."

Dr. Wallace picked her up. "Certainly I won't get your hat. You're big enough to reach your own hat. Can you get it now, chicken?"

"Yes, thank you." She pulled her hat off the shelf and stuck it on the back of her head. Dr. Wallace put her down and held her at arm's length. "You're growing fast, young lady. Can you button your coat yourself?"

"Yes." Cecily pulled her coat together quickly and struggled with the buttons. "I'm ready." She took Father's hand and they started out, Dr. Wallace following. "Where's Binny?" Cecily asked. "She isn't crying, still, is she, Father? She isn't still crying?"

"No, dear. She's in the kitchen with Cook," Father said, and slammed the front door.

They took a taxi. Cecily sat very still in between Father and Dr. Wallace, staring hard ahead of her, her mind confused and numb with the strangeness of the day, and was frightened because the people they passed in the street didn't know she was frightened. The taxi stopped in front of a tall, clean building, and they went in, and up, up, up, in the fastest elevator Cecily had ever seen, and down along corridors that seemed filled with people in stiff white dresses, holding trays or wheeling little carts filled with white towels or strange-looking silver things, people in white dresses walking rapidly, silently. Then Dr. Wallace pushed open a door at the end of a corridor, and there was Mother lying in a white bed and smiling. Cecily stood in the doorway, solemn-eyed, uncertain.

Mother whispered when she spoke. "How's my baby?"

Father pushed Cecily towards the bed and she ran to it, flinging herself against it.

"Steady there, chicken," Dr. Wallace said.

"Shut up, Nick," Mother whispered, and put her arms around Cecily. "Look how you have your hat on, baby, all crooked. There, that's better. Did you like your presents? Did you like what Mother gave you?"

"I—I haven't opened them yet," stammered Cecily, clambering up onto the bed and lying against Mother, knocking her hat half off.

"Didn't Binny tell you to open them at breakfast?"

"Yes. But I thought maybe you were coming home. Are you coming home soon, Mother?"

"Of course, darling. Aren't I, Nick?"

"If you don't talk and behave like a good girl," Dr. Wallace said. "Come along, chicken, you'd better go home now."

"But I just got here!"

"I want your mother to sleep so she can come home soon. You go on back and open your birthday presents. I'm not going to give you mine, though, until we share our birthday together. Will you say goodbye now, and be a good girl?"

"Yes." Cecily kissed Mother quickly, slipped down from the bed, and stood beside Father, holding his hand tightly.

"Come along, darling," he said, and then, to Mother, "I'll be right back after lunch, dear."

"Goodbye," Mother said, and closed her eyes. Dr. Wallace opened the door and pushed them out.

"See you this afternoon," he said to Father, then bent and kissed Cecily on the top of her head and slipped back into the room with Mother again.

Father straightened her hat automatically. "Come along, dear."

When they got back to the apartment he asked her, "Don't you want to open your presents?"

"Not yet. I'd rather wait." Cecily wandered over to the window and stared down at the street.

Father sat down on the sofa, hunched over, and after a moment Cecily moved from the window and climbed up into the big red chair, closing her eyes tightly, and started to count to a hundred, because sometimes that helped. When she had finished she looked at Father, and he was still sitting in the same

14

position, hunched over, his hand in front of his eyes. "Father," she said.

"Yes, baby?"

"Did God make you and Mother, too?"

"Yes, dear."

"Oh. Father—"

"Yes, baby?"

"Does the balloon man you and Mother bought me from know God personally?"

"I expect he does, dear."

"Oh." She watched him for a minute longer, watched his fingers tighten on the arm of the sofa, watched them rub hard against it, pushing, but he had turned so that she could not see his face. She closed her eyes tightly again and started to count.

She slept soundly after lunch, falling asleep almost immediately, but she woke up just as Binny came in. "Well, and so you're awake," Binny said. "Do you want to open some of your birthday presents?"

"No."

"Aren't you ever going to open them?"

"I want to save them."

"What for?"

"For the birthday I'm going to have with Dr. Wallace. He said he'd share it with me, and I want to open my presents then. Would you put them in the top of the closet, Binny?"

"Oh, and you'll be wanting them tomorrow."

"No, I won't."

"All right. I'll put them up later on. Do you want to go to the park?"

"No."

"Well, what do you want to do, then?"

"I don't care."

"Do you want to come to church with me and pray to God to make your mother get well soon?"

"All right."

Binny dressed her quickly and put on her coat and hat and they walked up Park Avenue to St. Ignatius. Cecily watched Binny and saw her change as they went in the church door. She became a part of something strange and beautiful, like a bead on her rosary, as she genuflected, then pulled out her beads and began to tell them. Cecily knelt beside her and the smell of incense seeped through her like something magic. She felt that there must have been the smell of incense when Mother bought her from the balloon man. The light from the stained-glass windows fell across the nave and the motes of dust were colored. Cecily clasped her hands together and tried to count the lighted candles burning everywhere, round red ones, and blue ones, and little white ones, and tall white ones, one two three four, *un deux trois quatre, eins zwei drei vier*—

"Are you praying to God to make your mother get well quickly?" Binny whispered.

"Not yet. I'm going to," Cecily whispered back. "Ought I to pray to God when I'm in here?"

"Of course you should. And who else would you be praying to?"

"The balloon man."

"You pray to God. A balloon man can't hear prayers."

"Mine can."

"I never heard such nonsense. You pray to God and be quiet."

Cecily moved her lips slowly, "Now I lay me," and "Our Father," and "God bless." And then, defiantly, "Dear balloon man, please dear balloon man, Father says you know God personally, and maybe he wouldn't hear me because I'm not very big or important, so would you please make Mother get well and come home and sing me the song about the king of the cannibal islands?"

And as she prayed and smelled the incense and watched the colored light filtering across the nave, she felt long shivers go up her back like cracks up a pane of glass. And then she was sleepy and all she remembered was the jerky feeling when Binny buttoned her coat, and walking home very quickly, and eating supper, and being in bed. She woke up for a minute when Father came in to kiss her good night and told her that Mother was better. He was smiling and he kissed her good night three times and tucked all the covers in twice, but she was so sleepy she hardly knew he was there.

And then, suddenly, the middle of the night was surrounding her, black and strange and cold. She had kicked her covers off and she was shivering and her throat was scratchy dry. She pulled the covers about her quickly and they came untucked at the bottom and her bare feet stuck out, so she rolled herself up into a little ball and wrapped the blankets about her as closely as possible.

"Mother—" she started to call. And then she remembered that Mother was not here but in a white room where Dr. Wallace could make her well, and Cecily wanted a drink of water—she wanted a drink of water—

"Father!" Cecily called, and again, "Father!" And then she

stopped. For she was Cecily Carey, bought from the balloon man and guaranteed absolutely, and she had just had a birthday, and in the rooms across the court people thought when they went to bed and they didn't know about her. She was Cecily Carey with half a birthday coming in the summer and she was the little girl in the mirror and God owned the world and she was very thirsty. So she got up and put on her slippers and bathrobe and went into the bathroom and reached for her glass.

Gilberte Must Play Bach

Claudine stood at the window with her cheek pressed against the cool window pane and watched a grey cat move fastidiously along the wall at the edge of the garden. He was so thin that his ribs rippled against the side of his body as he slid along, and his whiskers stood out stiffly against the snow like little brittle bones. Claudine watched him and half listened to her mother playing Bach on the piano.

"He goes so smoothly," Claudine said aloud without turning, wanting her mother to stop the E Minor Toccata. But Gilberte Valdahon strained towards the music, her forehead puckered, her lips closed so tightly that the tense lines at the corners of her mouth showed white. Claudine moved slowly away from the window, clutching the end of a long braid in each hand, watching her mother out of nervous eyes. "He goes as though he had on skis," she whispered, "as though he weren't walking at all. Wouldn't it be funny if cats could wear skis, Mother?"

Madame Valdahon shuddered and let her cold fingers fall off the keys. "What, Claudine?"

"Nothing." Claudine walked slowly over to the piano and put a timid hand on her mother's shoulder. "Is the middle G sharp still sticking?"

"Not so badly," said Gilberte Valdahon. "Haven't you anything to read, Claudine?"

"I've read all morning, and my eyes hurt." Claudine rubbed her hand across her forehead and felt her eyes throbbing from strain. "Mother, you said once..." she started, and bit her lip.

"What did I say once, Claudine?" Gilberte put an arm about the thin little body.

"Nothing. I mean, I don't remember. Mother, when I'm undressed my ribs show almost as much as the cat's," said Claudine unsteadily. *(But she did remember. She could see their drawing room at home in Paris and Aunt Cecile sitting on the sofa with her furs carelessly and beautifully flung across one shoulder, Aunt Cecile sipping tea and listening to Gilberte with a slightly amused smile that Claudine resented. "I know it's sacrilege for a musician to feel the way I do," Gilberte Valdahon said to Aunt Cecile while she drummed out the theme of the Beethoven fugue with one finger. "To feel how, my angel?" Aunt Cecile asked. "I never, never, never," said Gilberte vehemently, swinging around and still drumming the theme of the fugue with her back to the piano, "I never play Bach unless I'm upset and unhappy. So you don't mind, do you, Cecile, if I refuse?" "That's perfectly all right, my dear. I don't mind at all. I quite understand," said Aunt Cecile, and Claudine knew she did mind, and wanted to run over and hit her with all the force of which she was capable. "And really, why Bach?" Aunt Cecile asked, putting down her tea cup and stretching. "Because," Gilberte Valdahon said, "because*

you can't think of anything else but Bach while you're working at him.
You can't think of anything else at all.")

"Your ribs show almost as much as that cat's, Claudine," Gilberte said. But Claudine stood silent, rubbing her finger against the threadbare wool of Gilberte's dress, staring at the piano, through the wall, into a drawing room in Paris. "Claudine!" Gilberte shook her gently and laughed a little.

"I'm sorry, Mother," said Claudine breathlessly. "I was just— just thinking."

"You think too much, darling," said Gilberte, hitting the G sharp in a puzzled manner, automatically trying to loosen it, hopelessly trying to see beyond the pale controlled mask of the child's face.

"There's nothing to do if you don't think," Claudine said.

"I know, dearest, but you don't go outside enough. Run and ask your father to go for a walk with you before lunch."

For a moment Claudine's face lit up. "Do you think he will? Won't you come, Mother, please won't you?"

"No, Claudine. I want to work at the piano. Run and ask your father quickly and don't forget your muffler and your rubber boots."

"All right." Claudine squirmed out from Gilberte's arm and ran to the door; but when she had opened it she stood very still, watching the tense lines about her mother's mouth become white and hard again. Then she hit her clenched fists hopelessly and noiselessly together and started down the passage. As she passed the kitchen, warm golden light and the hot smell of soup rushed out at her, and old Thomasine was singing as she stood at the stove:

J'ai perdu ma maîtresse
Sans l'avoir mérité
Pour un bouquet de roses
Que je lui refusai . . .

Claudine hugged the warmth and comfort to herself for a moment, and then walked on into the cold shadows of the passage outside her father's study. She tapped on the door timidly, and he shouted angrily, "Who is it?"

But it wasn't his anger that frightened her. She opened the door and slipped into the room. He was sitting at the unpainted table in front of the window, but she knew he hadn't been typing even though the typewriter was in front of him with a half-covered sheet of paper in it. Sometimes he would sit at the typewriter all day, until late at night even, before he could bring himself to write for a paper controlled by the Germans.

"It's me, Father," said Claudine.

"Hello." Michel Valdahon turned around, all the irritation gone from his voice. "Does Gilberte want me?"

"No. I do. Can we go for a walk, please?"

"Isn't it late?" Michel gathered up a sheaf of papers and clicked them against the table like a pack of cards.

"There's half an hour before lunch."

"All right. Run and put your things on."

"Can we go right away, Father? You'll hurry? 'Cause I'll be ready in a minute."

"Right away," Michel Valdahon promised, and got his big black galoshes out of the corner where they were lying in a puddle of melted snow. The polish on the floor looked white and strange from the wet, and Michel Valdahon was ashamed of the way he had flung them angrily into the corner as though he were Claudine's age. He looked to see if she had noticed the puddle and the stained floor, but she was running down the passage. He stood still for a moment listening to the barely perceptible irregularity in the *pat-pat* her feet made. Her limp had almost disappeared; no one else but Gilberte noticed it except when Claudine was tired or had been walking a great deal. By now she had almost forgotten being pushed down the stairs by a tall uniformed beast when the Germans first came to Paris. Here in the country she could almost forget that they were still a conquered nation, except that Michel's own limp from a German bullet would never disappear, would always be there to remind them.

Her footsteps stopped and he could hear her talking to Thomasine in the kitchen. He pulled his worn great-coat off the peg on the wall and slipped into it, bracing himself a little against its weight, for his left arm was very stiff; his shoulder rebelled against pressure.

Claudine came rushing out of the kitchen and almost ran into him before she saw him. He caught her up with his good right arm and swung her around. She was too thin, too light, but even so he felt an effort and his breath was short as he put her down.

"I'm almost ready, Father," she said, "truly I am." Breaking away, she pelted down the passage to the dark boot cupboard under the stairs. In a moment she had on her old rubber boots and was sliding into her heavy navy coat. "I'm ready now." She pulled a white knitted cap off the shelf, jamming it onto her head. "I'm ready, Father."

As they passed the living room Michel Valdahon shouted,

"Goodbye, Gilberte," and the E Minor Toccata stopped for a moment.

"Goodbye," Gilberte called. "Have you your muffler, Claudine?"

"Oh, I forgot," cried Claudine, and flew to get it.

While she was rummaging in the cupboard, Michel Valdahon opened the door to the living room and watched his wife begin working on the E Minor Toccata again. He wanted to cry out, "For Christ's sake, stop playing Bach!" but instead he asked quite quietly, "Can we get you anything from the village, dear?"

Once more Gilberte let her fingers droop hopelessly against the keys; but when she spoke her voice was light; she used almost the same tone she kept for Claudine. "Nothing—unless you could get a substitute for these dreadful red plush chairs. And this horrible piano. It looks like the rock of Gibraltar, and the G sharp is so tiresome."

Looking at Gilberte's fingers drooping against the discolored piano keys, Michel Valdahon likened them to flowers suffering from lack of water and sunshine, flowers dying in the evil-breathed neurotic room France had become. "Just the same," he said, "it's better than Paris. It's better for Claudine. She's beginning to forget. And as long as the mail takes my stuff to the paper . . ."

"Do you want Claudine to forget?" she asked. "I don't know whether she is forgetting or not. I never know what Claudine is thinking." Then, sharply, "Do go on, Michel. She's waiting and if you don't hurry you won't have time for a proper walk."

He turned and Claudine was beside him with a strange expression in her carefully guarded eyes. "Right. Come on, Claudine," he said.

They plowed through the garden, Claudine holding his arm and stumbling. Walking in the snow was difficult for both of them and they limped along together.

"Where shall we go?" Michel Valdahon asked as they came to the gate.

"I don't care." Claudine watched the empty sky above the wall where the cat had walked. "You can almost push it apart," she said.

"Push what apart, Claudine?"

"Today. It's so grey and heavy I think if I knew how I could just push it apart and find what was really underneath. There was a cat on the wall this morning, Father."

"Was there?" (He hardly listened. The heavy greyness of the day was pushing against him, pushing him down so that he could hardly stand up.) He shivered a little and a few stray snowflakes fell from his coat. "Let's go to the village and maybe we might get something to bring back to Mother."

"All right." She clung on to his arm tightly, more tightly than was necessary to help her through the snow. "Mother's been playing the E Minor Toccata. Bach," she said.

"Oh," Michel Valdahon answered.

"The G sharp isn't as badly stuck as it was," Claudine said.

"Good. Then maybe Mother can play us the Brassin 'Fire Music' tonight." She didn't answer, and they walked silently through the snow. Michel Valdahon felt her weight pulling on his arm. She seemed even heavier than when he had lifted her, and the feel of her leaning against him almost frightened him. It was as though she were trying to ask a question and was afraid of the answer, as though she were seeking reassurance in the heavy roughness of his coat and the slight swing of his arm as they moved along.

They walked through the almost deserted streets. There were very few Germans here. Very few Frenchmen, too. In the few shops that were not shut up, the proprietors drowsed over the counters, and in the corner of the church a beggar shivered against the steps. Michel Valdahon flung him a coin and limped on savagely until Claudine stumbled and almost fell. As they crossed the bridge and came up to the little cafe, Michel Valdahon stopped and would not look at Claudine's eyes staring up at him. He turned towards the door and said as lightly as he could (but he could not speak lightly with Claudine dragging on his arm and the weight of the day pushing him down), "Come on in, Claudie. We'll go in for a few minutes and you can have a lemonade before lunch."

"I don't want a lemonade." Claudine's voice was hard and she looked down at the ground, twisting one toe so that she scraped a little hole in the hard-packed snow.

"Come in and sit with me for a few minutes, then," said Michel Valdahon, walking towards the door.

Claudine pulled on his arm. "Please, Father—couldn't we go on walking? You know it isn't good for you to . . . You said we might get something to take back to Mother." Her toe was working at the hole in the snow and she tried to move him away from the bistro.

"We can do that later." Michel put his hand on the door handle.

"But please, Father, please—couldn't we go on walking? Mother—"

He answered sharply, angrily. "Don't be silly, Claudine. Are you coming in with me or not?"

"I'll wait outside." Her voice was so small that it was almost lost in the day that was close-pressed by the vast snow-covered mountains leaning about it. Michel Valdahon flung into the cafe for his cognac and Claudine watched him while the door slowly closed upon him and the heavy odor that had rushed out at her as he opened it vanished with him. She walked slowly away, back to the bridge, and stood leaning against it, watching the water swirl underneath—water so swift that it never became entirely ice; even when it seemed completely frozen over there was always the wild sound of water rushing along under the ice, blind, mysterious. She felt almost sick as she watched it, trying to make her mind move quickly, as quickly as the water under the bridge, trying to think of a hundred unimportant things. But always in the back of her mind like water running under the ice was the sound of the E Minor Toccata.

Beating her mittened hands together in the same gesture she had used in the passage, she walked back to the cafe. The heavy smell hit against her face as she opened the door, but she walked on quietly until she came to the table where Michel Valdahon was sitting. He smiled at her and stood up as she came near, and she reached out and caught hold of his arm. Already he had had a good deal to drink.

"All right, Claudine, we'll go now," he said, and they walked out into the cold air which pressed upon him, which made him hurt until he wanted to cry out. "Shall we try to find something for Mother?" he asked.

"No. Let's go home." She was afraid he might go back to the

cafe again and started to pull him along. They walked as quickly as they could up the hill. Claudine panted and her breath came out in round curly puffs of vapor. "Do I look as though I was smoking when I breathe steam?" she asked, trying to hold her mittened hand as though she had a cigarette.

"Yes, darling," said Michel Valdahon. "Almost." One of the clasps to his galoshes had come undone and flapped against his leg, stinging it. He leaned down to fasten it, and took Claudine's hand in his when he stood up. There was something about the way she clutched his arm even when she talked nonsense that made him afraid.

"Let's hurry. It's late." Claudine tried to stumble along more quickly. "There's soup for lunch, Father." They turned in at the gate and an emaciated cat slid along the wall and looked at them with secretive eyes as he moved. "That's the cat I saw this morning," said Claudine, and started to pull back. She slipped her hand out of his and bent down to pick up a hard black twig that had snapped off one of the trees.

"What's the matter, Claudine?" Michel Valdahon stopped and watched her.

"Nothing." Claudine broke the twig into small pieces, and dropped them, black and sharp, onto the snow.

Michel Valdahon watched her a little longer, then started for the door. He left it open, and Claudine could hear Gilberte still working at the piano. The notes stood out as sharply and clearly against the snow as the black whiskers of the cat or the specks of the twig. For a moment Claudine listened quietly. Then she followed Michel Valdahon into the house.

The Mountains Shall Stand
Forever

Ellen stood in the middle school common room with her
nose pressed against the window pane and wept. When she
unscrewed her eyes enough to look out for a moment all she saw
was grey fog and the branches of the plane trees, thick and furry
through it. The lake and the mountains across the lake were as invisible as though they weren't there at all. Ellen's stomach jerked as
she thought how strange it would be if the fog lifted suddenly and
the lake and mountains were gone, and there was nothing but a
great gaping hole with space showing through, all empty and
black. The idea was so startling that she stopped crying and tried
to imagine what it would be like without the lake and the mountains. The older girls listening to "Goodnight, Sweetheart" on a
tinny gramophone would all scream with terror, but Ellen would
just stand there quietly by the window and watch. Maybe no one
would notice her, and they would all run out of the room and she
would be there, all by herself. She would be really alone, and she
could break the record of "Goodnight, Sweetheart" and just sit

there quietly with no one to bother her. They would all run out and fall into the space and she would stand by the window and watch them disappear and smile.

"Ellen."

Ellen pressed her nose harder against the window pane. "What."

"Come away for a minute. I've got something to tell you. Oh, you ass, you've been crying again."

"No I haven't, Gloria."

"Hunh," the other child said. "Come along."

"What do you want?" Ellen stared out of the window.

"I said I wanted to tell you something. Something awful interesting. If you don't come along I won't tell you. I thought you'd like to know."

"All right," Ellen said. Gloria took her arm and led her out of the common room and up the back stairs. "Where are you going?" Ellen asked.

"To my room. It's the only place we can be alone."

"But we aren't allowed—" Ellen began.

"To hell with rules." Gloria shook her head violently, and her dull brown hair with the frizzy permanent clung about her face. She pushed it away and took Ellen firmly by the hand so that she couldn't escape. "Are you shocked because I swore?" she asked.

"No," Ellen said. "What do you want to tell me?"

"Wait till we get to the room." Gloria led her along the corridor and into one of the dormitories.

"Well?" Ellen sat on one of the beds and held the tip of a dark brown plait firmly in each hand.

"Good Lord, you'd think you were doing me a favor in listening," Gloria said. "Not many people would tell you things, Ellen Peterson. Nobody likes you."

Ellen flushed and kicked her feet against the edge of the bed. "Do many people tell you things?"

"I wouldn't listen." Gloria tossed her head again. "I'm getting out. That's what I wanted to tell you."

"What do you mean?" Ellen looked up quickly, and Gloria walked self-consciously over to one of the white bureaus between the beds and sat down by it.

"Just what I said." She opened the bottom drawer and began rummaging around in it. "I'm leaving next Saturday. Just one week."

"But how can you?" Ellen watched, fascinated, while Gloria pulled a compact out of the drawer and powdered her nose, and then smeared a little lipstick onto her lips. "You'll get into an awful row if they find that stuff."

"I should care." Gloria rouged her cheeks liberally. "I've only got another week of this dump. You've got to promise not to tell."

"All right."

"I just wrote home, as Mother says she'd come and get me." Gloria rolled her makeup in a uniform blouse and put it back in the drawer. Then she pulled out a pink lace brassiere and held it up. "Do you have any of these?"

"No."

"Gosh, you're young." Gloria sat back on her heels. "I'll tell you why I told you about my getting out."

"Why?" Ellen asked, wishing that Gloria would hurry.

"I think you ought to leave, too."

"But this is just the beginning of the term."

"You're awfully silly," Gloria said, beginning to file her finger-nails. She looked at Ellen's, which were cut short. "You're always paying attention to rules and accepting things. You didn't like it here last term, did you?"

"Yes."

"Don't lie. You know you hated it. You are always crying. You won't like it any better this term. Why don't you write your mother?"

"She's dead."

"Your father, then," said Gloria, looking away, a little embar-rassed.

"I don't want to bother him."

"Gosh, you *are* queer," Gloria said. "I should think your being unhappy would bother him."

"He doesn't know I'm unhappy."

"But didn't you tell him?"

"No." Ellen wandered over to the window and stared out. It had never occurred to her that it might be possible to leave the school.

"Wouldn't you like to leave school?" Gloria persisted.

"Of course."

"Then I think you're an ass if you don't write your father. Where is he?"

"New York."

"What does he do?"

"He's an artist."

"Gosh, I'd think you'd want to be with him."

"I do." Ellen turned away from the window and walked between the beds to Gloria. "Is your mother really going to take you away?"

"Of course. I don't tell lies, even if you do."

Ellen didn't get angry. It wasn't worth it to get angry with Gloria. "You mean all you did was write her and she said she'd come get you?"

"Of course. Isn't that what your father would do?"

"I don't know. You'd better wash that stuff off your face, Gloria. If anyone sees you you'll get in an awful row."

"I'll take it off with cold cream," Gloria said, unrolling a jar from her gym bloomers. "It's awful bad for your face to use soap and water." She began to smear cold cream on her face, unconscious of the door opening and the stern stare of the matron. Ellen saw her first and backed towards the window.

"Well, Gloria!" the matron said, ignoring Ellen.

Gloria clutched the cold cream to her and glared at the matron. Ellen stood with her back to the window and looked apprehensively at the gold pince-nez perched on the matron's nose, and dropped her eyes down the white starched uniform to the floor.

"Go wash that stuff off your face immediately, Gloria," the matron said, then turned to Ellen. When she spoke her voice was softer. "What are you doing here, Ellen?"

"I was—I was just with Gloria, Miss Banks," Ellen said, tears rising quickly to her eyes at the note of kindness in the matron's voice.

"Well, run along to the infirmary sitting room and wait for me there. I want to have a talk with you."

Ellen left obediently and walked slowly down the corridor,

stepping carefully into the centers of the diamond patterns on the carpet. She timidly turned the handle of the door to the infirmary, but there was no one at the desk, and she slipped into the tiny sitting room unseen.

The fire was lit, but she went over to one of the windows and stared out into the fog. It was beginning to lift a little, and she could see the plane trees more clearly. Their bare branches looked ugly to her, and she stared beyond them, trying to see down the mountainside. But the lake and the mountains across were still invisible. She wondered if they were really still there. Was it possible for them to just disappear? People died and were never seen again. She did not hear the door open and she jumped when she heard Miss Banks's voice.

"What are you thinking of, Ellen?"

"Nothing."

"Oh, but you must have been thinking of something." Miss Banks sat on the couch in front of the fire.

"Just that it looks cold and you can't see the lake."

"Come over and sit down," Miss Banks said.

Ellen walked slowly over to the couch and sat stiffly on the edge. "Is Gloria a very good friend of yours?" Miss Banks asked.

"No."

"You seem to see rather a lot of her."

Ellen shrugged her shoulders. She couldn't tell Miss Banks she didn't talk to Gloria from choice. "She's all right."

"I don't think she's very good for you," Miss Banks said. "Why don't you play more with the other girls in your form?"

"I don't know." Ellen looked down at her feet. Miss Banks put an arm around her tenderly.

34

"Why are you so stiff and distant, Ellen?" Miss Banks asked. "People would like you if you'd only let them."

Ellen pressed her lips together. Miss Banks's arm held heavy about her and she wanted to jerk away. The matron held her arm around the stiff little body for moments, then stood up wearily. "All right, Ellen. Run along back to the common room."

Ellen left without speaking and went downstairs. In the common room there was still a group around the gramophone and some of them were singing the words..."Goodnight, sweetheart"...Gloria wasn't there and Ellen was glad. She went over to her locker, not speaking or spoken to by the groups of girls she passed, and pulled out her writing paper. She sat cross-legged on a table near one of the windows and began writing a letter to her father.

She didn't have a chance to speak to Gloria again until after supper. Then she drew her aside and whispered, "I wrote my father this afternoon."

"Gosh, that's swell," Gloria said. "Do you want me to tell you a joke?"

"No." Ellen turned away in disgust.

In the common room a group of girls was playing jacks on the floor. Ellen stood and watched them for a moment. They were four of the most popular girls in her form, and she was half-afraid of them, even while she scorned them. She looked at them and wondered what there was about them that wasn't like her, why they should like each other and not like her. One of them looked up and noticed her. "What are you doing, Ellen?"

"Nothing."

She started to move away but the girl stopped her. "Your father's an artist, isn't he?"

"Yes, Violet." Ellen stared at the girl, avoiding the close-set brown eyes and watching the rather prim little mouth.

"She doesn't look like her father is a painter, does she, Ginny?"

"I don't know." Ginny looked up at Ellen a little impatiently. "I don't think you look like a lawyer's daughter. She's funny looking enough."

"What does your father paint?" Violet asked Ellen, an impish look coming into her eyes.

"All kinds of things."

"Well, our house needs repainting. I 'spect he'd do it cheap for my father, wouldn't he?"

Ellen flushed and didn't answer, and all four of the girls burst into loud laughter. She started to leave but Ginny leaned out and tripped her up, and she fell. As she scrambled up she began to cry, and she couldn't see whether they were laughing or not as she ran from the room. It would be four days before she could hear from her father.

On Wednesday there was no letter for her. But there would be one the next day. Surely there would be one the next day. On Thursday morning she stood by the mail table fifteen minutes before the earliest possible moment when she could expect the students' mail to be brought out. Violet walked by her and said, "Don't forget about that paid job on our house." Ellen didn't answer, but when she saw Miss Banks she wanted to leave, but she saw that the matron was coming straight to her, so she slid down from the table and waited.

"Miss Hubert wants to see you in her office, Ellen." Miss Banks looked at the child strangely.

"Oh. All right," Ellen said, turning away under the matron's stare. She felt Miss Banks's eyes following her as she went along the passage and knocked at the headmistress's door.

Miss Hubert was sitting at her desk with a letter in her hands. Ellen's heart jumped as she recognized her father's handwriting.

"Good morning, Ellen," Miss Hubert said. "Sit down."

Ellen sat in a straight chair by the desk and stared at the letter.

"I have a letter from your father here. He says you are unhappy. What's the matter?" Miss Hubert looked at Ellen's thin face and watched the small jaw set stubbornly. "He says that you don't like the girls. Are they unkind to you?"

Ellen said nothing and stared at Miss Hubert, but the head-mistress felt that the gaze did not stop at her eyes or meet them but went on and on into space.

"There must be some reason for your being unhappy," she persisted. Ellen's jaw set more firmly and her eyes became more distant. "Gloria Ingle is a good friend of yours, isn't she?" Miss Hubert asked.

"No." Ellen bit the word off and clasped her fingers tightly around the polished arms of the chair the way she did at the dentist when she was afraid he was going to hurt.

"Who is your friend, then? Isn't there someone you like especially?"

"No." Her mouth began to tremble no matter how tightly she pressed her lips together.

This wasn't fair. It had never occurred to her that her father might write to Miss Hubert.

The headmistress watched the child's eyes fill and wanted to take Ellen in her arms, but she remembered what Miss Banks had told her, and was afraid. "Who is unkind to you, Ellen?" she asked.

Ellen shook her head. But Miss Hubert persisted with questions until the child's brain felt heavy and dizzy. "But surely there must be some who tease you more than the others. Your letter made your father very unhappy. He wants you to stay here and have fun with other children your own age. And how can I help you if you don't help me a little? Who is the one who teases you most?"

Ellen looked down at the floor and felt worn out. "Violet, I guess."

"What did she do?"

"I don't know."

"Is she the only one? Isn't there someone else?"

"Maybe Ginny."

"Is that all?"

"Yes. Yes."

"Do you really want to leave, Ellen? It would make your father very unhappy."

Ellen shook her head and stared down at her feet. She wished she'd never written the letter, and that she'd done what she'd wanted to do and stayed in the common room on Saturday afternoon instead of going with Gloria.

Miss Hubert watched her and again wanted to gather the thin little figure up, and again remembered Miss Banks. "You'll try to stay and be happy, won't you, dear?"

"Yes."

"Run along, then, or you'll be late to your class."

Ellen turned and left the office, then ran to the mail table. She read the letter from her father quickly, and then turned and ran into the bathroom, choking with sobs. She did not understand why he was unhappy because she had asked to leave, but he was, and she hated Gloria violently for having made her write the letter. She tried to cry quietly but every once in a while a great sob would come out. She was desperately afraid that someone would come in. When she stopped crying the first class had already begun, and she stayed in the bathroom for the full half hour, washing her face with cold water. She could not bear the thought of going into the class late with her face all streaked with tears. She went up as the bell rang and slipped into her seat.

After supper she went into the common room and tried to read, but she had turned only a few pages before Gloria came up to her and tugged on one of her long plaits. "Come on up to my room. I want to tell you something."

"No."

"Why not?"

"I don't want to, that's all."

"Don't you want to hear?" Gloria stared at Ellen with astonishment in her little pop eyes.

"I don't care."

"Well, okay. It doesn't make any difference to me. I don't particularly want to tell you. I just thought you'd like to know."

"I want to read," Ellen said.

Gloria put her hand over the page. "Well, wait a minute. Can't you talk like a decent human being for a while? Listen, what do you suppose Ginny and Violet were doing in Hubert's room all afternoon?"

Ellen's stomach turned over. Oh, God, why did I write that letter, she thought. "I don't know. Were they there?"

"All afternoon," Gloria said. "I expect they're going to be expelled."

"Oh, no!"

"Yeah. They were crying awful hard, and they aren't here now. Oh, there they come. Gosh, I bet Hubert gave it to them. They still look blobby."

Ellen stared at the pair with terrified eyes. They stood in the door and looked over the room until they saw her. Then they came straight towards her, without pausing at the group by the gramophone. Ellen dropped her eyes to her book, jerked away from Gloria, and tried to read. Her heart was pounding violently.

"Well, Ellen Peterson," Violet said. Ellen looked up and they were staring at her with hostility. Gloria's mouth was open and her little eyes were filled with curiosity. Ellen didn't say anything. She looked up from Violet to Ginny and she felt cold all over.

"So you're a tattletale, too," Ginny said.

"No, I'm not."

"Yes, you are." Violet's prim little mouth was hard. "You got us into one beastly mess with your sniveling to old Hubert."

"Are you—are you going to be expelled?" Ellen whispered.

"Oh, so you thought you could expel us, did you?" Violet laughed. "Well, you were mistaken there, Miss Sneak. We are still here, and will make things pretty unpleasant for you from now on, I can tell you."

"We don't want tattletales around," Ginny said.

Gloria couldn't restrain herself any longer. "What'd she do?"

"Just wrote her father and said we weren't being nice to her, and then told Miss Hubert what beasts we were," Violet said angrily.

"Say, I call that dirty." Gloria looked Ellen up and down, coolly.

"Dirty's not the word for it," Violet said. "Come along, Ginny. I can't stand talking with such filth any longer tonight." They turned and went over to the gramophone. Ellen could hear them talking loudly.

"Gosh, they're going to make life fun for you," Gloria said. "I'm glad I'm getting out."

Ellen closed her book with a bang. Her voice rose shrilly. "Leave me alone for a minute, can't you?" She walked over to the window and looked down at the mountain. It was a clear night, and she could see the lake and the deep shadows of the mountains across the way. She wished that they would disappear, that in their place would be space, a great empty hole, all black. And she would run out of doors and leap into the space that had been mountains and lake, and be all alone, forever.

Summer Camp

The ground near the pond was hard and damp and Lise lay flat on it, pressing her nose against it until the patterns of grass and twigs were printed across her face and her tears were mixed with the wetness left from the morning's rain. Hard bits of stubble pricked through her middy and bloomers and jabbed into her, but she pressed against the ground even more closely, welcoming the pain, digging her toes into little tufts of grass and pushing, trying to concentrate her misery into physical discomfort.

"Oh, God," she whispered. "Oh, God." And then quickly she sat up, staring defiantly at the sky, and said, "Damn." And then, "Damn it to hell." She held her face up and waited, looking at one grey cloud floating just above her head. But it floated past her and nothing happened. She flung herself down again and began to cry loudly, angrily, gasping. "Oh, God, why didn't you strike me down? Why didn't you strike me down?"

Then suddenly she became conscious of someone near her, and she stiffened, holding her breath, checking her sobs by pressing her face even harder into the ground. Someone was standing beside her, watching her misery. She lay perfectly still, desperately trying to become invisible in the short stubbly grass. "Go away," she whispered. "Go away."

"Lise."

"Go away," she said savagely into the ground. "Go away, damn you."

"I don't mind if you swear," the voice said. Lise was not sure who it belonged to but she did not want it there. She wriggled a few inches nearer the pond and stretched her arm out so she could dabble her fingertips carelessly in the water.

"I'm watching a tadpole turn into a frog," she said.

"That's very interesting, isn't it?" The voice was light. "I'd rather they stayed tadpoles, though."

"Would you?" Lise asked. "I like the frogs." She rolled over and sat up and saw that the voice belonged to one of the counselors, a counselor nobody liked. "Hello, Miss Benson," she said politely, trying to pretend that her face was not covered with tears, covered with bits of grass and lines where twigs had pressed against it.

"You can call me Sunset, if you want to," the counselor said. "I'm not ashamed of having red hair." Her thin young face was suddenly hard and unhappy.

"I don't call you Sunset," Lise said.

"I wouldn't mind if you did. I think sunsets are pretty. Do you know that I came down to the frog pond just now for the same reason you did? Because I wanted to cry?"

"Did you?" Lise looked at her with interest, then added softly, "I'm sorry."

"Don't be," Sunset said. "It's good to have something to cry about sometimes. That's how you grow." She sat down beside Lise at the edge of the pond and put her hand in the water, swishing it back and forth. Lise watched it, a long, knobby white hand, the back covered with fine red hairs, the nails cut off short and a little dirty. Sunset followed Lise's glance and said quickly, "I know my nails are dirty. I've been digging. Up on the mountain. I've been digging Indian pipes and planting them in a shoe box. I suppose they'll die, though."

"Maybe they won't." Lise kept on watching the thin, unshapely hand. Then she asked a little timidly, "What happens when you swear?"

"Nothing. Sometimes it makes me feel better. Not often. Not unless I can really shout."

"Oh. I thought maybe if I swore, God would strike me down."

"No," Sunset answered sadly. "It doesn't work that way. It's too bad, isn't it. But sometimes it does help if you shout. Would you like to try it?"

"All right."

Sunset scrambled up, her long, top-heavy body looking grotesque on her short legs. Lise stared at the legs sticking bare out of a tight skirt. Like the hands, they were white and covered with fine red hairs. She felt a little sick and jumped up quickly.

"Let's stand over here, on this rock." Sunset took the child's hand and led her over to a flat gray rock at the end of the pool farthest from the camp. Lise jerked her hand away quickly, then slowly put it back. "You don't have to if you don't want to," the counselor said.

"I do," Lise whispered, and climbed onto the rock, clutching the thin white hand.

"Now!" Sunset climbed up beside her and stood with her feet apart. "We put our hands on our hips and throw back our heads and shout 'damn' three times as loudly as we can."

"All right." Lise put her hands on her hips and glared up at the sky.

"When I say 'one, two, three, go,' we scream," Sunset said.

"All right."

"One—two—three—go!"

Lise threw back her head and shouted, "Damn! Damn! Damn!" at the top of her lungs with Sunset.

"There!" The counselor took Lise's hand again and pulled her down off the rock. "Don't you feel better?"

"I guess so."

"And see here. I'd rather you didn't tell Mrs. Hedges, if you don't mind."

"All right."

"Even if I am leaving tomorrow I—I'd just rather you didn't."

"All right. But why are you leaving tomorrow?" Lise stared up into Sunset's unhappy, defiant face.

"I handed in my resignation half an hour ago," Sunset answered, "because if I hadn't I'd have been asked to leave in very short order anyhow. I don't seem to have the knack of making you children pay any attention to anything I say. As a nature counselor I guess I'm worth exactly nothing."

"I pay attention to what you say."

"You're different."

"I don't want to be different!" Lise said furiously, digging her fingers into the ground.

Sunset looked at her sharply. "It was meant to be a compliment. I shouldn't have been talking to you like this if you weren't."

"Oh."

"You won't tell the other kids about this?"

"Of course not."

Sunset looked at the child again, and then began pulling out the short blades of grass, saying lightly, "Now I've told you why I came down to howl, you ought to tell me about you."

"Ought I?" Lise began pulling up grass, too, laying the separate short strands across the toe of her sneaker.

"It's only fair, isn't it?"

"I—I guess so. It was only that Franny Morrison and I were the only new girls in our tent and she's always been my best friend and none of the other girls like me so she doesn't anymore, either."

"And that was why you were crying?"

"Yes, and because everyone was mad at me because I lost the race for our tent because I can't run fast."

"You have a bad knee, don't you?"

"Yes."

"Then it's not your fault you can't run fast."

"They were mad anyway."

"And do you still like Franny?"

"Oh, yes."

"Why?"

"I don't know. I just do."

"Then why don't you get her aside sometime and have a talk with her? Or write her a letter? If she's worth having as a friend she'll snap out of it."

"Maybe I will."

"Good girl. You'd better run along now. It's almost supper time and someone will be out looking for you if you don't get on back to the tent."

"Yes," Lise said. "Are you coming?"

"No. I think I'll stay and have my howl. You run along."

"All right." Lise started off, then turned back. "I'm sorry you're going."

Sunset looked at her, then back at the frog pond. "Thank you."

Lise went back to the tent quickly, pausing for a moment to splash cold water on her flushed face at the wash basins. The others were sitting on the floor of the tent, playing jacks. They didn't look up or speak to her, so she sat on her cot quietly, rubbing the palm of her hand nervously over the rough grey of the army blanket and watching Franny. And she knew that she couldn't speak to Franny. She couldn't go up to her while the others were around—and the others were always around. Everything that was wrong was because of the others. So perhaps she would write. Sunset had suggested that she write a letter and Sunset was a counselor. Perhaps if she wrote Franny a letter asking her why she was so horrid, perhaps then things would be all right again. She stood up and pulled down her writing pad and a pencil from her shelf, sat down on the edge of the bed again, and started writing.

"Who are you writing to?" Franny asked suddenly.

"Mother."

"You wrote your mother yesterday."

"I can write her again, can't I?"

"Oh, sure, if you want to. I suppose you're homesick again."

"No."

"Then what are you writing her for?"

"Because I want to. She's my own mother, isn't she?"

"Oh, sure, I suppose so. I never heard otherwise."

"Come on, Franny, it's your turn," Bobby Biggs said impatiently. "Leave baby alone."

Lise watched Franny turn back to the game, bit her lip hard, and went on writing. She sat there until the others had run off to get in line for supper, not waiting for her; then she folded the letter, wrote "Frances Morrison, Private" on it, put it under Franny's pillow, and ran off to join the supper line.

Down by the wash basins that night she brushed her teeth, light at heart. She had not felt as happy as she felt now since before she had come to camp, since the days when she and Franny had made plans together about the wonderful time they would have that summer. So Lise brushed her teeth and thought about Franny, who had already finished her washing and was back in the tent. Perhaps right now, while Lise was spreading a second long white squirl of toothpaste on her brush, Franny was reading the letter, and maybe when she went back to the tent they would smile at each other, and just start talking the way they used to, and she wouldn't be left out anymore.

She walked slowly on her way back to the tent; she must give Franny plenty of time to read the letter. And because she wanted to run back she made herself walk even more slowly, holding off the pleasure she wanted so terribly, tasting every moment of the anticipation. The air was cold and crisp and it slipped through her flannel bathrobe and made her shiver, but the needles of the pine trees looked warm where they brushed against the sky and the stars were just beginning to come. If only there were someone to walk with, it would be such a beautiful place. When you were alone you were too small and it was frightening. Maybe after this Franny would walk with her again.

She couldn't hold herself off any longer and she broke into a run, reaching the tent, panting. She jumped into bed without a word and then looked over at Franny in the next bed. Franny was sitting up in bed with a bright red woolen sweater over her pajamas, reading the letter by her flashlight. She was smiling a very little smile, and Lise's heart bounded with hope. She stared over at Franny, her mouth a little open, breathing quickly. Suddenly Franny turned to her and said, "Why did you lie to me this afternoon?"

Lise felt everyone in the tent looking at her. "What do you mean?" she asked breathlessly.

"You said you were writing to your mother this afternoon, didn't you?"

"I—I guess so." Lise clutched the edge of her cot tightly.

"You did. But you weren't, were you?"

"No."

"You were writing to me, weren't you?"

"Yes."

"Listen, kids," Franny cried, "I got a letter from Lise. Lise wrote me a letter."

"Please, Franny..." Lise tried to whisper, but Franny didn't hear.

49

"Read it to us, Franny, read it to us!" Bobby Biggs shouted gleefully.

Franny held her flashlight close to the letter. "It begins, 'Darling Franny,'" she announced.

Lise scrambled out of bed and hung herself on Franny. "Give me my letter—"

Franny jerked away. "'Darling Franny, why don't you like me anymore...'"

"Give me my letter," Lise screamed. "Give it to me, give it to me—"

Franny jumped out of bed, choking with laughter, and ran over to the other side of the tent. "'We've always been such good friends...'"

Lise rushed at her. "Stop it, Franny! Give it to me! Give it to me!"

Bobby Biggs and two of the other girls held her, and she kept on screaming, avoiding the hands they tried to clamp over her mouth, screaming to drown Franny out. "Stop it, Franny! Stop it! Stop it! Stop it!"

"What's all this noise?"

Franny stopped reading suddenly and Bobby and the others let Lise go and turned around. Mrs. Hedges was standing at the front of the tent, pointing a flashlight at them.

"I want my letter, I want my letter," Lise sobbed as the others climbed quickly into bed.

"What letter, Lise?" Mrs. Hedges asked.

"Here, baby," Franny said quickly, and shoved the letter into Lise's hand. Lise clutched it to her and got into bed slowly.

"I don't want to hear another sound out of any of you

tonight," Mrs. Hedges said. "Stop crying, Lise. Control yourself, child."

Lise pressed her hand tightly against her mouth to keep her lips from trembling and shut her eyes tightly.

"Now good night." Mrs. Hedges switched her flashlight out. "If there's any more disturbance from this tent for the rest of the week, not one of you will be allowed to go to the picnic on the big lake on Sunday. Remember that."

"Oh, we'll be good," Franny promised, and the others echoed her.

"Oh, we'll be good, Mrs. Hedges. Honestly we will. Good night, Mrs. Hedges."

"Good night," Mrs. Hedges said, and strode away.

Sunset was just finishing packing her little car and was ready to leave when Lise's tent came up from archery the next morning. Now that she was going they all crowded her, curious, shameless.

"Are you going, Miss Benson?"

"Oh, we'll miss you, Miss Benson."

"Oh, Miss Benson, why are you going?"

"Goodbye, Miss Benson."

They seemed to take a malicious pleasure in accentuating the "Miss Benson." Sunset turned from stowing her box of Indian pipes in a safe place in the back of the car and looked at them with a half-smile.

"Goodbye," she said, holding her hand out to Bobby Biggs, who was nearest her.

"Goodbye," Bobby said, and put her hand behind her back.

Sunset's smile disappeared for a moment. Then she turned to Lise. "Goodbye, Lise."

Lise looked hostilely at the outstretched hand, white and bony and covered with fine red hairs on the back. "Goodbye," she murmured, and turned away. She walked over to a pine tree and leaned against it, watching Sunset climb quickly into the car, not saying another word, not waving. The others waved for a moment, then ran back to the tent, while Lise stood still, leaning against the tree, and watched the car disappear.

White in the Moon the Long Road Lies

The door slammed behind Selina, and the dogs barked excitedly as she whistled to them. Old Japhet was spraying the flowers with a long shimmering stream, twisting the hose so that the water swirled in shining spirals. Selina waved as she ran past him, down the path to the beach, to the warm silver sand. The faint lavender of the sky was reflected on the shore still moist from the receding tide. The sea oats were waving gold about the dunes, and the palmettos and Spanish bayonets were stiff silhouettes. Selina let the soft, dry sand near the dunes sift through her toes, ran down the beach to the cold wet sand, ran into the water and splashed it high ahead of her, made deep footprints and watched the slow wet sand sift into them.

The dogs ran wildly down the beach, breaking the still of the dusk into echoing fragments with sharp barks, shaking the water off their backs so that the spray caught the light and shone silver. In the faint glow, the dunes seemed to rise high against the sky like white and blue mountains. Selina climbed up the shadow of one and flung herself upon its piled snow. The dogs tore up the beach, and Selina watched them, hugging her knees. A flash of light caught her eye, and she looked out over the ocean to the sweeping curve of yellow from the lightship. The fishing boats were coming home, and quite close to shore she could see the glistening leapings of a school of porpoises. She put her head down on her knees and traced off little figures in the sand with her finger.

In town at the garden party, the air had been heavy and the sun had beaten down upon the garden. It had tipped the grass and the petals of the flowers with dry brown, made the asphalt tennis court catch the heat and throw it off, even under the trees, to the gay painted tables scattered about; so it seemed as though the heat were a ball bounced onto the tennis court that hit awry and went soaring over the boundaries into the garden. The cool sound of ice clinking in tall glasses had been almost lost in a warm buzz of goodbyes, a buzz of mosquitoes, the buzz of the lawn mower next door, the buzz of a telephone ringing incessantly inside the house.

Selina felt that she had never been so "deared" and "darlinged" before (oh, Selina dear, are you really leaving tomorrow...But Miss Williams is *too* intelligent...Darling, don't forget us way down here in the South...I want you to meet Miss Selina Williams; she's going up north to teach this winter and I do think it's *too* clever of her...), and all the while she had been smiling and shaking hands and letting unintelligible words come out of her mouth in answer to those she had heard, she had been conscious only of her linen dress wilting and clinging to her (and what is worse than a draggled linen dress, she thought), and her white shoes, which were too tight and had somehow gotten grass stains on them in spite of the care she had taken to walk only on the paths.

The afternoon had dragged on interminably, and Selina felt little drops of moisture trickling down her back, and watched the tight fingers of sun holding the day down so that she began to wonder if evening would ever come—or had she somehow been dropped into an air pocket of time where there would be nothing but tired shrill voices and thick heat? She had to hold her fingers tightly together to keep back impatient exclamations at the insincere and half-derisive superlatives on her cleverness that were marking the air like a fugue, that had somehow gotten started and could not stop—a wild mingling of discordant themes in which she had to join while the one voice that could resolve the chaos never came.

She whispered to her brother, "Bill, I'm going to scream in a minute—really yell." A scream, high and sharp and long, would split the heat and noise like lightning. The heavy superlatives would be suspended in midair and the sun would lose its hold on the hot afternoon. There would be a moment of nothingness after the flash, and then the low rumble of voices again... "But really, my dear..." "But you know I always said she was... well, a little..." Selina almost chuckled and Bill had her by the elbow and was piloting her to their moist and shining hostess.

"Let me drive, Bill," she had said when they finally reached the car, and he grinned and got in beside her as she tossed her hat on the back seat and ran her fingers through her damp hair. He let her drive much too quickly, breaking the silence only to say, "I

55

didn't see Peter." And later, to ask abruptly, "Do you really want to go, Selina?"

"Of course I want to go," she said almost savagely. "It's stagnant and old and narrow-minded here and no one has survived the Civil War except Pe— except one or two people. You've got your hospital, but I haven't anything and I want to get out."

"That's not really why you want to go," Bill said, and Selina was vaguely thankful that he knew.

"Do you think I'm wrong?" she whispered at last as the sun became a molten ball behind the pines and a faint salt breeze reached them from the ocean.

"No," said Bill. "No, I don't think you're wrong."

"But I'll come back..." Selina tried to steady the alarm in her voice as she watched Bill giving shape to her thoughts.

"Yes, this summer, perhaps—oh, I don't mean that you'll stay in the school or anything—but you won't belong here anymore. You never have, really."

"But Bill—it's part of me—I feel as though I were tearing myself up—I'm breaking myself off at the roots—just going away for this year." Selina gripped the wheel and stared at the road, trying to steady her voice, and out of the corner of her eye she saw tenseness in Bill's form beside her and knew that it was hard for him to tell her this, to hurt her.

"You are part of this beauty, Selina, but it's because it's the only beauty you had. You clung to the ocean and all its moods because it's really the only thing you have to cling to, except the family— and you don't really fit with us, either. The only person, the only person in the world who could hold you here isn't going to stay— I know that, Selina. And you know it, too."

"How do you know, Bill? How do you know about all of this?"

"I'm not quite sure. I've been thinking about it for a long time."

"Why don't I belong..." asked Selina, clenching her teeth together, and taking the worst curves on the road as wildly as she could so that she would be able to think of nothing but the car, so that Bill should not see her cry. But he was silent until he took the car from her at the gates to put it in the garage. She tried to shake off her mood and ran up the path, pausing only for a moment to greet the wildly barking dogs, to shout to the children battling tennis balls against the side of the garage. Inside the house it was damp and cool, and her heavy tiredness from the heat and nerves too tight fell away. Melly was singing deep down her throat in the kitchen, and there were glasses of iced pineapple juice on the table in the hall. Selina closed hands around the sharp coolness of one and ran upstairs to her room, bare, with all her books and papers gone from the desk and tables, and her suitcases on the chairs and about the floor. Almost before she reached the room she was pulling her wilted dress above her head, tossing it in a crumpled heap in the corner, flinging her shoes under the bed, her stockings in the middle of the floor. ("Oh, Lawd, who gwine help dis chile; who gwine help dis chile" floated Melly's voice from the kitchen.) Selina ran her fingers through her hair and rumpled it until it stood on end. She heard the screen door slam and swift feet running up the stairs, and the children were at the door.

"Hi, Selina; you back?"

"Umm," she mumbled, delving into an almost empty drawer.

"Where's Bill? How was the tea? Was Peter there? Hi, Selina, was Peter there?" Their voices were shrill, unquenchable.

"Bill's putting the car away. The tea was all right but it was too hot in town and I don't like to have people make such a fuss over me. Peter—Peter wasn't there." ("Oh, Lawd, I'se gwine far away, Who gwine help dis chile" came Melly's voice, and Bill's feet thumped in rhythm as he climbed the stairs.) They were silent for a moment, and the cool sound of Bill's shower splashed into their thoughts. "I'll be back in time for dinner," said Selina, and she ran down the corridor, past the rushing sound of Bill's shower, past the low current of voices from her mother's room, down the steps.

(Melly's voice had come clearly, then. "Oh, Lawd. Help dis chile, bless dis chile what's gwine far, far away. Oh, Lawd, who gwine help dis chile." Her voice was deep, minor, monotonous as she beat up the cornbread.)

It would be a long time before she would hear Melly's voice again, Selina thought, and tried to shake off her recurring home-sickness for the things she had not yet left, sticking her fingers deep into the sand. The dogs climbed clumsily up the dune, slip-ping in the unsteady sand, and lay down beside her. She smiled, a little crookedly, to herself. The farewell walk—but how could one say goodbye to the ocean and the great stretch of silver beach, the white dunes and leaping wind?

No matter what Bill said, this was something that was part of her, something that she could never leave without leaving part of herself behind, and she knew now that it was part of her that she would have to leave forever, no matter how long it would take the wound to heal. And strangely she seemed to hear in the recur-rence of the breakers a new note, to feel in the wind an adequacy of farewell that could never be attained by words. And somehow she felt that she had reached the height for a moment, that something more potent than words was speaking through her, that for a moment she was fused into the solitary splendor of wind and wave and sky. It was as though her soul was being branded with a talisman of the night, something that would always be with her wherever she was, something that would always be pulling her, pulling her, with a relentless and inevitable force. It was a feeling so wonderful and so vast that her human frailness was too small to hold it. She raised her head sharply, and a voice behind her said, "Selina." She looked around and Peter was there. Dim and shadowy behind her, Peter was standing.

"Peter." (Until this minute she had refused to admit to herself that she had been hurt because he had not come to the garden party that afternoon to say goodbye to her.)

"I wanted to say goodbye to you, Selina," he said. "If I'd been at the garden party, I wouldn't have had any excuse to come now. One can't say goodbyes at parties."

"No." A dim star began to flicker behind Peter's head.

He sat down beside her, and she stared out across the ocean silently. "So you're going tomorrow," he said.

"Yes." She began to trace Peter's head in the sand.

"My wild Selina going to teach in a young ladies' boarding school…" His finger was making little swirls and holes in the sand, circles and triangles, lines and squares.

Selina laughed. "It isn't as bad as all that, Peter. Teachers don't have to be as staid and solemn now as they used to. I was awfully fond of some of mine when I was at school."

"Don't let it narrow your horizon. It is broad, Selina; keep it. Don't let it be squeezed in by the narrow walls of school," he said, looking out over the ocean.

"That's why I'm going—because of narrow horizons," said Selina in a muffled voice.

"And the snows—" Peter's voice was reflective. "I can't see Selina in ice and sleet and fog. You belong down here in the sun, with the wind and the waves."

"I shall probably love the snow," said Selina staunchly (but she rubbed out Peter's face in the sand and a stiff little palm tree with a round sun above it came in its place).

"It's a long time till June," said Peter.

Selina looked at him. "Haven't I been trying not to think about it?" She pressed down upon the sand with her fist. "It's eternities until June!" She shook the small grains of sand from her fingers. "I'm sorry, Peter."

"You're sorry, Selina?" Peter said. "I am the one to be sorry. I didn't mean to hurt you." He watched her toes digging in the sand. "I'll miss you."

She smiled at him; Selina smiled at him and his face once more appeared in the sand, and one of herself with large horn-rimmed spectacles and her hair pulled severely back. (The beam from the lightboat swung around, brighter with every turn as the last light faded and the stars came out, one by one, white and blue and yellow, throbbing above the ocean and the beach.) Peter jumped up. "Goodbye, Selina." He bent down and kissed her quietly and disappeared behind the dunes.

For a moment Selina did not move; then she called, "Goodbye, Peter—" and her voice resounded against the silence. (His footsteps stretched behind the white dunes, filling in with the faintly glowing sand.) "Goodbye, Peter—" she whispered; and "Goodbye, Peter—" her finger traced in the sand.

The moon peered above the edge of the ocean, large and crooked. "The waxing moon—" Selina whispered and stood up, shaking the sand off her like a dog. She plucked a long, sharp strand of beach grass, held it, rough, pliant, to her lips, and whistled piercingly. The winds caught up the sound and it shivered along the beach. From far over the dunes came an answering echo. And "Goodbye, Peter—" Selina whispered again. The gleam from the lightship made a white arc across the sand, and the moon seemed to leap above the ocean's edge.

"Goodbye, Selina—" she whispered, and watched the dim sand trickling through her toes. She bowed mockingly to her waiting shadow on the dune. "Introducing *Miss* Williams, instructress of history," she said, and thought, incongruously, of rolling sand dunes and heavy breaks; sandpipers strutting up and down the beach in early morning, and the sleek black of the porpoises' leap; the flowers of Spanish bayonets in early spring, and broken shells upon the beach after a storm. It's a long time till June, Peter had said. (The narrow path on the ocean became broader and brighter as the moon climbed higher, growing smaller, more crooked.) A long time till June—a long road to travel alone, thought Selina, looking out over the white moon path to the horizon. Keep your horizon broad, Peter had told her, and she let the broad white horizon at the edge of the glistening path reach into her mind. She walked slowly down from the sand dune, pushing her feet deep into the sand until she got to the hard moistness of the water's edge. Ahead of her, rolling over the edge of the horizon, the gleaming highway of water stretched wide and clear.

Madame, Or . . .

It was a perfect street for it, Walter thought as he walked along checking the numbers on the houses, a neighborhood that not too long ago had been highly select and that now was only slightly down at the heels. A few of the houses were still private, but most of them had been divided into small apartments, and at two of the street corners were two new apartment buildings. He paused at one of the brownstones, looking up, frowning and unexpectedly nervous, at the lace-curtained parlor windows. He thought he caught a glimpse of two girls' faces peeping behind the curtains: Was one of them Nancy? From somewhere in the building came the unexpected sound of violin exercises meticulously executed. He drew back his shoulders bravely and bounded up the steps, pausing again before ringing the bell to the front door. To the right was a polished brass plaque: MADAME SEPTMONCEL'S RESIDENCE FOR YOUNG LADIES. Walter read it carefully and smiled sardonically, and his smile gave him courage to push the bell.

The heavy front door was opened almost immediately by a

young girl with a mop of wavy black hair, unnaturally long eyelashes (though they were, indeed, all her own), and a figure blossoming tightly against a yellow cashmere sweater that was perhaps half a size too small. Her mouth was heavily lipsticked, her face otherwise free of cosmetics. She smiled radiantly at Walter.

"Won't you come in, please?" she said. "Who is it you wish to see and whom shall I say is calling?" Her speech was very correct, almost a little too precise, as though she had been taking speech lessons: her voice was too husky for her accent. From upstairs the sound of the violin came more clearly now, a difficult passage of a cadenza exquisitely played.

"I would like to see Nancy Burton, please," Walter said. "I am Walter Burton."

"Oh, of course!" the girl said. "I knew I'd seen you somewhere before. Do come in and sit down and I'll call Nancy." She led the way into the parlor, her little bottom bouncing jauntily in the tight brown tweed skirt. Walter went over to a love seat upholstered in lemon-yellow satin, but he did not sit. "But you haven't ever seen me before," he said. "At least I've never seen you, and if I ever had I'm sure I could never have forgotten it."

The girl laughed. "Well, aren't you sweet! Nancy has a picture of you in her room. So you're the famous Walter. Odd you both having the same last name, isn't it?"

"Not especially, since—" Walter started, and then stopped, remembering Nancy's proclivities.

"Since what?" the girl asked.

But Walter got out of it by asking, "Who's the violinist?"

"Oh, that's Natalia. Good, isn't she?"

"I don't know too much about it," Walter said cautiously, "but she sounds all right." He could not take his eyes off the girl's obvious charms and she spoke too quickly to cover his embarrassment. "I've never in my life seen such long eyelashes. Do you put them on with spirit gum every morning?"

The girl laughed again. She had a slow laugh that started deep down her throat and rose to a gay chuckle. "You're really as nice as Nancy said you were," she said. She bent down to fondle a sleek grey cat that came slinking through the door. The cat moved lasciviously under her hand, turned, and moved back again.

"Are you a friend of Nancy's?" Walter asked.

"I have the room next door. Oh, I'm Deirdre O'Hara, by the way. I know it's a silly name, but it's all mine. I'll go call Nancy. Is she expecting you?"

"No," Walter said. "I hope she's here."

"Oh, sure." Deirdre moved away from the cat, blowing hair off the palms of her hands. The cat bounded onto an amber velvet cushion on a lemon satin chair and sat there, turning its head from side to side as if ready to participate in the conversation. "Look, are you planning to take Nancy out to dinner or anything?"

"Well—yes."

"Then you'd better see the madame first."

"The madame?"

"Madame Septmoncel. I mean, you'll have to get her permission before Nancy can leave in the evening."

Walter frowned. Deirdre looked at him and laughed again. "What's the matter? Scared? The madame won't bite. Look, I'll go tell her you are here, and see if she can see you right away. She rests in the afternoon but—what time is it?"

"Five thirty."

"Oh, then she'll be up. And then while you're with the madame, I can tell Nancy to go put on her best bib and tucker." She smiled disarmingly again. "I'm really not terribly good at this. The madame asked me if I'd mind answering the door this afternoon because Aggie's sick."

"Aggie?"

"She's the maid. Now hold on a minute, Walter, and I'll be right back." She hurried off, with that provocative wiggling gait, Walter staring after her, the cat leaping off the chair and following her. The combination of bravery and timidity with which Walter had walked down the street and climbed the brownstone steps had both gone, leaving him with a simple sense of excitement. It might be a wild goose chase; he might be going to make a fool of himself; but you never could tell with Nancy and he owed it to her to come and find out what it was all about. He looked very carefully around the room. Coldly and exquisitely furnished. Lemon-yellow satin. Rosewood. Parquet floor. Aubusson rug. An Impressionist painting over the mantelpiece, an excellent one, though he could not place it, a young, voluptuous-looking woman in a green velvet dress. Maybe Renoir, though he did not think so. A green jade horse on the escritoire. Late afternoon sun coming palely through the curtains.

Deirdre returned. "Madame Septmoncel says that she will be delighted to see you, Walter. You don't mind if I call you Walter, do you? I feel I know you so well from the picture and all the things Nancy's said."

And what the hell has Nancy said?

"Come on," Deirdre said. "I'll show you the way. Am I doing this all right? The madame says my manners are deplorable. I suppose they are. She thought it would do me good to take the door today, though there haven't been too many people. She says swinging the hips isn't the answer to all questions and I suppose she's quite right, though anytime I'm stuck it's stood me in good stead. I'm reading *The Red and the Black* now. The madame thought it would do me good. Oh. That's a non sequitur, isn't it? The madame says I make them all the time. She'll make me over yet. Don't look so nervous, Walter, love, I told you she wouldn't bite."

He followed her down a long, dark corridor, a sepulchral darkness that lemon-yellow satin and sunlight had not managed to dissipate. Deirdre giggled and turned back to look at him. "Golly, it's dark, isn't it? One of the bulbs has gone out." And he shook himself, thinking—*See, it's only in my imagination, it's because of Nancy, it isn't so at all.*

Deirdre knocked on a door and opened it with a flourish.

"Walter Burton, please; Madame Septmoncel," she said, and gave Walter a little shove, so that he had, whether he would or no, to advance a few steps into the room.

It was a study, and Madame Septmoncel was sitting in a blue velvet chair at a Regency desk. There was a fire burning in the fireplace against the autumn chill, and one or two lamps were already lit. A different cat, a tiger-striped one, lay on a sheaf of papers on the desk. Firelight and lamplight flickered against the backs of books, pictures, rose brocade curtains, mahogany, and Madame Septmoncel's silver hair. Walter took a few more steps towards the desk, and Madame Septmoncel came towards him, holding out her hand.

Walter took it and was astonished at the power of the grip,

for she was a tiny, exquisite woman, delicate-boned, fragilely appointed. "Good afternoon, Mr. Burton." Her voice was low and cultured, the voice Deirdre O'Hara emulated. "Deirdre said you wished to see me?"

"Well I—that is—" Walter stammered.

Madame Septmoncel returned to her blue velvet chair. "Please do be seated," she said, gesturing to a straight chair opposite hers.

Walter sat and looked across the desk at Madame Septmoncel. Gray eyes, their lucidity only slightly clouded by years, looked with amusement into his; he had never felt so young. "I'm Nancy Burton's brother," he said, "and I wondered if it would be all right if I took her out to dinner."

"Her brother?" Madame Septmoncel raised amused eyebrows.

"Well—yes."

Madame Septmoncel sighed. "Your sister has already made a place for herself here," she said. "We're all very fond of her, the girls and the staff and I. Yes, I can see that you are her brother. You have the honey-colored hair, and there is the same look of innocence between the eyes, and the timid line of jaw is similar. Yes, there is a definite sibling resemblance."

"Why—" Walter asked, "why shouldn't I be her brother?"

Madame Septmoncel offered Walter a cigarette, pushed matches and a cloisonné ashtray towards him, and then leaned back in her chair, one hand reaching up to touch the pearls at her neck. "You were not present when your father brought Nancy to me."

"No," Walter said.

"He told me that sometimes—sometimes her imagination runs away with her."

Walter looked unhappy. "Yes. You see, our mother died three

years ago and there's really been no one to—to understand Nancy since. Father's a terribly busy man—"

"Yes," Madame Septmoncel said. "And you, I believe, started in the business with him this autumn?"

Walter nodded. Madame Septmoncel laughed. It was, Walter thought, Deirdre's laugh with a foreign accent; so Deirdre had gotten her laugh as well as her speech from the madame. But not her walk; Deirdre's walk, he was certain, was her own, and he did not want it changed. But then again, if Nancy was right, perhaps Deirdre's walk was as assumed as her accent and her laugh. He looked across the desk at Madame Septmoncel. Her face was half in shadow, but he could see the delicate modeling of her bones; the arch of her brows, still dark under the silver hair; the thin, patrician line of her nose; the delicate, compassionate mouth.

"Your father told me Nancy had an older brother but somehow I did not connect to Nancy's Walter—it was stupid of me."

"Nancy's Walter?" he asked.

She smiled. "Don't judge her harshly. She knows no one here and she hasn't had time yet to make outside friends. Several of the girls, particularly the ones who were here last year or who already have friends in the city, have had young men come to see them, or to take them out to dinner or to the theatre. So Nancy had her picture of Walter. Walter who just happened to be a Burton, too, who was a musician, a violinist."

"I do play the violin," Walter said rather stiffly.

"But not nearly as well as our Natalia, unless I'm very much mistaken."

"No." Walter grinned. "I play abominably."

"And you are Nancy's brother, aren't you?"

"Oh. I see," he said.

"Now, please. Don't say anything to Nancy if you can help it. It will spoil her evening. Did she expect you to come so soon?"

"I don't suppose she expected me at all," Walter said unwillingly. "Dad just happened to have some unimportant business to be done here in the city and I managed to talk him into letting me do it. It *is* all right if I take Nan out to dinner, isn't it?"

"But of course. And you won't say anything about what I just told you, will you?"

"Not if I can help it," Walter said.

"But you *can* help it, if you choose. Nancy is more sensitive than she would like us to know. That is why she had to make up a second Walter for us who is not her brother, and that is why you will bruise her most unnecessarily if you uncover her little deception."

"Surely you don't approve?" Walter demanded.

"Is this a matter for approval or disapproval? This lack of discipline of the imagination is something that can do Nancy a great deal of harm and we will try to help her control it. But gently, Mr. Burton, and with care. I would be very grateful if you'd leave it up to me. You can hardly accomplish anything except damage if you take her to task for it over the dinner table."

Walter felt that the interview was over, but instead of rising he leaned back in his chair. "Do you take this much interest in all the girls?"

Madame Septmoncel smiled again. "But of course. That is what I am for. That is what the school is for." She reached towards a silver tray on her desk on which was a slender silver coffee pot and a cup and saucer. "I was about to have a cup of coffee. Will you join me?"

"Well—" Walter looked at the single cup. "Yes, please."

Madame Septmoncel touched a bell on her desk, and almost immediately there came a knock at the door and in answer to her call there entered a tall blond girl in a blue satin cocktail dress.

"All ready to go out, Barbara?" Madame Septmoncel asked.

"Yes, Madame."

"And who is it this time?"

"Harry. I've written it down in the book. We're going to the opera and then if it's all right with you, we'd like to go somewhere and have something to eat."

"Of course, Barbara. You're a senior this year and you have proved yourself worthy of my trust. Don't forget to sign in the book when you come in, and leave the key in the blue Canton bowl."

"Yes, Madame, thank you."

"Would you be good enough to get me another cup and saucer for Mr. Burton? Mr. Burton, this is Barbara Greene. This is her fourth year here and I can't imagine what it will be like next year without her."

From a mahogany cabinet Barbara brought a second delicate cup and saucer and set it on the silver tray. "Is there anything else, Madame?"

"No, thank you, dear. Aggie says she feels much better this afternoon and will be up and about again tomorrow. Have a pleasant time at the opera."

"Thank you, Madame. Good night. Good night, Mr. Burton."

Barbara left, moving with a gliding grace completely unlike

Deirdre's bounce, but in its cool way equally effective. Madame Septmoncel smiled across the desk at Walter as she poured coffee and handed him a cup. "You would never believe, seeing Barbara now, that four years ago she was so clumsy she could hardly enter a room without knocking into something."

"Good heavens, no!" Walter exclaimed.

"She is a brilliant girl," Madame Septmoncel said. "In the four years she has been with me she has done her last two years of school and four years of college. Four years ago you might have been aware that she has brains, but her beauty was not yet visible."

"It is now," Walter said, dutifully and truthfully.

"You see, that is part of what we are for," Madame Septmoncel said. "Barbara could have shared an apartment with another girl, or lived in a dormitory, or in one of those residence clubs that are solely for the purpose of chaperonage. We try to give our girls much more than that."

"Yes," Walter agreed. "I can see that you do."

"There is no longer any such thing as a finishing school in the old sense, and in any case I am not interested in girls who do not wish to use their brains as well as their bodies. A truly cultured woman is charming both mentally and physically. Some of my girls come from wealthy families but have gone to school in the middle west where English is an unknown language. They have to learn to speak it almost as though it were French. Your sister, of course, had none of the obvious problems. She's considered very highly at her dramatic school, and I don't think she will need her imaginary Walter for very long. But the fact that she *does* need him right now shows that she has her own particular needs that we hope to fill. I limit my girls to fifteen in number, so that I am able to give each one the personal counsel she demands. As well as their regular courses the girls are given lessons here in music and art appreciation, in French, in diction, and in deportment, if that is needed. We go to the theatre, to the opera, to museums. What we aim for is a rounded, integrated personality."

"I see," Walter said. Now the violin was playing a melody, its tone lush like velvet, like firelight. Natalia's violin was quite a different instrument from the one Walter had dutifully sawed at—and not touched in six months.

"We tend to forget," Madame Septmoncel was saying, "in our feministic and emancipated world, that a woman is more than a voter, a stockholder, a highly paid executive. She should also be a work of art. She must have the ability to excite and surprise, to give pleasure and to exert over us a charm that has both sweetness and strength. Otherwise, regardless of her position or bank account, she has failed as a woman."

"I see," Walter said again.

Madame Septmoncel looked up, as though she, too, was listening to the winding notes of the violin. "Natalia," she said softly. "If you know anything about music, Mr. Burton, you can hear that Natalia is one of the very special artists. I believe that she will be one of the great artists of our time. But more than that, Mr. Burton, she is also becoming a woman and she has the wisdom to realize that that, too, is an art, and that it takes as much work as does her violin."

She stood up and Walter had perforce to rise, too. The interview could be prolonged no longer. He took Madame Septmoncel's hand and again was surprised at the strength in the delicate, ringed fingers, and yet he felt that he should not be shaking these fingers but raising them to his lips and breathing in the subtle fragrance that came from the—what was she, the headmistress? Of this—school?

Deirdre was waiting with Nancy in the lemon satin room, a Nancy somehow less gauche and coltish than the child he had waved goodbye to a few months ago. She wore a dark wool dress he did not recognize that gave her a new assurance, and he felt a sudden pride as he saw that her childish prettiness was maturing into beauty. She flung her arms about his neck in spontaneous affection, then looked at him imploringly.

"Walter, it was so terribly sweet of you to come. Deirdre says you're as nice as your picture but I told her you're really ever so much nicer. Have you seen Madame?"

"Yes," Walter said.

"Isn't she gorgeous? I mean isn't she the most beautiful woman you've ever met in the world?"

"Well," Walter said shortsightedly, "I suppose for an elderly lady she's quite good-looking. Have you signed in the book or whatever it was you're supposed to do?"

"How did you know about signing in the book?"

"A girl came in while I was talking to your—to Madame Septmoncel, and said something about it."

"Who was it?" Deirdre asked eagerly.

"I think she was called Barbara. Quite a looker."

"Oh," Deirdre said. "One of the madame's pets. Of course, if you like that ice cold sort of look—"

"Oh, she's gorgeous, all right, even if she is a snob," Nancy said impatiently, "and I guess she was pretty much a slob before Madame got hold of her. Fifty pounds heavier at least. Come on,

Walter, let's go. I haven't got Barbara's privileges and I'm supposed to be in at a reasonable hour unless I get very special permission."

Walter held out his hands to Deirdre. "It's been a pleasure meeting you, Miss O'Hara."

"Oh, just call me Deirdre. I've been calling you Walter. Anytime you're in New York and you don't feel like seeing Nancy, just give me a buzz." She took his hand and smiled up at him, batting the long lashes he had earlier remarked on.

"Quite a girl, your friend Deirdre," he said to Nancy as they went down the brownstone steps.

Nancy looked a little sulky. "Yes, and she was all ready to snatch you right out from under my nose."

"Why shouldn't she?" Walter asked pointedly. "After all, I'm your brother, and I do have dates with girls, you know. As a matter of fact I'd like to have one sometime with your friend Deirdre."

Nancy looked deflated. "Okay," she said vaguely. "I'll see if I can arrange it sometime."

"Will you? But you don't have to arrange it for me, do you, Nancy? I can just call or write Deirdre myself, can't I?"

She stopped still on the darkening street, looked up at him with an anxious expression. "Walter, are you mad at me or something?"

Walter hailed a taxi and said nothing until it had drawn up. Nancy ducked into it, and as he sat beside her all he said was "Where do you want to go?"

"Oh, I don't care."

"Well, think of someplace, quick. You know I don't know this place too well."

"Oh, well, the Penthouse Club, then. Barbara is there all the time."

"Will she be there tonight?"

"No. Harry is going to take her to Cavanagh's before they go to the opera. It's *Pagliacci* tonight. Barbara loves it."

"Who's Harry?"

"Her elderly beau. He's loaded, though. Walter, you're mad at me, aren't you?"

The taxi jerked its way through the crowded street, stopped behind a truck at a red light. "I don't know whether I'm mad at you or not," Walter said at last. "I just want to know what this is all about."

"I tried to tell you in my letters," Nancy said. "But it's such a *difficult* thing to explain. You didn't say anything to Father, did you?"

"No. I would have, but then I got this chance to come down on business, and knowing you I thought I'd come see for myself."

"What do you mean, knowing me?"

"Well, I didn't want Father after you with a cordon of police unless there was a real reason."

Nancy laughed, but it wasn't an anxious laugh. "That's silly about the police, Walter. After all, it's not like white slavery or anything."

The last of the daylight was disappearing behind the buildings and lights were going on in streetlamps, shops, offices. In the gloom of the taxi Walter tried to read Nancy's expression. Finally he said irritably, "Nancy, you're my sister, and I've known you all my life, and this autumn is the first time you've ever been away from home, but I'm damned if I know anything about you."

"You said damn!" Nancy exclaimed.

"So?"

"It just sounded so grown-up, coming from you." She leaned back in the cab, crossing her legs so that they showed, long and slender, under the dark skirt.

Walter closed his mouth tight to keep from shouting back an angry retort, to keep from fighting as though they were brother and sister in the nursery again. "Nancy," he said, "did you really expect me to believe that cock-and-bull story?"

Nancy lowered her head and all she responded was a whisper. "Yes."

"Well, I don't believe it."

"Okay, Walter," Nancy said softly, "don't, then. It makes it easier."

Now Walter shouted. "It makes *what* easier?"

"Oh, everything. You see, it was all such a surprise to me when I first wrote to you, but now I'm more used to the idea, and it doesn't shock me anymore, and if you don't believe me then I don't have to worry about shocking you."

"Nancy, you haven't—"

"Haven't what?"

"You know."

"Then you *do* believe me!" Nancy exclaimed triumphantly.

"I don't!"

The taxi stopped and this time it wasn't a red light but the restaurant. Walter paid the driver, then opened the door for Nancy. She stood there in the light of a streetlamp, wearing a dark coat with a little fur collar and a hat with feathers, and he thought that she was much prettier than he had remembered. He took her arm as they went to the lobby and then up in the elevator, and now he had lost the sense of excitement and pleasure that had come to him talking with Deirdre, and wished that Nancy had never written him, or that he had had the sense to show the letter to his father.

He turned to her in the elevator and saw that she was staring with a serious, considering expression at her reflection in the long mirror. "Nancy," he said, "Father hasn't shown me any of your letters to him, but I know you've written. What have you said to him?"

"What do you suppose I've said?" she asked. "What he wants to hear. How I'm loving dramatic school."

"And aren't you?"

"Yes, of course I am," she said impatiently.

"Go on."

"How we all adore Madame. What terrific school spirit we have. All perfectly true. We do. And I told them how we love the concerts, the dressing for dinner every night, and how we take turns serving coffee in the drawing room afterwards. We'd be at home in Buckingham Palace after a year or two under Madame."

"Or?" Walter asked.

"Yes, or." She grinned. "You do believe me?"

"No," Walter said. "Why should I? Ever since Mother's death your life has been nothing but a web of lies."

"Do you think that's when it started?"

"Isn't it?"

"Walter darling, I'm an actress. I'm not going to dramatic school for fun, no matter what you and Father may think. Part of my life has always been make-believe. Part of it always will.

77

It's one of the most important pieces of an actress's luggage. As long as I know which is fact and which is fiction, that's all that matters."

"But do you know?"

"Yes, Walter, I do. What I wrote you about is hardly a joke."

"Nancy," he said. "Maybe you can keep fact and fiction clear in your own mind, but how do you expect other people to do it, too? How can anybody know when you're telling the truth?"

"Anybody who really knew me would know," Nancy said sadly. "But then of course you've never bothered to understand me, Walter. We've had a lot of fun together, we've had our share of sibling quarrels. I suppose we love each other quite deeply, but we don't really know each other at all."

"Do any two people?"

"I think Madame knows me," Nancy said. "I'm sure I know Deirdre far better than I do you. And most of the other girls. I'm not sure about Barbara or Natalia. They are Madame's specials and they *are* special."

"Would you like to be one of Madame's specials?"

"Of course. And I will be. I just haven't been there long enough."

"And how does what you wrote me about fit in with this?"

Nancy smiled dreamily at the waiter as he removed her hors d'oeuvre plate. "I feel differently about it now. Then it was only from things Deirdre had said, and she isn't one of Madame's specials, in spite of all that Madame has done for her."

"Does Deirdre think Madame has done so much for her?"

"Oh, sure, Deirdre's no fool. She's just jealous." Now the waiter put a dish in front of her, removing the lid with a flourish and looking at Nancy for approval. Nancy smiled at him again. "It looks just beautiful," she said. "Thank you so much."

A few months ago, Walter thought, waiters were not looking to Nancy for special approval. Had she acquired the ability to excite and surprise that Madame Septmoncel had spoken about, the charm that has both weakness and strength?

"Of course," she said seriously to Walter, "if you look at it objectively, it can be a tremendous help to my career. I'm going to be a *great* actress, Walter, and I've learned enough in the past couple of months to know that this takes ruthlessness as well as talent. Contacts can be used quite cold-bloodedly, you know. It isn't necessary to get emotionally involved. A lot of money can be quite useful, too."

"Is this the role," Walter asked in distress, "or is this Nancy?"

"Which?" she asked, smiling at him, spoiling it by batting her eyes in a manner too reminiscent of Deirdre's.

"And what about marriage," he asked, "and children, and all the things a normal woman wants?"

"Am I a normal woman?" she asked back. "Or do normal women really want these things? Isn't it something we've been made to think we want simply for the preservation of the species?"

"Nancy," Walter Burton said desperately, "if any of these things is—or should become—true, you'd have to give up all ideas of marriage. You're young and ambitious now, but you may feel differently later on and then it would be too late."

"But why?" she asked gaily.

"Don't you know? Don't you know that no decent man would have you?"

"I don't know any such thing. Many of Madame's girls have made excellent marriages. And most of them have her to thank for them, too. And they do, you know. There's hardly a week one or two doesn't come for dinner, and usually with their husbands, so I've had a chance to see just how well they've done."

"Nancy," Walter said sharply, "I hate to see you getting so under the influence of any one woman. It's a spell, really."

"Oh, no," Nancy said definitely. "I know exactly what I'm doing. Madame isn't using me. I'm using her. She knows it, too. That's why I am going to be one of her specials. She doesn't like blind adoration. Natalia's going to be a famous violinist and it's mostly thanks to Madame and she knows it, but she isn't thanking Madame, she's simply using her as a stepping stone."

"And how much help would Madame be if Natalia didn't have talent?"

"Oh, talent," Nancy said impatiently. "Thousands of people have talents. Thousands of actresses have talent but they'll go on having milkshakes in a drugstore when I'm having champagne and caviar."

"And for this you are willing to—to let yourself be bought and sold?"

"Whenever an actress signs for a part, what else is she doing but selling herself? What else is the management doing but buying her? I'm just making myself more—more interesting. Maybe you might say more available. Walter, I'd like some wine with this dinner."

"You're not twenty-one," Walter said.

"Oh, you're so stuffy. I could pass for twenty-one without any trouble, couldn't I?"

"I don't know," Walter said grimly, "but you're not going to try. Nancy, when I said goodbye to you in September you were still wet behind the ears—" He flung his fork against his plate with so much force that the waiter came hurrying up, asking, "Anything wrong, sir?"

Nancy smiled up at him again. "Everything is just lovely." She looked over at Walter tolerantly and raised her lovely brows ever so slightly. She did not look at the waiter, but he smiled at her as though they had a very special secret between them.

"Now what are you so furious about?" Nancy asked as the waiter discreetly withdrew.

"Believing you. I don't mean to, but you've always managed to make me, no matter how outrageous your stories." Then he pointed a sudden angry finger at her. "But hey, what about me, Nancy? What about your dear friend Walter Burton who just happens to have your surname?"

Nancy laughed merrily. "Oh, Walter darling, that was just sort of self-defense. All of the other girls have someone and you just came in so handy."

"What about Arnold?"

Nancy laughed again. "Him? I keep his picture hidden in the bottom of my suitcase."

"But he writes you three letters a week at least, doesn't he?"

"Oh, sure."

"Do you answer them?"

"Oh, just often enough to keep him hanging on, as sort of insurance."

"Nancy, that's—that's dastardly."

Nancy grinned. "Sure. I'm a dastard."

"Nancy, you didn't have to make me up. There isn't only Arnold. There are half a dozen other boys at home who pant whenever they see you."

"Callow infants."

"But you've let Madame Septmoncel think there isn't anybody, haven't you?"

"But there *isn't* anybody. Nobody that counts. Only Walter Burton. And that's true, Walter. You're not in the same class with these other idiots. You're the only one worth making up a story about."

He tried not to be pleased; he couldn't believe her flattery any more than anything else she said.

"But why must you make up a story, Nancy? Why can't you just take things as they are?"

"Because I don't like things as they are. Well, at any rate I never have until this year. I don't think I'll be making up stories very much longer."

Walter looked away from her, down at his plate where his dinner still lay, almost untouched.

"Did you tell your Madame Septmoncel how Mother died?"

"No. It's far too fantastic." Suddenly she pushed back her chair. "I want to go home."

"Home?"

"Not home, you idiot. To—to the school."

"The school?"

"It is a school—in a way. I'm learning something for the first time in my life. I'm going to the ladies' room, Walter. I'll wait for you by the elevator."

He paid the bill to a disapproving waiter, feeling that he had handled neither Nancy nor the situation as they should have been handled, and that he knew no more than when he had first gone down the street and climbed the brownstone steps and seen the polished brass plaque: MADAME SEPTMONCEL'S RESIDENCE FOR YOUNG LADIES.

Nancy was waiting for him by the elevator, her face composed and freshly powdered, but, he thought, rather pale. They went down in the elevator in silence and stood out in the street, waiting as the doorman blew his whistle for a taxi. No, Walter thought, looking at Nancy with her soft, honey-blond hair shining out under the hat with feathers and falling softly against the little fur collar of her coat. She wouldn't get away with saying she was twenty-one, that she couldn't do, except for her eyes, and her eyes had always been ancient, even when she was a tiny child.

"So what are you going to do?" Nancy asked as she leaned back against the leather seat of the taxi.

"About what?"

"About me. About what I wrote you."

For a long time Walter was silent. The taxi moved like a small bug through the streets, wriggling past cabs, past buses, past trucks. At last he said, "Nothing."

Almost imperceptibly she relaxed. "Nothing?"

"No."

"Why not? I thought you'd come to save me."

"But you don't want to be saved, do you, Nancy?"

She smiled again, the smile that was meant to be far more than twenty-one. "Not particularly."

"And I can't do it to Father," he said. "I can't say anything while I'm not sure. You've done that at least, Nancy; you can have at least that satisfaction. You planted a doubt in my mind. I'm not sure."

The passing lights illuminated her face, let it fall into shadow, and then brightened it again. She sat quietly, relaxed, her brow clear and innocent, the tender corners of her lips just faintly turned up. "Darling Walter," she said gently, "you don't want to believe it. You'll be much happier not believing it. That's best for us both, I see it now. But you'll come again and take me out to dinner, won't you?"

"I suppose so. If there's any reason for me to leave the office."

"And you'll just be Walter Burton who happens to have the same name that I do?"

"If it's that important to you."

The taxi turned down the quiet street. "Where are you staying?" Nancy asked.

"At the Y."

"Don't get out with me. I'll run on in. You keep the taxi and go on."

Surprisingly Walter agreed; he felt old and tired and the thought of climbing the brownstone steps with Nancy, of going into the building, seemed a physical effort of which he was not capable. "I'll wait to see that you get in safely."

She leaned to him and kissed him gently on the cheek. "Good night, big brother."

She slipped out, slammed the taxi door, and ran up the steps. The streetlights cast a pale glow on the brass plaque. She stood for a moment searching through her small velvet bag for the key, found it, put it in the door, and opened it. As she closed it behind her she heard the taxi drawing away and she sighed with satisfaction. It had been a most successful evening. She wondered if Deirdre was asleep.

She paused at the mahogany table under the mirror to sign her name and the hour in the book. The door to the lemon satin parlor was closed and voices came from it, masculine laughter and girls' giggles; a couple of the girls must be having dates there. The door to Madame Septmoncel's drawing room opened and out came a man in evening clothes, carrying a top hat in his hands. He was followed by Madame herself in pearl-gray chiffon. As he passed Nancy he looked at her appraisingly and whispered something to Madame. Madame merely smiled and nodded, saying as she passed, "Wait just a moment before you go upstairs, Nancy, dear." She went to the front door with the impeccable gentleman, and stood there a moment talking to him. They were speaking in what Nancy took to be French, and so low that the girl could not understand their words. Then the gentleman kissed Madame's hand (as Walter would have liked to have kissed it that afternoon) and left, and Madame came back to Nancy.

"Well, and did you have a nice evening with your Walter, my dear Nancy?"

"Yes, thank you, Madame."

"You're in a little earlier than I expected."

"Walter was—Walter was tired, Madame."

"And you? Are you tired?"

"No, Madame. I'm never tired."

"That's my Nancy. Well, come on into the drawing room, then, and sit in front of the fire and have a cup of coffee with me. Since we didn't expect you back so soon I told Natalia she might use your room for a little while tonight. It's been a busy evening."

Nancy stood very still in the dark hall, trying to stare through the gloom at Madame.

"You mean she's practicing?"

Madame laughed. "If you want to call it that. But Natalia is so finished at everything she does one can hardly call it practicing, can one?" She moved slowly down the hall, moving with a grace that Barbara only imperfectly and Deirdre never would be able to copy. Nancy stood still, for the first time uncertain, her heart beating rapidly, a faint tremor of suspicion tingling her flesh. Why hadn't Walter come in with her, bringing with him the safe fabric of lies? Why had he left her? What was happening?

Madame turned around. The tiger-striped cat slid out of the drawing room and down the hall, brushing deliberately, smoothly, against Nancy's ankles.

"Come, Nancy," Madame said. "I think we'll find we have a good deal to talk about."

One Day in Spring

Every life has a turning point. Several turning points, probably, but there's always one that stands out as *the* turning point, without which the course of life would be totally different.

For Noel Townshend it came on a day in spring. Without that day, none of the summer, the working in the theatre, the knowing Kurt, the beginning of a completely new life, would have been possible.

Even then she had been aware of it. Sitting there she had thought, *How strange to know that the whole course of my life can be changed in a dingy room smelling of cigar smoke and cheap perfume!*

But it was true. It was so frighteningly true that her hands felt cold with fear and her heart beat so fast that for a moment she was afraid that she might faint in the hot stuffiness of the little room. Although it was unseasonably hot for an April day, steam hissed in the radiator, and there was no window in the ante-room. There was not even an open door.

Because she had not been able to sit still another moment she went over to the receptionist.

"My appointment with Mr. Price was at two o'clock and it is after three now."

"Yeah?" The receptionist looked at her with a hot, annoyed face.

"I mean—he's still going to see me, isn't he?"

"You've got an appointment card, haven't you?"

"Yes."

"Okay then, relax. Sit down. Though why you want to see him I don't know. I'm sure he doesn't want to see you."

Noel sat down again. She felt miserable and young, and more than snubbed. She looked down at her feet because she was afraid that if she looked at the others she would find scorn in their faces.

"Don't let it get you down," the girl next to her said. "I've been in an office where the receptionist said, 'Thank you for coming in' after she told me the cast was all set. They're not all like sourpuss here—though with a second-rate theatre like Price's running, I don't know why we're all hanging around here like a lot of trained seals waiting for him to throw us a fish."

The door to the hall opened and a young man entered. The moment he came in, a slight, pleasant smile on his face, Noel saw that there was something different about him, that he was not like anybody else in the room. And then she realized what the difference was: he was the only one who was not nervous.

He walked over to the receptionist's desk: "Hi, Sadie, how's my duck today?" He had a slight accent.

The sour face was amazingly pleasant when it smiled. "Oh,

dying of heat, Mr. Canitz. Otherwise I guess I'll survive. You want to see Mr. Price?"

"If he's not too busy."

"Oh, he always has time to see you, Mr. Canitz. Go right in."

The young man smiled his pleasant smile at the roomful of hot, nervous people and opened the door to Mr. Price's office. Noel looked in quickly and saw a room very like the ante-room, except that it had a large opened window and a brief, welcome gust of cool air blew in at her. Mr. Price was sitting at his desk talking to a young woman with blond hair, and he waved his hand genially at Mr. Canitz. "Oh, come in, Kurt. I want you to meet this young lady."

Then the door shut and heat settled back over the room. "If I had sense," the girl next to Noel said, "I'd leave this hell hole and go home. So would you."

"Home," said Noel, "is the last place I'd go."

"Well, then, I guess you have a point in hanging around. Why don't they open the door or something? Why don't they at least open the door into the hall? Why don't they turn off the heat?" She appealed to Sadie. "Couldn't you turn off the heat or something?"

"No, I can't," the receptionist snapped. "The radiator's broken, and I'm just as hot as you are. Hotter. If you don't like it here, why don't you get out? I tell you, he isn't going to hire anybody else. He's got the whole season set. You're wasting your time."

The girl turned back to Noel. "That's the way people get ulcers. People with vile natures always get ulcers. If I stay here much longer, I'll get ulcers, too."

"But is it true?"

"What?"

"That the whole season is set."

"Of course it isn't true. She only said it because she's in a vile mood. What's your name? I'm Jane Gardner."

"I'm Noel Townshend."

"Listen, I don't mean to butt in," Jane said, "but don't be so nervous. You're practically making the bench shake. After all, the world isn't going to end if Price doesn't give you a job. Nothing is that important."

"But it is," Noel said, "for me it is."

The door to the office opened again and Kurt Canitz and the blond young woman came out. Mr. Canitz had his arm protectively about her. He ushered her gallantly to the door. Then he smiled at Sadie and looked around the room. His eyes rested on Jane, on Noel, on a little man in a bowler hat. Sadie picked up a stack of cards and called out, "Gardner."

Jane rose: "That's me—well, it's only the fifteenth office I've been in today. What've I got to lose?"

Noel watched her as she walked swiftly into the office, shutting the door firmly behind her. Yes, Jane was obviously a person who knew her way around theatrical offices. She had a certain nervous excitement, like every actor waiting to hear about a job, but it was controlled, made into an asset; it gave a shine to her brown eyes, a spring to her step. Noel felt Jane was dressed correctly, too. She wore a pleated navy-blue skirt and a little red jacket. Her hair was very fair, a soft ash blond, and on it she wore a small red beret. Noel felt forlorn in the other girl's absence, and suddenly foolish. She herself wore a simple blue denim skirt and a white blouse, and she felt that she belonged much more on a college campus than she did in a theatrical office on Forty-Second Street in New York. If someone as desirable as Jane had been in fifteen offices that morning and still did not have a job, then what was Noel thinking of when she was letting everything in the world depend on whether or not Mr. J. P. Price took her into his summer theatre company?

But Mr. Price was the only one who had sent her a possible answer to Noel's letters of inquiry about summer stock companies. Many of the managers had offered her opportunities to apprentice but at two or three hundred dollars' tuition fee. Mr. Price had simply sent her a card telling her to be at his office at two o'clock, April 14th, and he would see her then.

She looked around the office and thought, with an odd combination of defiance and forlornness, *Well, even if nothing comes of this, I've seen something of how the professional theatre works, anyway.*

She looked around her at the dingy ante-room; the buff-colored walls were cracked and some of the cracks were partially covered with signed photographs of actors and actresses of whom she had never heard. There were no familiar names like Judith Anderson, Katharine Cornell, Eva Le Gallienne, Ethel Barrymore. The air was thick with smoke, cigarette smoke overpowered by cigar smoke from the little man in the bowler hat who sat stolidly on a folding chair, surrounding himself with a cloud of heavy fumes. The small room was full of hot and heavy smells: smoke, perspiration, Sadie's perfume, the humidity of the day.

She noticed Kurt Canitz sitting across the room from her writing busily in a small notebook. He looked up and stared directly at her for several seconds, then scribbled something else in the notebook, tore off the page, and gave it to Sadie with a radiant smile, and left. Noel wondered what his connection was with the theatre—was he an actor, a director, perhaps a producer?

Again the door of the office opened, and Jane came out. She grinned at Noel.

"Did you get the job?" Noel asked eagerly.

"Well, not exactly the job I went for, but at this point it'll do. I'm going as an apprentice, which I swore last summer I'd never do again, but this time at least I got a scholarship."

"Oh, I'm so glad!" Noel exclaimed. "That's wonderful!"

"Thanks," Jane said. "Good luck to you, too."

Sadie was looking at her cards again. "Townshend," she called. Noel stood up.

Jane took her hand. "Good luck, *really*. I hope I see you there."

"Thanks," Noel answered, and went into the office.

"Well, what do you want?" Mr. Price asked her, looking her up and down until Noel flinched. "What can I do for you?"

"You can give me a job," Noel said, and was surprised at how calm her voice sounded.

"And what kind of a job are you looking for, my dear?"

"A job in your summer theatre. As an actress." Noel felt that her voice sounded flat and colorless; anxiety had wiped out its usual resonance.

"And what experience have you had? What parts have you played?"

Noel ignored the first part of his question. "I've played Lady Macbeth and Ophelia, and I've played Hilda Wangel in *The Master Builder* and Sudermann's Magda, and the Sphinx in Cocteau's *The Infernal Machine*."

"A bit on the heavy side, wouldn't you say?" Mr. Price asked her. "And aren't you a little bit young for Lady Macbeth or Magda? How about something more recent—perhaps a little gayer?"

"Well, I've played Blanche in *Streetcar*—Oh, I know that's not very gay, but it's recent—and—I've done some Chekhov. One-acters, they're not very recent, but they're gay."

"And where did you get all this magnificent experience?" Mr. Price asked her. "Why, after all this, have I never heard of you?"

"At college," Noel said, looking down at her feet.

"My dear young lady." Mr. Price sounded half-bored, half-amused. "Perhaps you do not realize, but I am running a professional theatre. I am sure you were very charming and very highly acclaimed at college, but I am really not contemplating producing *Macbeth* or *Magda*, or even *The Infernal Machine*. So what have I to offer you?"

"All I want is," Noel said desperately, "anything."

"Anything what?"

"Maids, walk-ons, working in the box office. Anything."

"I take a certain number of apprentices," Mr. Price said. "The fee is five hundred dollars."

Noel shook her head. "I borrowed the money to come to New York to see you today. I—I—"

"And I suppose if I don't give you a job you'll jump off the Empire State Building? Or into the Hudson River? Or perhaps the East River would suit you better?"

"That's not funny!" Noel said with a sudden flare of anger. "Would you really laugh if you were responsible for someone's death?"

"If you did anything so foolish as to kill yourself, I wouldn't be responsible, you would." Mr. Price's voice was calm and reasonable.

"As it happens," Noel said, anger still directing her words, "I agree with you. And I do not approve of suicide under any conditions. However, a weaker character in my circumstances might."

Now Mr. Price smiled. "Are your circumstances so very particular?"

"To me they are. You never know what people's circumstances are."

"Perhaps I can guess some of yours. You go to a good college and major in drama. Your family has a thoroughly adequate income."

"Wrong," Noel said. "I go to a good college but I major in chemistry and I am on a scholarship and I have no parents."

"I stand corrected."

Noel looked at him, tried to smile, and said, "And now, since you haven't a job to offer me, I'll say goodbye and go and throw myself under a Fifth Avenue bus."

The door to the office opened and Sadie thrust her head in. "Say, Mr. Price, I almost forgot, Mr. Canitz left me another note to give to you."

"Kurt is far too fond of putting his opinions down on paper. Someday it's going to get him into a lot of trouble," Mr. Price said. He read the note and handed it to Noel.

Kurt Canitz's writing was strong and European-looking. He had written, "Give the tall girl with glasses a scholarship. I have a hunch about her."

Mr. Price looked at Noel. "You're tall—rather tall for an

actress, incidentally—and you wear glasses, so I assume Kurt means you. By the way, how does it happen that you don't take off your glasses for an interview?"

"I can't see without them," Noel said. "I meant to take them off, but I forgot. I don't wear them on stage, of course."

"I suppose I'll have to answer to Kurt if I don't at least have you read for me. All right, read for me."

"If you like me, will you give me a scholarship?" Noel asked.

Mr. Price looked at her as Kurt Canitz looked at her, as though she were a horse he was appraising. "I'm known for being—shall we kindly call it being shrewd—about money, but as far as the theatre is concerned I also have a conscience. I collect as many hundred dollars' tuition as I can. If a girl can offer it, why shouldn't I take it? However, if I think a kid has possibilities I take her for the summer and I work her like a dog and I give her at least a couple of walk-ons and maybe a part if I think she can do it—or he, as the case may be—and for the benefit of these budding young workers in the theatre, I create scholarships. Usually two for young men and two for girls. I have both my men set and one of my women. You might possibly fit the other scholarship. Of course there's room and board, but perhaps you could manage that? The apprentices and most of the resident company live at a cottage a few blocks from the theatre. The scholarship apprentices pay the minimum of twenty dollars a week. Could you manage that?"

"I'll have to," Noel said.

"I have the feeling that you're a hard worker," Mr. Price told her. "Also, believe it or not, I have a healthy regard for Kurt Canitz's hunches—and also for his dollars, which help finance the theatre. More of a respect for his dollars and his hunches than

I have for his acting, I might add, though I could pick a worse director. Okay, now read something for me." He picked up a dog-eared copy of *The Voice of the Turtle*. "This is pretty much of a classic in its own way," he said. "Maybe you won't feel too much above it."

Noel stood up. "Mr. Price, I know you're laughing at me, and I know you have a perfect right to. Maybe the parts I've played are silly. I didn't do them because I expected to replay my college triumphs on Broadway, but because they're parts anyone who really cares about becoming an actress ought to study, and because it was my one real opportunity to work on them—until I'm an established actress and can really do them if I want to. Perhaps I won't want to then. But I'll have learned a lot from them that I can apply to anything I do."

"Pretty sure of yourself, aren't you?" Mr. Price asked her.

"No, but I have to talk as though I were."

Mr. Price sighed: "Darling Miss Townshend—it is Townshend, isn't it?—there are so many like you. So many who believe in themselves as potential great ones—and many who don't have the handicaps of being tall and wearing glasses—so many who have real talent. Do you know that with ten young women of equal talent only one of them can possibly succeed? And of those who succeed only one out of ten is honorable, only one out of ten puts theatre above herself?"

"I'm willing to risk it," Noel said.

Mr. Price sighed again. "All right—read for me."

"What shall I read?" Noel took the book from him.

"Just hunt for a couple of longish passages. One of Sally's, one of Olive's. Are you familiar with the play?"

"We did it in college. I directed it, though; I didn't play in it."

"Good. That means you ought to know it pretty well, but you won't be giving me a rehash of an old performance. Found something?"

"Yes. Here's a speech of Sally's." Noel read the speech slowly, not trying to force a quick characterization. She made her voice low and pleasant, her words quick and clear and well defined, but she felt that she was failing thoroughly, that Mr. Price expected a performance. When she had finished the speech she said, "I'm sorry it was so bad. I don't work very quickly. I mean, I can't plunge into a character right away."

"No, and you had sense enough not to try," Mr. Price told her, and for the first time his smile was for her, not at her. "One of the great banes of my existence is the radio actor who gives a magnificent first reading and then deteriorates until his performance is thoroughly mediocre, if, indeed, it is possible at all. Many of my headaches have come from replacing a radio actor with a legit actor who gave a mediocre initial reading but ended up with a magnificent performance. Each time I cast a show I say that I won't be fooled, and each time I am fooled. Okay, Miss Townshend, don't bother to read any more. If you want to come under the terms I've outlined—as a scholarship apprentice—you may."

Noel sat down abruptly. "Yes, I want to," she said, and her voice sounded as though Mr. Price had punched her in the stomach.

"Good. Give Sadie your address and she will drop you a line as to trains and when to arrive and so forth. Also I will have her send you a note confirming all this so that once you get back to that good college of yours you won't worry about my forgetting you. Goodbye, Miss Townshend. I'll look forward to seeing you at the end of June, and you, in the meanwhile, may look forward to a summer of hard work."

"Yes, thank you," Noel said, still sounding winded.

Mr. Price smiled at her again. "And one more thing: I hope you realize that I'm offering you this opportunity not because of your reading but because of Mr. Canitz's hunch and my own whim. The theatre is not a reasonable place. You may as well learn that now." He held out his hand to her.

Noel shook it and left the office. She almost missed Jane Gardner, who was standing in the dim corridor leaning against a fire extinguisher.

"Hello. How did you make out?" Jane asked her. "I thought I'd wait and see."

"I've got a scholarship," Noel told her, beaming and very pleased at Jane's friendly interest.

"Oh, good. I'm awfully glad. Look, let's go have a cup of coffee at the Automat to celebrate."

Noel hesitated and then said, "I don't think I want any coffee, but I'd love to come while you have yours."

"Fine."

They went in the elevator, both smiling with a vague and dreamy happiness at the prospect of the summer ahead of them. And to Noel, New York was no longer frightening, but suddenly full of excitement and glamor, and the starkness of the Automat was vested in glory because Noel Townshend and Jane Gardner were going there and perhaps one day other struggling young actresses would say, "Do you know, Noel Townshend and Jane Gardner used to come here!" The great and famous Noel Townshend and Jane Gardner.

Noel sat at one of the tables and waited until Jane came back with two cups of coffee. "Just thought you might have changed your mind," she said casually. "If you don't want it, I'll drink it—or, look, if you're broke or something at the moment—and heavens knows almost everybody in the theatre is—you can pay me back sometime."

"But that's just the trouble. I probably can't," Noel said. Her voice sounded rather desperate.

Jane looked at her with friendly curiosity for a moment, then said lightly, "What's a cup of coffee between friends? Anyhow, I was referring to the golden future when we're both rich and famous and have our names in lights. Look, let's get to know each other. I'll give you my autobiography and you can give me yours. Though as for me, I'm a lot more exciting than my autobiography."

Noel laughed. "Me, too."

"I'm just a damned good actress," Jane said. "How about you?"

"I'm a damn good actress, too."

"Good. Now we know the most important things about each other. As for the unimportant details, I was born in New York and have lived here most of my life. My father teaches higher mathematics at Columbia, and I can't count up to ten. Neither can my mother, who is highly beautiful, but has never made me feel like an ugly duckling. I've graduated from Columbia, against my will, and on my parents' insistence, though they're both very nice about my wanting to be an actress, and last winter I went to the American Academy and fell madly in love with a great young actor named John Peter Toller, who also—and for this I get down on my knees and it's why I took this scholarship because

I'd rather have a scholarship with John Peter than a job anywhere else, though I honestly did try to get a job; I told you I'd been to dozens of other offices this morning—anyhow, where was I? Oh, yes, John Peter has a scholarship with Price this summer, too. He's been away for two weeks visiting his parents and during these past fourteen days my life has been blighted. I feel as though I weren't breathing when I'm out of his presence. He's the oxygen in my air, the sun in my universe, the staff of my life. From this you may gather that he means a great deal to me, but please don't tell him because he knows it far too well already. Now, tell me about you."

A sober, rather sad look crossed Noel's face. Then she said lightly, "There isn't much to tell. My parents are dead and I live with my aunt in Virginia. She doesn't approve of the theatre. I've graduated from college this spring, I'm foot-loose and fancy free."

"Well, let me warn you of one thing, my dear young woman," Jane said, finishing her coffee and leaning back in the chair. "Don't let your fancies fall on Kurt Canitz."

"I don't think I'm going to let my fancies fall on anyone, but why not on Kurt Canitz?" Noel asked.

"Too many fancies have fallen on him and his have fallen on too many."

"I think I'm safe," Noel said. "Men never make passes at girls who wear glasses, and anyhow, right now, I've no idea of letting an emotional entanglement hamper my career."

Jane laughed. "Now, if that doesn't sound like a college graduate. My emotional entanglement, if you want to call it that, hasn't hampered my career one bit. It's helped it. I know more about life and humanity and understanding and compassion and knowledge—and therefore about acting, too—since I've known my darling John Peter than I've ever dreamed of knowing before. Just you wait, my girl, you'll see."

"So?" Noel asked. But she sounded skeptical.

Jane pushed back her chair. "I've got to dash now. I promised my mother I'd meet her and do some shopping. Maybe we'll room together this summer. I hope so. Anyhow, I'll be seeing you at the end of June."

"Right," Noel said. "Good luck until then."

"And good luck to you, too."

They shook hands. Noel watched Jane walk swiftly out of the Automat, erect, graceful, assured, and somehow more alive than anyone else in the restaurant. Noel realized that Jane was probably well in advance of her as an actress, and then she thought happily, *But I'll learn!*

Now there was no need anymore for the Empire State Building, the East or the Hudson Rivers; life for her was not coming to an end; it was beginning.

Prelude to the First Night
Alone

All the lamps were on, and the shades to all but one had brown burnt spots where that red-headed Nicky Gatti had let the bulb press against the cheap parchment. The top of the in-laid mahogany table that stood in front of the red couch was covered with rings from the cold wet glasses of Cuba Libres that Nicky and his friends drank every night. The maroon velvet winter drapes were nailed up at the windows; Nicky hadn't even bothered to fix them properly.

So Paul looked at the burnt lamp shades, the ruined table top, stained rug, disarranged bookshelves, nailed-up curtains; and the anger that he had been holding back flared up inside him; a flame shot up in his stomach; fire filled his whole body; his cheeks burned crimson. He walked over to the window and jerked at one of the red velvet curtains, coughing as it came down in a cloud of dust.

Sitting curled up in the blue wing chair, trying not to show that she was uncomfortable, Estelle laughed. "I'll have to teach you to be neat, Nicky," she said. Paul stared out of the window, felt Nicky walk over to Estelle, put his arms around her, kiss her, tall and handsome in his uniform, his red hair bright above the khaki; Nicky secure with an easy desk job, Nicky secure in New York, Nicky secure with Estelle.

The afternoon autumn sun hit against the warehouse that faced the window, and some of it came back onto Paul, its reflection mocking his fair hair, his angry face that he would not let them see. With his back to them (Estelle and Nicky leaning close in her blue wing chair), Paul walked over to the sofa and lifted down from the wall the Renoir lady forever holding her green plaid rug about her shoulders, forever looking just a little like Estelle, the enchanting Renoir lady framed in voluptuous gold. Still with his back to them he leaned the picture against the sofa. "You bought her, Estelle. She goes with you."

"Oh, Paul, she goes with the apartment." Estelle pushed away from Nicky just for a moment, started to get up and go over to Paul, then leaned back in the chair again, resting her cheek against Nicky's hand. She had washed her hair the night before and it looked soft and lustrous. Nicky ran his fingers through the curly bangs. In a few days the hair would seem thin and oily, and she would have to wash it again. Tonight it would be up in bobby pins, little round flat curls each pierced with a small crucifix of two bobby pins, lying very flat against her head, making her face startlingly clear and large. She would sit on the bed in the sheer white nightgown with the strawberries embroidered on it and rub oil into the soles of her long feet; but it would not be the bed in the next room, it would be a bed in a hotel eight blocks away, a double bed in a small hotel room, a sordid room because Nicky deliberately loved sordidity no matter how much he talked. God damn Nicky for taking a room with a double bed, Paul thought; the whole business would not be so unbearable somehow if only Nicky had taken a room with twin beds.

"You and Nicky will take the picture, Estelle." Still not facing them, he went to the bookshelves and started taking out books, putting them in a pile on the floor.

"Oh, Paul, must you, darling?" she asked, and this time she got out of the blue chair, crossed the room, put her arms about Paul, turned his face around so he could see the tears in her large eyes.

He knew about those tears, how well he knew about those tears, but he wanted to put his arms around Estelle and press her close against him, to stroke her hair, kiss her tenderly, draw her into the bedroom and lie down next to her, kissing her softly, left eye, right eye, forehead, left ear, right ear, nose, left cheek, right cheek, chin, left shoulder, right shoulder, lips. When Nicky was gentle it was because he knew Estelle liked it, because he wanted to own her completely; not because gentleness and love and protection came welling up out of him like a fountain let loose at the sight of the too-easy tears brimming in Estelle's eyes.

Paul stood still while Estelle put her arms around him and showed him her tear-filled eyes. "Don't cry," he said, his voice that he wanted controlled suddenly seeming to crumple up. Then, "They're your books. I can't be a storage house for you and Nicky." He went about the apartment, collecting everything that belonged to Estelle and piling it up in the center of the rug. When he had finished he turned to them, Nicky still sitting on the edge of the blue wing chair, his arm around Estelle. "All right," Paul said, "clear it all out, will you? I want to get settled."

The bookshelves were gaping with empty spaces, empty spaces like missing teeth. The wallpaper showed dark squares where pictures had come down. Estelle got up and ran her finger over the gold frame of the Renoir lady. "Couldn't I just leave this for you, Paul?"

"No."

Nicky had bought a bunch of yellow chrysanthemums. They were in the blue ginger jar on the tail of the piano. Paul wanted to take them out and put them in the pile on the rug, but he left them spilling their golden stain onto the dark mahogany of the piano.

Nicky said, "You can't think you're going to get away with this, Paul. We're not going to let you. You'll see us every day."

"No."

"But why does this happen all of a sudden?" Nicky asked, putting his hand on Paul's shoulder, pressing five strong fingers into Paul's shoulder, peering with anxious eyes into Paul's face that tried to look composed and empty, but that was tight and angry and hurt, Paul's face that looked like a puppy's who has been beaten and kicked for something he has not done.

"What's the matter, Paul?" Nicky asked, and Paul wanted to laugh, to shout, "What's the matter, you damn fool!"

But Nicky was asking it seriously, his freckles standing out strongly with his intensity. "Nothing," Paul said, pulling away.

"But you weren't like this at first. Why now all of a sudden?"

"I'm supposed to meet someone for dinner in half an hour." Paul looked at his watch with the luminous dial and the second hand that had belonged to Estelle's father. "Start taking your things downstairs, for heaven's sake, Nicky." He didn't want to call him Nicky. He wanted to call him Gatti, by his last name, to spit at him, "Get the hell out of my home, Gatti. You've done your thieving. Now get the hell out."

But he just said, "Please," very hard, and picked up the picture of the Renoir lady and handed it to Nicky.

When Nicky had started down the stairs with the Renoir lady (forever hugging her green shawl about her shoulders), Estelle got up from the blue wing chair and put her arms about Paul. "Darling," she said. "You do understand that I love you dearly and tenderly? I always will. This is just something none of us could help. I wish you wouldn't behave this way, but if you must I know there isn't any use trying to force you. But it won't last. You'll see. I love you too much to let you go."

"All right," Paul said. "You have the icon, so I'll keep the records. That's fair, isn't it? Anyhow you and Nicky haven't a gramophone."

"Well, I don't know." Estelle looked at the records in the bottom shelf of the bookcase. "Some of the records are really mine."

"But the icon belonged to both of us." He had bought most of the records, paid for half the icon.

"Well, we'll see," Estelle said. "Because you mustn't forget I love you, darling, and I'm not going to let you become a hermit."

"I haven't any intention of becoming a hermit." He turned away from Estelle's warm body, jerked down the other maroon curtain Nicky had nailed up so casually. The dust from the curtain went up his nose as he folded it, and he thought of an afternoon long ago when he had gone to the museum with his aunt Barbara, who wore a coat made of two different kinds of fur, a huge coat that reached almost to her ankles. She wore heavy garnet earrings and a hat with ostrich feathers and a diamond dog collar about her throat that showed where the coat fell open in front. She looked the way the curtains smelled, and she had taken him to see the mummies. Holding his thin fingers that were never still, that were always picking at something, holding his hot fingers in her cold blue-veined hands, she said, "Your little hands are solid flesh and bone; but when they uncovered Egyptian boys who had been dead for thousands of years the skin and bone of their perfect little hands turned to dust. Because their bodies were there, preserved, for thousands of years, does that mean their souls could find no new home until their bodies were uncovered and turned to dust, until their old houses of bodies were gone forever? What do you think, Pauly? Tell me what you think?"

And Paul had looked up at her, answering solemnly, "I shouldn't think they would like to have their bodies turned to dust. I wouldn't."

That night he woke up in bed and called for Aunt Barbara in terror because he felt dust in the sheets and he was afraid for his body, afraid his soul would lose its comfortable home. But now, he thought, now that I am older I have learned that the soul can have its home in more than one body, and my soul is losing the home it loved so dearly for five years.

"What are you thinking?" Estelle asked sharply.

Paul finished folding the curtains. "I suppose I'll have to have these things cleaned." He went out to the hall and put them in the corner.

"Paul," Estelle called.

He stood still in the hall looking through the doorway into the living room, the two white china dogs next to the blue pickle jar lamp, the warm curves of the piano. Estelle's hair was the same shade as the mahogany piano but there was an aura of coldness about her even when her eyes filled with tears, even when her full mouth curved into a smile and she held out her arms. The piano stood in the lamplight, lamplight shining through burnt shades, red candles in the silver candlesticks on either side of the music rack, red wax drippings on the base of the candlesticks and on the mahogany of the piano. Paul opened the piano and the anger that surged through him as he saw the grimy piano keys made the tears break the surface. Estelle and his aunt Barbara who took him to see the mummies were the only women who had ever seen him cry and Estelle would never see him cry again. He sat down jerkily at the piano and began to play. "God damn the filthy bastard!" he shouted. "He let it get out of tune!"

The small square gold clock stood on the mantelpiece, its fingers pointing to after six. Too late to phone the piano tuner and God knows when he'd be able to get a tuner anyhow, with everybody in the army. Everybody but Paul. But without a spleen they won't have you in the army. Without a spleen people are apt to think of you as a freak. Estelle's face had gone very white when he told her how it happened. She held him close to her and rocked back and forth, spilling her tears onto his cheeks, saying over and over, "Oh, my darling, I can't bear to have you hurt, I can't bear to have you hurt. Please God I'll never hurt you."

There were the snow-covered hills, the heavy low-hanging grey sky occasionally dropping a feather of snow, the three fir trees at the top of the hill, and the single silver birch halfway down. He had flung himself onto his sled and started down the hill; as he started to gather speed, the rope that controlled the steering broke, and down he went flying wildly. For a moment he thought he should roll off, but then he thought another of the flying sleds would collide with him and he might as well go on to the bottom since he had been the first to start and there was no one ahead of him. The speed with no steering to control it frightened him and he closed his eyes; he closed his eyes forgetting about the single silver birch halfway down the hill, not remembering the silver birch even when he suddenly seemed to have become part of a clap of thunder, to be caught in the center of a fork of lightning, not remembering the birch even when he heard voices around him and pain such as he had never imagined shot through him. He kept his eyes tightly closed. He would not open them until his aunt Barbara was leaning over him in her coat made of two kinds of fur, until his aunt Barbara was leaning over him to make everything all right.

"Oh, Pauly, Pauly, don't die, please don't die," he heard his younger brother wail, and fear that was even stronger than the pain made him open his eyes. His younger brother and the other boys, some older, some younger than he was, were crowded around him. Their faces were all white and frightened, and his younger brother was crying, tears streaming down his cheeks and freezing there, a thin wet dribble freezing under his nose. Then a light grey blanket that slowly became black covered their faces, and a loud voice came in his ears, "The skin and bone of their perfect little hands turned to dust"—and then the voice became lost in thunder.

But the skin and bones of his hands had not turned to dust. His fingers were moving angrily over the piano keys. He did not apologize to Estelle for what he had said about Nicky. He simply repeated more quietly, "God damn him."

Estelle picked up an armful of books and went out. He wanted to fling his head down against the piano and howl with rage and misery but he thought, even if it weren't for Estelle and Nicky, once you start doing that sort of thing you're finished. So he went to the hall closet and took down the two green and lavender blankets that belonged to Estelle. He put them on the rug by the other things, looked for a moment around the mutilated room, and went downstairs. At the first-floor landing he met Estelle.

"I have to go out," he said. "When you and Nicky finish getting your stuff out you can drop the keys in the mailbox." He didn't wait for her to answer, but pushed out the red-painted front door.

The September evening was hot after the damp coolness of his north-facing apartment. The sun was still up and it seemed to burn as it fell on the top of his thick, neat blond hair. Lines rushed into his mind:

For though my soul disputes well with my sense,
That this may be some error, but no madness,
Yet doth this accident and flood of fortune
So far exceed all instance, all discourse,
That I am ready to distrust mine eyes,
And wrangle with my reason that persuades me
To any other trust but that I am mad.

Aunt Barbara had read Shakespeare to him, and other Eliza-
bethan plays. Estelle had cried because Aunt Barbara was dead and
she would never meet her.

This is the air, this is the glorious sun, I am not mad, and yet I
do not believe that upstairs my home is being torn apart, Estelle's
Renoir lady down from the wall over the sofa, great gaps in the
bookshelves, dark spots on the wall, her closet empty.

But why, why had he sublet the apartment to Nicky for the
three months he and Estelle had gone on the road with the
small opera company, Estelle understudying the prima donna and
singing in the chorus, Paul playing the piano in the orchestra?
Why had he let Nicky have the apartment? He had known then
what was going on between Nicky and Estelle, but he had written him frequently, even affectionately; he had let him stay in the
apartment.

It was because he hadn't believed it, hadn't believed anything
could change the relationship he and Estelle had had for five
years, because only this afternoon when they had returned from
Chicago and he had seen Nicky's personality splattered all over
his home, because only this afternoon had he realized that
Estelle was going to be with Nicky and not with him from
now on.

He had let Nicky stay in the apartment because he was sorry
for him, because he pitied Nicky having to stay in New York
during the hot summer while Paul and Estelle were on the road.
Nicky had always been *his* friend. Nicky had warned him that
Estelle was a bitch, that she was cold, that she would never really
love anyone but Estelle. But you've brought that out in her,
Nicky, Paul thought, my Estelle, with whom I was so happy, was

warm and loving. You've pandered to her Narcissus complex, that's how you won her, the weekend I went out of town on an accompanist's job.

The minute he let himself into the apartment after he came back from the three-day accompanist's job, his blue shirt wilted from the heat, his hair moist, beads of sweat across his upper lip, the minute he opened the apartment door and they came to greet him, he knew that something had happened. They put their arms around him so lovingly, they were so solicitous, and there was something new in the way they looked at each other.

"'Stelle and I are taking you out for dinner, Paul," Nicky had said.

Paul sat down on the blue wing chair, and pulled Estelle down with him. He told them about his trip. They talked about music, the theatre, movies. Finally, his heart beating violently and a hollow feeling in his stomach, Paul pulled Estelle's head close to his and whispered, "Have you let Nicky touch you?"

And she nodded, then added, "But don't worry, darling. It's not going to make any difference to you; it won't change anything with us. I promise you."

He had tried to believe her as he always believed Estelle when she looked at him and widened her eyes solemnly and said, "I promise you." They hadn't tried to hide anything. They had been completely open about it all. Estelle had insisted on that. After watching the course of Nicky's other affairs, she said, she had decided it was the best thing to do, the fairest to everyone.

The next day he and Estelle had signed their contracts for the tour with the opera company, and he had thought, we'll be gone three months, it will make everything all right; and he had pitied

Nicky for getting himself into another of his emotional tangles. During the three weeks of rehearsals, he had given in to Estelle's pleading that Nicky be allowed to stay at the apartment; he had been even more sorry for Nicky than he had been for himself. It might have been all right if Nicky hadn't gotten a week's leave while they were playing in Philadelphia, if Nicky hadn't come to Philadelphia tall in his uniform, his red hair shining, Nicky making a great fuss over everyone in the company, making a great fuss over Estelle in public, not trying to hide from anybody that they were together. When they left for Pittsburgh and Nicky went back to New York, Paul delivered his ultimatum to Estelle. They sat leaning back wearily in the day coach crowded with the company and soldiers and sailors and untidy-looking girls dirty from too much traveling around after their men. Paul had had a cold all during the two weeks in Philadelphia; now his throat felt raw and he sucked one cough drop after another until he felt sick, but if he stopped, the dust irritated his throat so that he had to suck another cough drop. He sat next to the window because Estelle almost always let him sit by the window. When he spoke to her he kept on staring out of the window, at the trees covered with thick hot dust, at the sky covered with thick hot dust, too. "If you want to go on living with Nicky," he said, managing to keep his voice quite controlled, "you can't go on living in the apartment." She didn't say anything and he took another cough drop out of the battered cardboard box and sucked it. After a while he said, "I've supported you almost completely for five years now. We have a very pleasant home. You won't be able to live nearly as comfortably with Nicky. I'm not trying to bribe you. I'm simply trying to be practical. Because you don't love Nicky. This business is still just sex with you. If you stay with Nicky any length of time you'll get under his spell and be lost, but you're not lost yet."

Estelle had not answered at once. She had picked up a magazine and finally said into it, "This isn't any place to talk, Paul, except to say I don't agree with you. We'll discuss it later." But they never had, and after a while Estelle began to talk about Nicky's looking for a place for them, and Paul didn't write Nicky Gatti any more letters because he was sorry for him.

> Yet doth this accident and flood of fortune
> So far exceed all instance, all discourse,
> That I am ready to distrust mine eyes
> And wrangle with my reason that persuades me
> To any other trust but that I am mad.

One day in Philadelphia, Nicky had drawn Paul into the bathroom and said to him, "I really love you far more than I love Estelle. I know you're a much nicer person. It's just that you can't do anything about sex."

Paul stared at the shelf with his shaving things, the shelf with Estelle's slightly soiled makeup and Jet perfume, and thought, You're evil, Nicky, you're the most completely vicious person I've ever known; you're sick of soul and you're all the more danger-ous because you yourself are thoroughly convinced of your own purity. You've caught Estelle in your web and you had me caught in it enough so that I didn't do anything about it while I had the chance. But he stared at the shelf in the hotel bathroom until Estelle pounded on the door and called at them to hurry up.

Philadelphia was halfway through the tour, but still Paul's emotions did not grasp what had happened. He could not realize, for instance, that from now on when he talked he would have to say "I" instead of "we." When he talked about his plans for the coming winter he still said "we" and had to correct himself, reddening with embarrassment. He did not realize with his emotion that when he had finished working on one of his compositions there would be no one to criticize it. Estelle had been a good critic for him; she had known how to make him work, to rewrite; it would be difficult to fight his tendency for too-easy composition alone. He did not realize that if he was ill, if he had the attacks of flu that came on him every winter, there would be no one to take care of him, no Estelle to read to him, to sing to him.

Only when he walked into the apartment with Nicky's personality smeared over it like the lipstick on Estelle's mouth did any of it touch him at all, inside, beyond his mind. Walking down the street the moment of realization was gone again. He stared at the converted brownstone houses, although converted, he thought, was hardly the word for them; disconcerted, betrayed, degraded brownstone houses. Hardly converted, more like apostated, or was that the right word...

A car passed along the street and light reflected from it flashed across the windows of the betrayed brownstone house, and loneliness flashed across his mind. I can't bear it, he thought, I can't bear to be alone.

He turned and hurried back to the brownstone house where their apartment—where his apartment—was on the top floor. Outside the house was a small tree. Its leaves, already grey and dry from heat and dust, were turning brown and dry from autumn. He did not look at the tree, but opened his mailbox. The keys were there. So they had gone. He took the keys out of the mailbox and clamped his hand over them, walked slowly up the three flights of stairs to his door, put the key in his lock.

Please Wear Your Rubbers

"Get my hat," cried Nana, "my big green hat! What time is it? What time is it now?"

"Ten of two." Vicky pulled the hat down from the high shelf.

"I should have left five minutes ago!" cried Nana. "Damn it!" She flew about angrily, pausing at the bureau to look at herself, pausing at the mirror in the hall, rushing, rushing, while Vicky brought her the hat.

"It's snowing. Wear your boots," said Vicky.

"No."

"Please," Vicky insisted. "Wear your boots. You can take them off when you get to the theatre."

Nana started flying about again. "My umbrella! Where's my umbrella?"

"It's hanging on the knob of the closet door. Here. Hurry."

Nana grabbed the umbrella and ran to the door. "What time is it now?" she asked tragically, as though she were saying "Is he dead?" and of course he would be.

"Five of two."

"I shall be at least ten minutes late!" she screamed, and rushed out the door.

Cold wind struck Vicky's face. She closed the door and locked it. They had told her always to lock it when she was in the apartment alone. She went and stood in front of one of the long windows and watched the snow dropping between the two rows of houses and an old man trudging along, holding a newspaper gray and wet over his head. Down the street Nana was walking under the green silk umbrella. She turned the corner towards the subway and Vicky left the window—and there, in the middle of the room, were Nana's rubbers. So she picked them up and put them in the bottom of the closet and sat down on the dilapidated studio couch that pulled out into two comfortable beds at night, surprised to hear that she was whimpering the way she used to years ago when she woke up in the middle of the night and there was no one to call.

She thought of Nana in the subway, smiling a little in the secret way that always made people smile back at her, but never rudely; Nana reaching the theatre and hurrying in, calling hello to everyone, and everyone really glad to see her; now making up, smoothing greasepaint and soft shadows into her skin; Nana dancing behind the musical comedy star ("It's an awful job, Vicky, hateful as humiliating when I'm so much better a dancer than she's an actress, but my God, it pays more than your schoolteaching and we've got to live"); Nana coming home for dinner so that Vicky shouldn't be lonely, then off to the theatre again and out with Frederick afterward—Vicky was asleep before Nana was home. Long before. She had to be if she was to get up and go to school in the morning.

Vicky shivered in the chair by the window and felt the radiator. It was warm, but the wind and even the wet from the snow came in around the edges of the window. Lighting the fire—Nana wouldn't live in a room without a fireplace even if they were too poor to have a bed—she crouched in front of it. Tonight she would sit up for Nana, and tomorrow night and the next night, too, if she felt like it. (*"I'm sorry, Miss Craig, but there aren't enough students enrolled for German to continue the course this semester." Vicky, panicky: "I speak French as well as I speak German—couldn't I help in some of the French classes?" "No, I'm sorry. We can't have anyone new in the French department. How about Spanish? Do you speak Spanish?" "No. No Spanish."*) Nana had simply raised her eyebrows when Vicky told her. "It's a good thing the show's going to go on running indefinitely, my lamb," she said.

The fire blazed high and burned Vicky's cheeks as she crouched there and cried. Getting more and more like a child, she thought. I mustn't lose control of myself all the time like this, I mustn't!

But she cried until she was exhausted, and then lay there on the floor and fell asleep. It was after five when she woke up. Nana would be home soon and the meal must be ready. Vicky looked out the window into the dark, and the snow had turned to rain as people were slushing by, cross and unhappy. She closed the blinds quickly, then pulled open the curtains that shut off the kitchen equipment from the rest of the apartment and looked at the few cans on the shelf. Soup. Nana hated soup. But it was so horrid out. There was nothing Vicky wanted less than to go around the block to the grocery store. There was nothing Vicky wanted less than to get dinner for Nana. Though it was only for Vicky's sake that Nana came home between shows at all. Frederick would take her anywhere she wanted. Every night. But Nana came home to have dinner with her sister. Poor Vicky all alone. All alone. "I won't!" Vicky said to herself and again out loud, "I won't!"

Pulling her brown coat out of the closet she thrust her arms into the sleeves angrily, reached up to the shelf for her brown beret and couldn't find it. Oh hell, oh damn. She pulled a silk scarf out of one of Nana's drawers, Nana's best blue silk scarf, and tied it over her head, fished in Nana's top drawer for lipstick. Nana's lipstick was darker than hers and smelled exotic. On it went thickly and out of the door went Vicky. No rubbers. No umbrella. And all the lights left burning. The rain blew into her face and beat against her ankles. She hailed a taxi. "Where to, miss?" Where to? Where shall I go? I'll be a nurse and go to London. I'll sing for the soldiers in Paris. My feet are soaked. I'll go to my death. "Where to, miss?" the taxi driver asked again, and grinned at her. "You look kind of wet."

And Vicky's teeth were chattering. "I'm drenched. Algonquin Hotel, please."

Against the glass window in the roof of the taxi the rain dropped. Vicky leaned back on the cold leather seat and shivered, and wondered if they'd give her a room when she carried no suitcase.

But they gave her a room. Two nights in that room. Two days of meals, and the last of her money would be gone. All right. It would be gone. She had to look for another job. What a fool she was. Of course she could get another job. Anybody could get a job nowadays. But she didn't want to work in a factory. Couldn't type. Wouldn't Nana raise that eyebrow if she got a job on the stage? She'd never told Nana about that. About wanting that. It had always been men and her dancing. Because Nana'd always talked about it. Nana'd always let everyone know what she wanted.

"Room service, please. Hello, room service? Will you send a dinner up to room 601? Yes, I'll have a cocktail first. A—a—" (What does Nana order?) "Oh, I think I'll have a whiskey and soda. Yes. Then the shrimp cocktail, roast beef, peas, baked potato, and coffee. Yes, that's right. Thank you."

After she had eaten—and she ate everything, and ordered French pastry for dessert, too—she sat down at the desk and wrote Nana.

Dear Nana,

Don't worry about me. Pat Conway, you remember, she was at school with us, dropped in unexpectedly and asked me to spend a few days with her in the country, and I couldn't resist the temptation. Frederick will be glad to have me out of the way, anyhow. Take care of yourself while I'm gone. Don't forget you need a quart of milk a day and eight hours of sleep and if it rains *please* wear your boots.

Love,
Vicky

She went out in the rain to post the letter, then she came back to a long hot bath and to bed. And to sleep. She slept until almost eleven the next morning, waking up and not opening her eyes for a moment. Because it was a few minutes before time for the alarm clock to go off, a few minutes before time to get ready for school, and she was still sleepy. But all at once she realized that she didn't have her pajamas on. Her arms were quite bare. And her legs. Her eyes still closed, she rolled over and remembered. She was wearing her slip. She sat up and opened her eyes and here she was in the Algonquin Hotel, where she'd always dreamed of going on her honeymoon. All right. She'd marry three times and collect millions in alimony. She'd have affairs with all her leading men. Then she'd stick to the last one and they'd be known as the new Lunt and Fontanne.

★

"We're not casting today.... Sorry, you're not the type.... We want a beautiful blonde. Sorry, no blondes.... All cast.... Too tall.... Too thin.... No experience? Sorry, no chance.... No women in the play.... No women under forty.... No women over eighteen.... No casting.... Not the type."

Two days of that.

Then—"You might do for an understudy. Come back tomorrow at three. We're sending *Stage Door* on the subway circuit."

So no food for a day and one more night at the Algonquin. Sleepless. The subway circuit. An understudy on the subway circuit. It would be a job, a job as an actress. Would she have to join Equity to be an understudy? On the subway circuit? That would more than take her salary. But she wouldn't worry about that till she got the job. Maybe she could borrow it somehow. She'd manage. Mustn't give up the job even if she had to go out and sell herself on the streets.

In Rosenbaum's office there wasn't a seat, though she got there half an hour early. She stood against the wall. In the chair nearest her sat a girl whose red hair showed dull brown at the roots. The heavy smell of her perfume made Vicky feel like she was covered with thick dust. Next to her sat a dark girl with a blunt nose and full lips, and lipstick so dark it was nearly black. She offered a cigarette, and smoke filled Vicky's eyes and made them water. Half an hour. Rosenbaum came out and put his arms about the redhead's waist and led her into his office. Vicky sat down in the empty chair.

"Geez," said the thick one as Vicky sat down. "You got to know someone. And she won't introduce me to nobody."

"Oh," Vicky said.

"I'd be swell for Terry. I'm just the type. But I won't get a look in because Rosenbaum don't know me. You got any experience?"

"Not yet," Vicky said.

"That's tough. You can't get experience till you got it. How long you wanted to go on the stage?"

"Always, I guess."

"Me, never thought about it till last week. Been ushering at the St. James. And then all of a sudden I thought, geez, if I was acting on the stage instead of passing out programs I'd be making a lot more money than I do and not much longer hours. Bet I make a good actress, too. I'm the type."

The door to Rosenbaum's office opened and the redhead came out, smiling and carrying a script. Rosenbaum took his cigar out of his mouth, closed his eyes, and looked around the room through lowered lids. Then he pointed his cigar at Vicky. "You," he said, "come here."

Vicki got up and followed him into his office. Rosenbaum sat down and looked her over.

"So," he said. "I told you to come back?"

"Yes."

"What for?"

"For—for the understudy."

"You could understudy what?"

"You just said I might understudy."

"I said that?"

"Yes. And to come back today."

"Oh. Well, I got somebody for understudy."

"Oh." Vicky watched him for a moment. He was looking through some papers and puffing on his cigar. "Well—" she said. He didn't look up. She left quietly, shutting the door behind her.

"Any luck?" asked the thick girl.

"No," she said, and she wanted to cry, to have someone comfort her, pull her close, tell her it didn't matter, give her a hot bath, put her to bed and bring her some milk toast and maybe even feed it to her, and then rub her head gently until she fell asleep. But who was there? Nana would just laugh.

"Tough luck," said the thick girl. "I don't expect much out of this joint myself. Hell, who wants the subway circuit?"

"Please—" Vicky almost whispered. "How do you get a job as an usher?"

"You just go around to Ms. Duffy's office in the Shubert, hon. They need girls right now. Don't pay you much, though. Geez, if you're an actress in Equity the least they can give you is fifty-seven fifty a week."

"Oh," said Vicky, and went out. She walked quickly down

Forty-Second Street. What if ushering didn't pay enough so she could keep up her share of the apartment? Nana'd have to pay more than her share for once. Vicky had never asked for anything before. And ushering would give her time to make the rounds of the producers' and agents' offices during the day.

She walked over to the Shubert's office.

When she got back to the apartment Nana wasn't there. The curtain into the kitchen was open and the sink was full of dishes. All of Nana's bureau drawers were pulled half out with clothes hanging over the edges; the closet door was open and clothes piled on the floor, the studio couch unmade. Vicky hung her coat up, folded Nana's blue silk scarf, and put it on top of the bureau. Then she went into the bathroom and sat on the edge of the tub, not looking at the towel on the floor, not looking at the dusting powder spilled everywhere, the ring around the tub, the unwashed stockings in the basin—not thinking. Just sitting and looking at nothing, feeling nothing. After a long time she began to clean up, slowly, methodically. It was eleven when she had finished. She took a hot bath and got into bed. If Nana came straight home she ought to be back any minute. But at two o'clock Nana had not come home and Vicky fell asleep. It was just beginning to be daylight and she woke up to hear the key in the lock. She kept her face pushed into the pillow.

"Oh" came Nana's light voice. "Vicky's back. You'd better not come in, darling."

And Frederick's voice: "Well, we had a nice holiday. I wish it didn't have to be over. You're too conscientious."

"Shh."

"She's asleep."

"Shh anyhow."

"When will I see you tomorrow?"

"At the theatre."

"Not before?"

"Not tomorrow. Good night, my sweet."

"Good night, my love." And a long kiss.

Nana locked and bolted the door, and came over to Vicky's bed. "Vick?"

Vicky rolled over. "Hello."

Nana sat down on the edge of the bed and slipped her arms out of her coat. "Did you have a nice time in the country, darling?"

"Lovely."

"How was Pat?"

"Oh, fine."

"You cleaned up my mess."

"Mm-hm."

"I meant to do it before you got back."

"It doesn't matter."

"When did you get back from the country?"

"Just this evening."

"You know it's a funny thing, darling, but I was sure I saw you in Times Square yesterday."

"Oh."

"Were you there, sweet?"

"Yes."

"Not in the country?"

"No. And I won't be able to pay my share of the apartment for a while."

"Oh?"

"You make enough to pay the extra for me, and Frederick gives you everything you want."

"Do you think it's quite fair of you, darling?"

Vicky turned over, away from her. "I don't much care."

"How much will you be paying?"

"I guess I'll make enough to give ten dollars."

"That's not very much."

"Personal maids usually get good salaries. Please leave me alone now, Nana. I'm tired and I want to sleep."

"Oh, all right, if you feel that way about it."

She lay very still while Nana got ready for bed. It always took Nana at least an hour and a half to get ready for bed. Tonight it was half an hour.

"Vicky," Nana said as she climbed into bed.

"What? I don't want to talk. I'm asleep."

"Maybe we'd better give up the apartment."

"Why?"

"Well, I mean, I don't think it's very fair to keep it this way, you not paying your share in everything, darling, and I sort of decided while you were away that now's as good a time as any to marry Frederick."

"Oh."

"You can easily find a job that will support you. Anybody with a college education can get a job nowadays. Or you could be a WAC or a WAVE."

"I'm a nurse's aide. That's just as important."

"Well, you can get a good job anyhow. And if I'm married to Frederick you won't have to clean up for me anymore. What was your job with the magnificent salary?"

"I was going to be an usher at the Booth."

"Oh."

"You needn't say 'oh' in that tone of voice."

"I wasn't using any tone of voice, darling. Well, I must say I think you can easily get a better job than that. From German teacher in a good girls' school to usher isn't very dignified."

"It's what I want."

"Well, I think it's just as well. You certainly should be doing something better than that. I'll see if I can't get Frederick to lend you enough to take a secretarial course. You could probably get a big paying job in Washington. God. I'm exhausted. Good night, Vick darling."

"Good night." Vicky opened her eyes wide and stared at the ceiling, and at the cheap chandelier in the middle of it. Then the chandelier blurred as her eyes filled with tears.

After a while Nana spoke again. "Where were you if you weren't in the country?"

"That's my own business."

"Oh, all right, darling, if you want to have secrets it doesn't bother me . . . Why are you crying?"

"I'm not."

"Go to sleep, then." Nana yawned. "You want to be fresh to look for a new job in the morning. Good night, my sweet."

"Good night."

"And don't wake me up in the morning."

"Do I ever?"

Nana didn't answer. In a moment her breathing came slowly and rhythmically. Vicky raised herself on one elbow and stared at Manhattan in the early morning light. Nana lay curled up like a kitten, her face pillowed on her arm, rosy and childish. Vicky watched her for a long time. Then she lay down and closed her eyes and pressed her face into the pillow. But she didn't cry.

A Room in Baltimore

It was about eight thirty when the train, several hours late as usual, pulled into Baltimore, and we were starved because we hadn't had anything to eat since breakfast. No stop long enough for us to dash to a station lunchroom, nobody coming through the train with paper cups of coffee and sandwiches, no dining car. We were tired, too, because we'd just done a lot of one-night stands, and the prospect of a week, of seven whole nights, in one town, was very welcome.

I left my roommate, Fiona, at the information desk. Hugh and Bob, our two best friends among the men in the company, took our suitcases along to their hotel so we wouldn't have to carry them. Fiona and I were the only two in the company who weren't settled in a hotel, and Fiona wasn't settled solely out of kindness to me. I wasn't settled because of Touché.

Touché is a very small silver French poodle, and she had quite a big part in the play, far bigger than mine. Touché had three curtain calls and I only got in on the big general company one.

Touché shared the stars' dressing room on the stage floor while I was always several rickety flights up. I don't know whether it's a tribute to my noble nature or to Touché's charm and undoubted acting ability that I didn't mind her having a juicy role while I was just several walk-ons and general understudy, and that I never wished she didn't belong to me when no hotel would accept our reservations or I had to spend ten hours in a freezing baggage car when the conductor didn't melt at the sight of her lovely little face, or when I didn't get away with holding her under my coat in the general position of my middle, and looking wan and in an interesting condition.

I got Touché out of the baggage car now and joined Fiona. She had once played a summer of stock in Baltimore and had stayed in a boarding house where she was great friends with everybody, so we weren't, for once, worried about finding a room.

It was quite dark and starting to snow, which meant I couldn't find a star to wish on. This depressed me a little, since I'd almost had a quarrel with Hugh on the train over a game of double solitaire called Spite and Malice which we played on a suitcase balanced on our knees; but I knew that with no hotel to be depressed in, and on an empty stomach, I had better squelch my superstitions. Besides, Hugh was trying to teach me not to say "bread and butter" when something came between us, or to go back around the block when a black cat crossed my path; and every time I came to his dressing room he started whistling.

Touché was as hungry as Fiona and I, so one of the first things we did was to stop at a lunch wagon and buy her a hamburger. We had some coffee but resisted the temptation to get a couple of hamburgers for ourselves because we had decided to get settled first, and then meet the boys for a real bang-up dinner, bottle of wine and all. We had to get the room first anyhow because we couldn't go into a restaurant with Touché—though in emergencies I'd found the *enceinte* trick worked very well, and Touché never gave it away by moving or barking, but lay, far quieter than any baby, born or otherwise, with her little grey head under the table cloth, nudging my knee gently if I didn't slip her a bite often enough.

Now, anyone who knows Baltimore knows that there are two stations, each one at opposite ends of the city. Of course, Fiona's boarding house was very close to the station we *hadn't* arrived at. So Fiona led the way. I'd played Baltimore once before but I never did have any bump of locality, so I just followed her blindly, and wherever I went, Touché went, too. The only thing I was sure of was that I would *never* go back to the dreadful hotel where four of us had stayed on two very dirty double beds and where there was a bathtub bang in the middle of the room with a screen around it—but no toilet. The fact that we paid four dollars a week apiece didn't make up for the filth that even the bottle of Lysol that was our constant companion from hotel to hotel couldn't make us forget.

"It won't be long now," Fiona said comfortingly after we had tramped for blocks and blocks and blocks and Touché was beginning to drag on her leash. "It's a lovely boarding house with great big rooms and it'll be a lovely change after all those awful hotels." Fiona's full name is Fiona Feanne (pronounced for some reason Foy-een-ya) O'Shiell, and she is a creature almost as ravishingly beautiful as Touché (than which there could be no higher praise) with masses of red hair and alabaster skin and a body so lovely that most people, learning that we were in the theatre, asked if we were playing the Gaiety, or whatever was the name of the nearest burlesque house. She walked along now, her face held up to the soft white flakes of snow that were beginning to fall, humming a little, and Touché and I dragged along, and finally Touché deliberately held up one forepaw and started limping along pathetically on three legs until she got her own way (as usual) and I picked her up and carried her under one arm.

We walked and we walked and we walked and we walked, and Touché, for all her beauty and grace, grows heavy after a while. Finally Fiona said, "Funny we aren't there yet. This doesn't look like a very nice neighborhood." She hailed a passing man and asked for the address of her boarding house. The man leered at us both, his eyes going suggestively from our heads to our feet and back up again, in a most unpleasant manner, but he did make it clear to us that we had walked all the way across Baltimore for nothing; Fiona's boarding house was a few blocks from the station at which we had arrived.

Fiona turned red and then white and then red again. "I don't know how it could have happened—I could have sworn—Oh, please, forgive me!" she gasped.

If it hadn't been for Touché and me, Fiona would have been safely settled in the Lord Baltimore with Hugh and Bob and most of the rest of the company. How could I help forgiving her? I stamped my very wet, very cold feet, in shoes that needed resoling. "It's okay, Fifi, but let's get going. I'm starved and frozen."

Fiona flung her arm around me. "Tonight I'll give you a ten-dollar back rub," she said. "That's a promise."

Touché growled as Fiona touched me, but she just pulled the curly grey puff of bangs. "Angel, I am not molesting your mistress, so shut up. What on earth are you going to do with Toosh on your wedding night?"

We tried to take a taxi but it seems in Baltimore dogs are not allowed in taxis and she kept slipping out from under the front of my coat. We knew it would do no good to try a bus, so we walked. In about a weary hour and a half we were back in what, to Fiona, was familiar ground, and soon we went up the brown stone steps of a very nice-looking house. I didn't care what sort of a room they gave us. I didn't even care much about dinner with wine with Hugh and Bob. I just wanted to take a hot bath and get into bed and have one of Fiona's ten-dollar back rubs.

The boarding house keeper gave one look at my beautiful, my sweet, my adorable Touché, and said they didn't take dogs and couldn't make an exception even for a dog who worked to earn her own living. Fiona cajoled and wheedled with all her Irish charm, and Touché, true to her histrionic nature, stood on her hind legs and danced, but the boarding house keeper (who shall be nameless) was a hatchet-faced old sour-puss and there was no getting around her. As she was gently pushing us out the door she started to coo over Touché. This was the last straw.

"If you refuse to allow my dog in your home, please stop gurgling over her," I said coldly, and stalked out. Fiona hurried down the steps after me.

"Angel, that was rude of you, you know," she said softly. I was ashamed of my temper as I always am once it's lost, but I wasn't going to admit it. I reached in the pocket of my old trench coat and pulled out the typewritten list of Baltimore hotels that Al

Finch, our advance manager, had posted on the call board. We started by trying all the hotels in the neighborhood. They were without exception expensive, but that needn't have bothered us because they wouldn't take Touché anyhow. Finally we decided to forget the size of our weekly paychecks and try the frightfully expensive hotel where Miss Le Gallienne and Mr. Schildkraut, our stars, were staying.

"I'm sorry," the manager said, "but we don't take dogs."

"Look here." I was almost in tears. "Miss Eva Le Gallienne is staying here and she has two cairns and a combination Manchester terrier–Chihuahua. And Mr. Joseph Schildkraut is here, too, and he has *three* Chihuahuas. I know because I walk them every day."

At this point the hotel orchestra, which we could hear playing dimly in the distance, for some reason began to play "The Star-Spangled Banner." This was also played at the end of the overture and we had taught Touché, waiting on stage with the rest of the company, to stand at attention. As she heard the familiar strains her grey ears pricked up, and, tired though she was, she rose to her hind legs and put one small grey paw to her forehead. I relaxed, certain that now we would be shown the bridal suite.

The manager didn't change expression. "I'm very sorry, but we take *no* dogs."

Now, I think Miss Le Gallienne and Mr. Schildkraut deserve every possible consideration a star can get, but this hotel business was beginning to burn me up, not to mention my rage at anyone crass enough not to appreciate Touché. Also, I was having a hard time to keep from crying with anger, hunger, and fatigue. I looked up at the manager with brimming eyes. "If you keep on telling lies like this, someday God will strike you down. Come, Fiona. Come, Touché." And we stalked out again.

This time Fiona did not scold me for being rude. Back in the street I turned up my collar and blew my nose. Fiona quietly took the list of hotels from me. "Here's one that says theatrical rates only a couple of blocks from here. Come on, angel."

"Look, Fifi, Toosh and I will understand perfectly if you go on back to the Lord Baltimore. Do go on, please, and we'll call you when we find a place and tell you where we are."

Fiona said nothing to this and walked determinedly down the street, and Toosh and I staggered after her. We got to the corner where the theatrical hotel was supposed to be, but at that number was an imposing-looking building with a canopy leading to the front door and we guessed with sinking hearts that the management had changed and the rates would no longer be "theatrical."

"Well, let's try anyhow, it's only money," Fiona said. We went up to the door and were just about to go in when Fiona clutched my arm in a frantic manner and pointed to a brass plate on the door. In chaste letters it announced: CREMATORIUM.

We turned and ran down the steps and I started to roar with laughter. "What," demanded Fiona, "is funny?"

"I was just thinking," I explained, "of how they'd have looked if we'd gone in and asked if they took dogs, and could they put us up for the night!"

Well, we started back to the center of town to the hotels that were nearer the theatre. It was a good bit after eleven o'clock by now and even the inexhaustible Fiona was on her last legs.

We looked for a phone and I finally went into a bar and called the boys at the Lord Baltimore to tell them to check our suitcases downstairs and go on to bed. We'd probably sleep in the station or maybe find a church that was open all night. Hugh was properly sympathetic but agreed to leave the bags downstairs, saying they were very tired and they'd already had something to eat anyhow because they hadn't heard from us.

They were tired! I thought furiously, and hung up just as a large cockroach crawled across the telephone box. I am terrified of cockroaches so I dropped the receiver like a hot coal and dashed out to Fiona and Touché, quite certain that my name would *never* be changed to Mrs. Hugh Franklin. (Funnily enough, it is.)

It took us a good half hour to get into town through the falling snow that at least had the grace to be getting drier instead of wetter. My feet were so cold now that I couldn't feel anything, even the blisters on the backs of both heels. Touché lay like a pathetic lump of lead in my arm, and I thought wistfully of all the pleasant autumnal walks we'd had earlier in the tour, when Hugh would walk me back to my hotel after the performance.

We always walked until Touché had done a final wee wee for the night, and on the evenings that I was not with Hugh she would always head for the nearest lamppost (because it was a spotlight, not because it was a lamppost) and perform; on the nights when Hugh, of whom she approved, was with me, we would sometimes walk for over an hour before she would finally have to give in and squat.

"What about the hotel you stayed in the last time you were here?" Fiona asked tentatively.

"Fifi, we simply can't stay there. It's too awful to describe and Toosh would never agree to it."

By midnight we had tried all the hotels on the list except one. The remark after this was "Cheap, but certainly wouldn't recommend it for the girls."

It was only a couple of blocks from the theatre so we decided to try it anyhow. The exterior didn't look too prepossessing. Outside a dirty brown building a large sign in lurid red lights said, ONE DOLLAR A NIGHT.

Fiona turned to me. "At this point we'll try anything, but this looks like A House, not a hotel."

We went into the lobby. The floor was tiled with the kind of small white tiling you usually find only in bathrooms. A few exhausted-looking soldiers and sailors were sprawled in chairs whose springs sagged through the torn upholstery. Both Fiona and I did a double take when we looked at the man behind the desk; his face was the color of parchment; he looked as though he'd been embalmed and then they'd decided he wasn't dead after all. On his head he wore a wig, which was pale pink. I suppose it was meant to be blond but it had faded to baby pink. Out from under it strayed a few damp grey hairs. Touché looked at him and growled with great disapproval. I closed my fingers firmly around her muzzle and she stopped.

"Do you take dogs?" Fiona demanded bluntly of the man in the pink wig.

He just grinned foolishly. "Do I take dogs?"

I held Toosh out towards him. "Do you take *this* dog?"

"Do I take dogs?" he asked again. "How many beds? One? Two? Three? Four?"

"One bed is cheaper than two?" Fiona asked. He nodded. "All right. How much for a double bed for one week?"

"Six dollars apiece for the young ladies. The dog can share it with you."

"Okay," Fiona said brusquely. "Let's see it."

The little man took us up in the elevator himself. I don't think they had anyone else to run it. It was one of those elevators where there aren't any doors and only two walls. They make Touché and me nervous.

"What do you girls do?"

"We work in the theatre," Fiona said.

"At the Gaiety?" the little man asked—as usual.

"No." Fiona was very indignant. "We're playing Chekhov's *The Cherry Orchard* at Ford's Theatre with Eva Le Gallienne and Joseph Schildkraut."

The little man looked disappointed, but then his eyes flickered hopefully. "Either of you by any chance Eva Le Gallienne?"

Fiona and I imagined Miss Le Gallienne staying in that particular hotel and laughed heartily.

The little man looked hurt and took us down a dim and dirty corridor and flung open a door with a flourish. "Some sailors been sleeping here today," he said, "but we'll change the sheets for you." He made this sound like a great favor.

Buff wallpaper with a spider design was peeling off the walls. The ceiling was about to fall. A lumpy-looking tumbled iron bed stuck out from one corner, a wardrobe huge enough to hold any number of murderers or skeletons from another. There was a chair that had evidently actually become so shabby it had to be taken out of the lobby, and a three-legged desk. The floor was covered with cigarette butts, matches, ashes. Touché pressed closer to me so that she would not be contaminated by coming in contact with anything. Fiona and I looked at each other and our hearts sank.

"Let me see the bathroom," Fiona said bravely. We were astounded to find the bathroom reasonably clean and reasonably modern. We thought of our bottle of Lysol and nodded.

"We'll take it," Fiona said to the little man. "Please see that the floor is properly swept. We'll go down and sign the register now."

While the little man was carefully studying our signatures Fiona said, "Now we'll go get our suitcases."

"Suitcases!" the little man with the pink wig said. "What would two pretty girls like you want with suitcases?"

I was about to make an appropriate remark but Fiona pushed me out the door. Fortunately it wasn't far to the Lord Baltimore. We picked up our bags and they felt as though they were filled with lead. We thought of Hugh and Bob, having had dinner, asleep in comfortable twin beds, and felt very sorry for ourselves and not very kindly disposed towards anyone else who had not shared in our troubles. We knew we'd never be able to stagger back to the hotel with our suitcases, so we stood and flagged a taxi.

Fiona did a last act of *Camille* for the driver, coughing pathetically and looking beautiful; I stood and glowered, and Touché held up one paw and tried to lick it, limped a few steps, and finally stood on her hind legs and pressed her forepaws together as though in prayer, and the driver succumbed, whether to the histrionics and beauty of Fiona and Touché or to both combined, I'm not sure.

It was after one when we finally got up to our room. Normally this is pretty early for us, but that night it didn't seem so. We were far too tired, hungry though we were, to think about dinner. Besides, what would have been open in Baltimore so late on a Sunday night?

Fiona got out the Lysol and we wearily scrubbed the bathroom and the foot- and headboards of the bed and all the doorknobs. We opened one bureau drawer and found it filled with more dirty cigarette butts and a handkerchief that Fiona said had been used for not very nice purposes, so we decided to live out of our suitcases.

They had put clean sheets on the bed while we were fetching the suitcases, but the blankets and spread hadn't been changed since the opening of the hotel a couple of centuries before. I knew Touché would never consent to sleep on that dirty floor, or even on the counterpane, so I spread my coat out on the foot of the bed and put her blanket over that.

We took baths and then I took Touché's dog biscuits out of my suitcase and the three of us each ate several and fell asleep, counting, instead of sheep, the days till we could leave Baltimore the next Sunday morning for seven weeks of one-night stands.

Julio at the Party

Now Julio was trying to balance the knife on the tip of his nose. He was being very clumsy about it and everybody was laughing, everybody was shouting and encouraging him.

"Julio, will you be careful!" Rebecca cried, but she was laughing so hard that the tears were running down her cheeks and nobody heard her.

Thank God Julio was drunk at last. Not drunk from alcohol, because Rebecca had seen him pouring most of his drinks into the big glass aquarium of tropical fish that she and her husband, Johnny, had inherited from the last tenants; but drunk from excitement, from adulation; drunk because with Julio it was a question of the wildest gaiety or the most complete agony of brooding.

John passed by with more drinks, his glasses slipping lopsidedly down his nose. "Johnny," Rebecca said, still laughing, automatically pushing his glasses back up for him, "all the fish are going to be dead tomorrow morning." She laughed and laughed at the thought.

"That's fine," John said, "and tomorrow morning you'll be in tears over them. Why will they be dead?"

"Julio's drowning them in alcohol."

John looked over at the aquarium just in time to see Julio surreptitiously pour two-thirds of a high ball into the aquarium. "I thought the water level was getting rather high. Well, thank God Julio's high at last, too, even if he's getting it vicariously from the fish. That first hour when he sat around like the tragic muse and everybody else sat around respecting his mood..." He stroked her hot dark hair back from her cheeks. "Listen, sweetheart, go speak to old Lindstrom, will you? He's looking lost."

"Oh, darling, of course!" She started to move away from John, drying the tears of her laughter and remembering her duties as a hostess.

The apartment was a cold-water walk-up. They paid twenty-two dollars a month for it and they had five small rooms, the largest of which was the combined kitchen and bathroom. This was sometimes difficult when they gave a party but they always managed, and when there were complications they contrived to keep them funny, even the time when they had the very serious party (if you could call it a party) for some of John's colleagues at the university and one of the professors' wives burst open the easily yielding bathroom door and found her husband happily sitting in the bathtub with one of the young art instructresses. Rebecca rushed in and turned on the cold water and everybody laughed and somehow it became funny instead of serious, and the evening became a party.

Now Julio was sitting on the floor by the piano, still trying to balance the knife on his beautiful nose, his delicate and aristocratic nose, led on by the applause of the group around him. Oblivious to the laughter and the noise, Leda Oliver, Rebecca's sister who had the apartment under Rebecca and John, was standing by the piano in gold lamé pajamas and an orange Chinese blouse, singing *Lakmé*. Her upswept blond hair was beginning to come down, her nose was shiny, and her lipstick was smeared; but the notes poured from her quivering throat as delicate and cool as the fountains at Versailles. As she finished her song, the group on the floor, still with their attention on Julio, clapped heartily. Leda smiled with her gently vacant eyes at the applause, those very round, very light blue eyes with the small pupils that never changed their mild, slightly bewildered expression.

"No, never," Walter had said once. "Leda's eyes never change. Not even when—"

"Walter, shut up," Rebecca snapped. "Let Leda keep her private life to herself. And you keep yours, too."

Now Walter was clapping loudly for Leda and egging Julio on. Julio was beginning to look very silly (though even silliness could not destroy the passionate beauty of his face), sitting there, his feet stuck out in front of him, trying to balance the cumbersome knife. The grey-haired man at the piano ruffled through the music, found something that interested him, and placed it on the music rack, looking at Leda. She smiled obediently and prepared to sing.

Walter had said, "Leda is much too obedient. I don't like obedient women. That's why you once held such charms for me, Rebecca darling. You never did anything I told you to, or anything I expected you to do. Nobody'd know you and Leda were sisters. Even I wouldn't know it."

The grey-haired man struck the opening chords and Leda opened her mouth. When she was singing she always seemed a little surprised that the effortless crystal music pouring from her throat was hers; she sang whenever possible, even at parties like this when the smoky air tore into her throat, not caring whether or not anyone listened. Often Rebecca and John would wake at three or four in the morning to hear Leda, in the room below them, singing, singing.

Rebecca picked her way through the rooms, heading for the furthest and smallest one, which John used as a study, and where she had last seen Dr. Lindstrom, John's old professor; but she was stopped by a couple who had pulled a volume of John's stories out of one of the bookshelves and were arguing over it.

"I never interpret Johnny's writing. I just feel it," she said. "You'll have to ask him, if you want to know anything about it. He's in with the tropical fish, I think."

A red-headed girl who had appeared from nowhere but was presumably somebody's friend clutched her arm. "Do tell me about your Spanish friend—what's his name? Hoolio?" She fumbled for the Spanish pronunciation.

"Julio, that's right," Rebecca said.

"Yeah, but, is he really the one who wrote that wonderful poem?"

"Did you like it?" Rebecca asked eagerly.

"Well, I haven't quite read it yet, but I'm going to get it tomorrow. Now that I've met the author it makes it so much more thrilling. Besides, he's so divinely handsome."

"Johnny—my husband—translated it," Rebecca could not help adding.

145

"But why didn't you tell me before! Now of course I shall get it. What did you say his name was? His first name?"

"John, or Julio?"

"Oh, either one would be divine. I must go talk to him!" the red-haired one cried, and rushed away, stepping on fingers, on peanut butter sandwiches, overturning drinks as she went.

Now at last Rebecca sat down on the sagging arm of Dr. Lindstrom's chair. "Hello, darling," she said, stroking his sleeve, because he was more like a father to them than an ex-professor or even one of Johnny's colleagues. "Have you read Julio's poem?"

Dr. Lindstrom jumped. He had been napping. "Truly magnificent!" he exclaimed, waking up with enthusiasm and smiling into the cloudy night of Rebecca's eyes. "An honest blend of the poet's art and the reformer's zeal without the latter intruding, killing the poetry and weakening its own message by its protuberance. How on earth did you find him?"

"I've known him for years, in an odd sort of way," she explained, as Horace somebody, one of John's students, approached. "Mostly through letters, as a matter of fact."

"I'd like to see those letters," Horace said. Rebecca remembered that Johnny always called him "Horrors."

"I have them all," she answered. "Now that his long poem's such a success I think Julio ought to bring out a volume of letters. They're wonderful."

"I admired his poem," Horrors said pompously. "I thought it was terrifically politically sound. You know, I couldn't think of a thing to say against it except that it hasn't any sense of humor."

Dr. Lindstrom spoke, his pipe clenched between his teeth as he waved a match over the bowl and sucked both at the pipe and at his words. "A sense of humor in that poem would have weakened its intensity, but we'll go into that another time. How did you meet him, Rebecca?"

"We spent a year in Barcelona when I was ten. I met Julio then and we decided at once that we were going to get married. He was eleven, and he'd written reams of poetry already. He used to read it to me and I thought it was wonderful. But he always burned it because he said it wasn't good enough." Through the open door she could see Julio still seated on the floor by the piano. He had put his knife down and was no longer trying to clown. "Oh, good Lord, now he's looking miserable again. I'll have to go cheer him up."

"That large friend of yours, I think his name is Walter," Horrors said, "is arguing with him."

Julio raised his voice excitedly, and they heard him saying in faltering English, "But you cannot say you are anti-fascist and then say you were a Francoist. That is a—a—contraception."

The group on the floor roared with laughter. Julio looked wounded.

"Hoolio, Hoolio darling," the redhead said. "You mean 'contradiction.'"

Julio looked bewildered. "But that's what I said."

"Honestly," Rebecca said, giggling, "I could shoot that big hunk of a Walter. He has no right to upset Julio with his reactionary talk, especially when the poor guy can't speak English well enough to fight back properly." She shouted over to Leda in the golden trousers and the orange shirt, "Leda, my swan, sing 'Caro nome' for us."

Walter broke off arguing to call back. "Leda wasn't the swan. You've got your mythology wrong."

"Or your anatomy," the redhead shrieked, flinging herself against Walter with choking hiccoughs of laughter.

"Horrors, darling," Rebecca said without thinking, "would you be adorable and get me a drink? Rhine wine and seltzer, please."

John's student looked startled for a minute, but he smiled politely. "Of course." He hurried through the rooms. Rebecca saw him burst into the kitchen-bath, and then withdraw, crimson with embarrassment.

Leda began to sing, and Walter continued to talk quietly, smiling at Julio, but she could not hear what he was saying. But she remembered that the only time she had been afraid of Walter was when he had that look of ineffable tenderness on his face.

The redhead was lying with her head in Walter's lap, pulling at one of his ears. Rebecca wondered how long he would stand for it; Walter did not like having his ears touched.

"Excuse me for a moment, darling, will you?" Rebecca asked Dr. Lindstrom, and started to pick her way towards the piano. No political arguments at parties; that was the rule.

"I am a very strong, very firm Catholic," Walter was saying in his quiet, beautiful voice.

John signaled to Rebecca. He was standing by the aquarium. He looked pleased and excited, his glasses askew again. "Beck, the fish are all stewed. What do you bet they won't be dead tomorrow if we change the water? They'll just have terrific hangovers. Have you ever seen a fish with a hangover, sweetheart?"

She looked at the fish and started to giggle, too. "No, but

I've seen you with one." The fish were swimming drunkenly, bumping into each other and bumping into the glass sides of the aquarium. "Walter!" she shouted, remembering again Julio's distressed face. "Come and see the fish! They're drunk!"

People began to cluster about the aquarium, but Walter remained seated on the floor by Julio. Now the red-headed girl was stroking the back of his neck, but Walter did not seem to notice as he said, "It is because you are blind, because you are an idealist. It would have been better if you had died in Spain because you are living in a dream." His voice was gentle, loving.

"If I am living in a dream, then the only decent people in the world are living in a dream and everybody else is trying to make it a nightmare," Julio cried, waving his hands excitedly, his hands that had once been as soft and as sensitive as his face but which were now hardened and scarred.

"Perhaps not all of us are asleep," Walter murmured. "Perhaps some of us are awake."

The red-headed girl came surprisingly into the argument, sitting up with a jerk. "But Walter, darlingest, if you are a Catholic how can you be awake? Do you believe in Adam and Eve? All that stuff about Eve and the apple?"

"When I look at you, my sweet, I do," Walter said, and she flung herself into his lap again.

A delicate-looking woman, someone Rebecca remembered vaguely as being from the French department, pointed an accusing finger at Walter. "It is a crime that people like you are Catholic. You blacken a religion that should bring only comfort and joy to people. It is not for me, but why should you take it away from those it can help?" She looked at Julio for corroboration, but he was staring with dark fury at Walter's placid face.

"The dream again," Walter said to the girl, then turned back to Julio, laying one of his strong, beautifully kept hands on the Spaniard's knee. "Wake up, Julio. Wake up, boy."

"If I were awake," Julio started to grind between clenched teeth, "I would—"

Rebecca finally managed to cross to them and cut him short. "Walter, I shoot you. You're dead. Bang bang." She made a pistol of her fingers. "Go home, you louse. This is Julio's party, not yours."

"Ak ak ak," went the redhead like a machine gun, first at Walter, then at Julio. "Now they're both dead so nobody has to go home."

"Julio." Rebecca reached down and took his hand to pull him up. "Come and see Dr. Lindstrom. He wants to talk to you about your poetry. Don't pay any attention to Walter, the big oaf. He doesn't mean a word of it."

"But I do," Walter said. "I'm deeply serious. It is of the greatest interest to me to talk to these mistaken idealists."

"Come along, amigo," Rebecca insisted, tugging at Julio's hand.

He rose and followed her. As he reached Dr. Lindstrom he said, trying to be calm, to choose his English slowly and carefully, "This is the first time this has happened to me. This man is my enemy. In Spain I would shoot him if he did not shoot me first. But because I have come to America, because I am a guest here tonight in your house, I have to sit and talk to him."

"I'm sorry, Julio"—Rebecca kissed the top of his dark head,

her curls mingling briefly with his—"but I shot him for you so it's all right."

"But why is someone like him here!" Julio exclaimed. "I know you do not feel the way he does. So how can you have him in your home?"

Rebecca kept her voice light. "Oh, he's always been sweet to me. He paid my rent when I was broke. Before I knew Johnny. He's such a nice guy. You can't help liking Walter, you know you can't."

"Even before you knew John you knew what that man was like. You must have known. And you let someone like that touch you?"

"Julio," Rebecca said warningly.

Julio bowed his head. "I am sorry. But I do not like to see those I have loved behaving like—like—"

Rebecca cut him short. "Walter was in the army, too. He was a second lieutenant."

"Where did he fight?"

"He was in Washington. Please, Julio darling, please don't take it so seriously. He's just drunk. He really doesn't mean it."

"He is no more drunk than I am," Julio said. "He has been drinking nothing but ginger ale. And it is not possible to take such people too seriously."

"Rebecca!" someone called from across the room. "I've burned a hole in your carpet with my cigarette. I'm overcome with shame. And the fire in your potbelly's almost out." And then, as everybody shrieked, "I mean your stove. Oh, for heaven's sakes!"

"Take care of Julio," Rebecca told Dr. Lindstrom, and went to investigate the damage done to the rug and to put some more coal on the fire. Johnny's student, Horrors, found her, gave her her drink, and fixed the stove for her. She saw, with annoyance, Walter cross to Julio, then heard John calling, "Hi, Julio, come in the bathroom and help me make sandwiches."

"Oh, let me come, too," the redhead said, deserting Walter's lap. "I've never known such a divine kitchen. Or did you say bathroom?"

Bless Johnny for trying to help Julio, Rebecca thought as she pushed her way towards Walter, determined to get rid of him because now the girl from the French department was arguing with him.

"I'm hurt," Walter said to Rebecca in a low voice.

"Why?"

"Johnny's far more jealous of your crazy poet than he ever was of me. You're a cagey one, Becky. You never once mentioned him."

"I told you all about him when I asked you to the party." She did not lower her voice to meet his. "Walter, you reactionary scum, I thought I killed you dead, bang bang. Go home. Once you start arguing you can't stop. You've stayed long enough. You were practically the first to arrive. Now git."

He looked at her with a wounded expression. "All right. If I must, I must. I have to wait till Leda stops singing, though."

"Leave Leda alone for once. Scram. Vamoose."

He stood up and took her chin in his hand, giving her a quick, gentle kiss, giving her that look that made her afraid. "All right, little earnest one. I'll help you protect your poet."

She turned her mouth away. "Don't talk like that about poets. Johnny's a poet."

"But he doesn't write about politics."

"Now, I'm not going to make you happy by arguing with you the way everyone else does." She pushed him towards the door, and then leaned against the piano to listen to Leda sing the "Queen of the Night." Walter would go now while Julio was making sandwiches and everything would be all right. She was suddenly very tired, and she stood leaning there, letting Leda's singing pour over her as cool and refreshing as a shower in summer. There was the singing and the laughter and the tropical fish in the aquarium would be drunk and Johnny said they wouldn't die but they'll have an awful hangover...

Then the laughter stopped, and she heard Walter's voice, and Julio's voice. Walter was standing by the door. Julio, brandishing the carving knife, smeared with peanut butter and apricot jam, was talking in a high, unnatural voice.

John caught him by the sleeve. "Come back in the kitchen and let Walter go home."

It was Johnny's restraining arm that released Julio's fury. He flung it off and the knife swooped through the smoky air and into Walter's stomach. In the crowd around him, Walter could not fall, but without a sound he slumped to the floor, lying huddled on Julio's feet. The sound of the piano stopped and Leda broke off in the middle of a note.

"Oh," she said. "Oh, dear. Did something happen?" She could not see through the crowd around Walter. "Some of the fish are floating on top of the water," she said as she pushed her way through the people towards the kitchen. "Is something the matter?"

The Foreign Agent

W ell, in the first place he didn't ask me the same silly questions everybody else does. "How do you like living in the city?" "Don't you miss the country just terribly?" "Do the subways frighten you?" Stuff like that. And anyhow, the others aren't really interested the way he was. They don't listen to my answers on the rare occasions that I get a chance to give them.

But the truth is, as I told him, that I love the city. For instance, in the country I couldn't escape to walk the dog. I mean, there was absolutely no reason for me to walk the dog. We just opened the door and he ran out across the fields and then into the woods. I know that in the country people are *supposed* to go for long tramps with the dog, but this is when they don't really live in the country. People who go for long tramps with the dog are people who either live in or really have their roots in the city.

You've no idea what it's like to escape from the country at last! Now I can say, "I'd better take the dog for a walk," and I can get his leash and off we go. If my mother knew the places we walk! Actually I'm even beginning to pick up Spanish. I mean, I walk across the park to the West Side and I walk up and down the streets there where the people are all assorted and different, black, white, yellow, and the shops are all small and cluttered and fascinating, and you hear more Spanish than English. My mother doesn't like this, but I enjoy it. It makes me feel that maybe I'm in a European city. I mean New York is really a foreign city as far as I'm concerned. When you've never been out of a small village in Vermont in your whole life, New York is really *travel*. Well, I have been to Brattleboro, but you can't really count that.

Anyhow, back to the way he didn't ask me stupid questions like the others.

He's my mother's literary agent.

My mother writes cookbooks with comments. Regional stuff. If anyone looks unlike a native Vermonter it's my mother, though actually she *is* a native Vermonter, so if she wants to write folksy things with her recipes I guess she has a right to. But she isn't big and comfortable in an old housedress and clean white apron the way her cookbooks want you to think she is. She's tiny and has black, black hair, and wears peasant blouses and long dangle earrings and writes poetry. Her poetry doesn't sell but her cookbooks do. She went back to live in Vermont when my father died a few months before I was born. They lived in Greenwich Village (this is the part of New York where artists and other peculiar people live and that's where she got the idea for the peasant blouses and gypsy earrings).

Why are we in the city now? Well, because I graduated from high school this spring, and in the autumn I'm going to Barnard. I would have liked to live in the dormitories like everybody else, but my mother says I'm so naive that the sophisticated life of a college freshman would destroy me utterly if she weren't around to help me get adjusted.

Frankly, since I got adjusted to the island of Manhattan so easily, I don't see why I couldn't get adjusted to dormitory life. What I would like more than anything would be to be allowed to do things *on my own*.

Well, even being in Manhattan is a step. I mean, it gives me hope that someday somebody (like my mother's agent, maybe) is going to think of me as a grown-up. It's not that I want to go in for smoking cigarettes in long holders, or literary cocktail parties; I'd just like my mother to take it for granted that I'm old enough to ride the subway by myself.

I suppose the reason she still thinks of me as a baby in diapers, practically, is that we've lived such an isolated life. I don't want to give the wrong impression about her.

She's really wonderful. I mean, all those cookbooks! She's supported us with them. But since I'm all she has, I think she puts too much of her energies into creating me. And I want to create myself. Maybe if she sold more of her poetry instead of just the cookbooks she'd be happier.

Back to my mother's agent. He came up one afternoon to talk about the new cookbook. He wanted fewer recipes and more folksy talk. That way they could get two books instead of one.

But what a surprise he was! I'd heard Angel talk about him, and sometimes she used to go down for a week in New York, leaving me with the Gadsens on the neighboring farm, but I'd never seen him. (I'd better explain about calling my mother Angel. In one of her cookbooks she had four children, all of whom called her

Angel, and after that she got fearfully annoyed with me if I called her anything else. With a little effort you can get in the habit of calling people almost anything, but I've never pictured angels with black bangs and mascara.) Mother's agent didn't call her Angel, however; it was always, very respectfully, Mrs. Folger.

His name was Roscoe Whitelaw, and he was new. I mean, the man at the agency who used to deal with Angel—is that what an agent does? Deal with his clients? It doesn't sound quite right, but I think it's probably accurate as far as Angel's concerned. Anyhow, this man retired and she was assigned to Roscoe Whitelaw or he was assigned to her or something, and she was always complaining about him. He didn't treat her with enough respect; after all, she made a good deal of money for the agency, and so forth and so on, and he was just a new young squirt, et cetera.

Roscoe Whitelaw seems to me quite a good name for an agent and I had a very clear picture in my mind as to what he would be like. Or rather, an alternating picture. One was a man with black brilliantine hair and a striped shirt with a Yale tie with a flash stick pin and a checked sports jacket. And the other was really the same kind of man, only this time he was playing conservative and bought gray flannel suits at Brooks Brothers, and he didn't use nearly as much brilliantine and had a touch of gray at the temples.

So when the doorbell rang and I went to it, I thought it was a young man on some kind of survey. We've had quite a few of those. Do you know Linus in *Peanuts*? He looked sort of like a grown-up version of Linus. I'm sure when he was a little boy he had a blanket he loved and carried it around everywhere with him, and I'll bet you anything he was still sucking his thumb and rubbing a blanket against his cheek when he was using five-syllable words. I mean, he seemed so *vulnerable*, and agents oughtn't to be vulnerable. At least not agents who deal with my mother. He was quite tall, and had lots of straw-colored hair, no brilliantine. No mustache. Nice blue eyes. He looked as though he came from a neighboring farm in Vermont, but I believe it was Utah and his father was a big muggy-mug Mormon or something of that ilk.

So I said, what do you want, and he said he wanted to talk to my mother. Angel was working at her desk on folksy sayings for the cookbook, so I said she was busy and couldn't be disturbed. I mean, he came to the *back* door; how could I know he was her agent instead of the Fuller Brush man?

Well, then he explained to me that he had an appointment with Angel, that he was from Andrews, Parkinson, Mossberg Agency, and that he'd come to the back door because our front door had just been painted and we didn't have our name or the number of the apartment on it yet, and the back door *did* have the number, so I suppose he can't be blamed for having thought that was it. So I apologized all over myself, blushing from the roots of my hair right down to my toenails. But then he goofed, too, even goofier than I had, because he thought I was the maid. Well, I did have on an apron, because it was five o'clock and I was getting dinner. Angel hates to cook.

So I stopped blushing and he blushed instead.

"But you don't look in the least like your mother," he said.

No, I don't. I'm at least a head and a half taller than my mother, almost as tall as Roscoe Whitelaw, and I have red hair and gray eyes and too many freckles and I'm fearfully nearsighted and wear repulsive glasses. Angel is always getting me new, fancy frames, and telling me, "For heaven's sake, Amy, take off your glasses." And whenever there is a school dance she's always quoting me the tired old couplet of Dorothy Parker's, "*Men never make passes at girls who wear glasses.*"

But let's be honest, Angel. It isn't because I wear glasses that the boys at school didn't make passes at me. I never wore glasses to school dances. Angel would take them from me and not even let me carry them in my evening bag, because she said the minute her back was turned I'd put them on again. And it isn't Angel's fault they never made passes at me. She was actually a great help. She made me take dancing lessons, so at least I got danced with even if I didn't get pawed. And she helped me work out a line. We sat down and created a set of questions aimed at making the boys at the dance think I thought they were fascinating because that's the way to make them think *I'm* fascinating. I memorized the questions, there wasn't any trouble about that, and I found it was quite easy to ask them and to sound as though I really cared about the answers, and at the next dance I thought it was working just beautifully when one of my partners said, "Hey, what gives? That's the fifth time you've asked me those same questions."

That's what comes of not wearing glasses.

But it's become a conditioned reflex by now, so when I realized that this wasn't someone from the SPCA but Roscoe Whitelaw, I grabbed off my glasses and stuck them in the pocket of my apron, so I never really knew when he stopped blushing.

"My mother's in her study, Mr. Whitelaw," I said. I hate calling her Angel in front of people, though she loves it. "Just follow me," and I led him through the kitchen and pantry and into the living room, where he stopped me just in time to keep me from walking into a chair.

"Hold on," he said. "Let's not disturb her for a few minutes. Give me time to get adjusted to you."

"But you don't need to get adjusted to me," I said. "I'm not your problem. I don't write cookbooks or poetry or anything else."

"I thought you were a small child," he said. "I thought you were mother's baby girl."

"I'm seventeen," I said.

"And your name is Amy."

"And I'm going to college next year. To Barnard."

I *think* he smiled at that. A smile has to be awfully big before I can see it without my glasses. "Well, what do you know," he said. "I went to Columbia. Class of '57."

Well, then he was still in his twenties. I mean just the right age for a college woman, which is what I was about to be.

Angel came out then. "Amy, who on earth are you talking— Oh, hello, Roscoe, I didn't hear the doorbell."

"I came by the back door, as a matter of fact," Roscoe said.

"Amy, for heaven's sake, put on your glasses," Angel said, and I almost fell over backwards in amazement, because, as I said, Angel's always telling me to take them *off*. I took them out of the pocket of my apron and held them in my hand. For the first time, I didn't want to wear them. I cared.

"Put them on," Angel said impatiently. "You know you are blind as a bat without them. Come on in the study, Roscoe, and I'll show you what I've done."

She sailed off in the direction of the study, and Roscoe stood aside for me. "Coming, Amy?" he asked.

"Amy has other things to do," Angel said grandly, so I went back to the kitchen, but I didn't put my glasses on till Roscoe had followed Mother into the study, and then I'd managed to get fingerprints all over the lenses and I had to wash them with soap and water.

That night I sat up in bed and wrote some poetry. In the apartment I had the maid's room and bath, which is all the way at the other end of the apartment from Angel's room, so I'm lots more private than I was in the country, where I was just across a narrow hall. Also Bruce, the dog, sleeps with me, and he growls the minute he hears a step, so I always know if Angel is coming.

Do I sound as though I resent my mother? Well, I do. I do. But don't get me wrong. I love her, too. I love her very much. She needs me to take care of her, no matter how much she thinks it's the other way around. She needs me to call her Angel and do the cooking and to give her a feeling that she's living in a world of people and not just recipes. But at this particular time I was resenting her more than I ever had before, because I didn't want her to hold my hand while I went to college. I wanted to do it all by myself. Because it was really her hand I'd be holding; I'd be giving her self-confidence, not the other way around, and going to college and being with completely different people was enough of a big thing to cope with, without having Angel tied to my apron strings, too.

I wrote poetry for several nights in a row, and some of it was pretty good, if I do say so myself. I wrote it in my head while I was walking the dog, or when I was riding the subway, and then put it down on paper after I'd gone to bed at night. I thought that maybe if I wrote enough poetry, then I could show it to Roscoe.

Then one day the telephone rang and I answered it, and a nice man's voice said, "May I speak to Miss Folger, please?"

Often people call Mother Ms. Folger, so I said, "Just a moment, please, I'll see if she's busy."

Then there was a laugh at the other end of the line, and the voice said, "Is this the maid?" And I knew it was Roscoe.

"Yes," I said. I meant to say something witty and provocative, like, Yes, this is Parthenope, to show him I knew poetry, but all I said was plain yes with sort of a catch in the back of my throat so it sounded like a frog's croak.

"Well, dear maid, I don't want to speak to Mrs. Folger, I want to speak to Miss Folger. In other words, I don't want to speak to Angel, I want to speak to Amy."

"Hi," I said, brilliantly.

"Amy, I have two tickets for the new Rodgers and Hammerstein musical; the author is one of my clients. Would you like to have dinner with me and go?"

"I'd adore to!" I said. "I've never been to the theatre, except school plays, and I was always in those." And falling over the scenery, I didn't add, because I couldn't see the furniture without my glasses.

Angel helped me get ready. I couldn't tell whether she was pleased or annoyed because Roscoe had called me.

"Amy," she corrected me, "you're far too young to call him Roscoe. It's Mr. Whitelaw."

"Yes, Angel."

"It was very thoughtful of him to call you. Of course, he did it as a favor to me. Now, about your glasses. I think you'd better wear them."

I had no intention of wearing my glasses with Roscoe. "You're always telling me to take them off," I said. "In fact, most of the time you grab them right off my face."

Angel spoke slowly, emphasizing each word. "Amy, Roscoe Whitelaw is not a local yokel from Vermont. He is a man of the world. I'm afraid you wouldn't have the slightest idea how to handle him. I'm not at all sure I should let you go out with him unchaperoned. I wonder if he could get a third ticket? I think I'll call him." And she went to the phone and dialed.

At that moment I hated Angel.

But Roscoe, darling Roscoe, told her that the show was completely sold out, and it was only through the utmost pull that he'd been able to get two tickets.

"You will wear your glasses, Amy," Angel said firmly.

"Yes, Angel," I lied.

Roscoe came for me and as soon as Angel let us go and we were standing, waiting for the elevator, I took my glasses off and put them in my bag. I was determined not to wear them all evening, even though I knew I wouldn't be able to see a thing on stage.

Suddenly the door of the apartment opened and my mother stuck her head out. I reached for my handbag to grab my glasses but I wasn't quick enough.

"Amy!" Angel cried. "Put your glasses on immediately!" She smiled fulsomely at Roscoe. "The silly vanity of young girls. Poor little Amy can't see a thing without her glasses and it's very bad for her eyes to go without them."

To be betrayed by one's own mother!

The elevator came just then and the elevator man stood waiting, and Roscoe and I stepped into the car. I couldn't say: "She's the one who makes me take them off." I couldn't say anything. I clutched my hand back with my glasses still in it and went from white to red to white again.

"You do whatever you like about your glasses, Amy," Roscoe said kindly. "I think you look very nice either way."

But the evening was spoiled. I had been humiliated beyond endurance. Roscoe was wonderful; I mean he just kept on growing more and more wonderful every minute, but at dinner I just sat there as though I were tongue-tied.

He wasn't, though. He talked and talked. He told me about Utah, and he told me about Columbia, and then he told me about how he'd studied for a year at the Sorbonne, and how he'd been in Japan in the army. It was almost like going out with somebody really foreign, since we were in an Italian restaurant eating food I couldn't pronounce. It was like going out with a foreign agent. Gradually I began to relax as I listened to him, though I still couldn't talk. Anyhow, I'm not in the habit of talking a great deal. Angel is a great talker and I learned early that I couldn't hope to compete with her. I mean, she's witty and clever and gay and sarcastic, and I can never say anything except what I feel. This is a great drawback.

I compromised about the glasses and put them on at the theatre, but I took them off at intermission. After the theatre we stopped at the cafeteria for a lemonade, and then he took me home on the subway. I suppose if it had been Angel it would've been a taxi. Angel doesn't like subways. I do.

That night for some reason I couldn't write any poems at all.

The next week I didn't go walking with Bruce nearly as often as usual. I kept hoping that the phone would ring, that it would be Roscoe, that it would be for me.

Well, it was Roscoe once, and Angel got to the phone before I did, and it was for her. He was sending the manuscript in to the publisher. So there wouldn't be any reason for him to call again until Angel had a new book ready, or unless he sold some of the old ones to a women's magazine or something.

What was I to do?

I wanted to see Roscoe again more than anything in the world.

I wrote poetry.

I wrote poetry until I had twenty-five poems out of about fifty that I thought were reasonably good.

My chance came one evening when Angel went to a cocktail party at her editor's. "I hope you don't mind staying in the apartment alone, Amy," she said. "They urged me to bring you with me, but really, these literary cocktail parties are no place for a child."

I assured her I didn't mind staying alone in the least. It would be a good opportunity for me to finish the new skirt I was making.

As soon as Angel had gone—and I waited not only until I saw her step into the elevator, but until, leaning out the living room window, I could see her leave the building and get into a taxi—I ran to the telephone and took off my glasses. It was a few minutes after five, but I hoped that maybe Roscoe didn't leave the office promptly. I had the office number memorized, but I had to put my glasses back on to dial.

I must've gone through at least three secretaries before I got Roscoe. "You just caught me, Amy," he said. "Now, what can I do for you?"

I told him about the poems.

There was a funny sort of hesitation at the other end of the line.

"Does your mother know you're calling me about this?" he asked.

"No," I said. "She doesn't even know I've written the poems."

"Amy," he said, "I don't want you to be disappointed, but we don't usually handle poetry."

"Oh," I said.

"But look, Amy, I'd like to see it anyhow. Do you want to come in with it tomorrow?"

"Sure," I said. "I'd love to. What time?"

"Let's see. I have an appointment for lunch. Make it around three."

"Three," I said. "That'll be fine, Roscoe," and then I almost fell off the bed, because Angel was standing in the door.

"I forgot—" she started, and I never did learn what it was she had forgotten, because then she said, "Well, Amy, and to whom are you talking?"

"Roscoe," I said. "Mr. Whitelaw. Excuse me, Ros— Mr. Whitelaw," I said into the telephone. "Angel is here. I have to hang up now."

"Just a second, Amy," my mother said, smiling brightly. "I'm going to have to call Roscoe this evening, anyhow," and she took the phone out of my hand. "Put on your glasses," she commanded, but she was still smiling, the same kind of smile she used at cocktail parties when she wanted to impress someone. Why was she using the smile on me? Or was it really for Roscoe? It was the kind of smile you can *hear* as well as *see*.

Oh, Roscoe, darling Roscoe, in spite of Angel's pumping he didn't tell her about the poetry. He just told her he'd asked me to come in so that he could show me around the agency.

"It's really very thoughtful of Roscoe," Angel said.

So the next afternoon I got ready with great care. I finished the new skirt, and I wore it with a freshly washed and ironed white blouse with a little lace at the neckline.

"You'd better let me wash your glasses for you," Angel said.

She didn't do it on purpose, this I am quite sure of. But somehow the glasses fell into the sink and broke. Why on earth they chose that particular moment to break I'll never know. I'm constantly dropping them, and they never break. But this time there was a large crack right across the left lens. Oh, this was tragedy compounded on tragedy. Because these weren't just my glasses, these were my spare pair. The regular pair had been leaving an ugly red mark on the bridge of my nose, and they were being fixed.

Angel was sorry, she was truly sorry. This I know, because she had planned to do a lot of work on the new cookbook that afternoon, and instead she said, "I'll take you down in a taxi, Amy. You can't possibly go by yourself without your glasses."

To go see Roscoe with Angel would be much worse than not going at all. "No, Angel, it's all right, truly it is. I can manage."

"How can you possibly manage?" Angel demanded. "You know you can't see two inches in front of your face without your glasses."

"I won't go till tomorrow, then. My other glasses will be ready tomorrow morning."

"You don't seem to realize," Angel said, "that Roscoe is a very busy person. He can't just shift appointments around to suit your convenience. Roscoe works on a very tight schedule and it was exceedingly kind of him to work you in at all."

"But he always sees you whenever you want him," I said.

"After all, that's a very different matter. I provide a good deal of butter for Roscoe's bread," Angel said smugly. "Come along, child, and let's go."

"I'll go alone," I said stubbornly.

"You know perfectly well that it's not safe for you to be out alone without your glasses. You'd probably walk right in front of a truck. I said I would take you, whether it disrupts my schedule or not, and take you I will."

And take me she did. It was awful. She made Roscoe show us all over the agency, and I kept having to shake hands with people I couldn't see, and Angel kept beaming because they all said I looked like her sister and so forth and so on, et cetera, ad infinitum. We walked through a large room with lots of desks, and I banged right into a filing cabinet.

"What happened to your glasses?" Roscoe asked.

"She broke them," Angel said. "You've no idea how much money I spend on Amy's glasses. Children are so thoughtless."

Just as we were leaving I felt a slip of paper being shoved into my hand. I looked up and there was Roscoe's shadowy form. Angel was talking animatedly to someone else, and Roscoe raised his arm in a gesture that I realized must be putting his finger to his lips. I closed my fingers around the paper and put it into my pocket. When we got home and Angel had gone into her study—she said we'd go out to dinner because I couldn't see to cook and

I might put cockroach poisoning on the chops instead of salt—I went into my room and held the paper up close to my eyes and read in Roscoe's small, tidy handwriting, "Meet me on the back steps of the Metropolitan Museum at 10 o'clock tomorrow morning with your poetry, Princess Amy."

The old glasses weren't to be ready till eleven, but I determined I would meet Roscoe anyhow. After all, it wasn't very far away. I could walk. I wouldn't have to take a bus or subway. That wouldn't have been possible, anyhow, because I couldn't see where to get off without my glasses. So I could walk, and I could take Bruce; that would be my excuse for getting out; and the Metropolitan Museum was big enough for even me to see.

So after breakfast I said to Angel, "I'm going to take Bruce for a walk."

Angel was irritable. "How can you take the dog for a walk? You can't see where you're going." Angel had made the coffee for breakfast herself and it wasn't nearly as good as mine. I told her I could make it with my eyes shut and they didn't need my glasses for coffee, but she wouldn't believe me, and that made her crosser than ever.

"I'll be fine. He's practically a seeing-eye dog anyhow," I assured her. This is not true. Bruce is sweet and he is large, but he is also dumb. I'm always having to haul him out of the paths of taxis and trucks. But fortunately Angel doesn't realize this and she is convinced that any dog of hers must be exceptionally intelligent, so she was satisfied.

So about nine thirty I set off. I wanted to give myself plenty of time, and I wanted to be there first, so that Roscoe would have to recognize me instead of the other way around. People who aren't nearsighted themselves are apt to think you're awfully rude if you stare right through them. But if I got to the back steps of the Metropolitan first, I could be sitting on them and reading, and Roscoe would have to come up to me and say, "Hello, Amy," or whatever it is he would say, and then I'd know who he was.

It didn't take me more than ten minutes to get there. I had my pages stuck in the pages of a *New Yorker*. I certainly didn't want Angel to find out about them. As it was, she couldn't understand why I was taking a *New Yorker*, but I said I might just sit on a bench in the park until time to go pick up my glasses, and she knows I can read if I put the page right up to my nose.

I sat on the steps and reread my poetry. I was surprised at how good it was. It had never occurred to me that I, Amy Folger, could write poetry. It was a darned sight better than Angel's, if I do say so myself.

I was absorbed in one of my poems when a voice said, "Hello, Amy."

Roscoe! My heart thumped in two flip-flop syllables.

"Oh, hi," I said. "I got here early because I thought I'd go over things a little." I glanced up at Roscoe's shadowy form, but even without my glasses I didn't dare look right at him. You know that story about the Greek woman who is very beautiful, and Jupiter—oh, golly, is it Jupiter in Greece and Jove in Rome or the other way around? I never can remember. Anyhow, he comes down from Mount Olympus in human form and makes love to her, and she wants to see him not in human form but as he really is, and he keeps on warning her and everything, but she insists, and finally he reveals himself, and the sight of a god is too strong for human eyes, and it kills her. Well, that's sort of how I felt about looking directly at Roscoe.

"And what would you have to go over, young lady?" asked this voice, and suddenly I was suspicious. I squinched up my eyes and looked as hard as I could and realized he wasn't nearly as tall as Roscoe. My heart did another flip-flop, but this time it didn't say Roscoe, it just plummeted down into my stomach and then managed to get back up into place again.

"I'm terribly sorry," I said, "but I've broken my glasses and I don't know who you are."

It was a lawyer we met a couple of times at parties. Oh, woe. Very nice and everything, and it would be just lovely if Angel would marry him so she has somebody else to worry about, but I certainly didn't want to see him right now when I was waiting for Roscoe.

"Are you waiting for somebody?" he asked me.

I hoped that I didn't look too disappointed when I realized it wasn't Roscoe. "Oh, sort of," I said stupidly.

"A gentleman friend?" I could sense the amusement in his voice. Angel's baby girl playing at being grown-up.

"An acquaintance," I said frigidly.

"Hi, Amy" came a voice, and this time it was Roscoe's voice; there was no mistaking Roscoe's voice when it really came.

"Well, I'll be running along now," Angel's friend said. "Oh, hello, Whitelaw. Robbing the cradle?"

I could've killed him. And he'd probably go running to the nearest telephone and report to Angel. Well, at least Bruce growled. He was on my side at any rate.

"Where are your glasses?" Roscoe asked me, patting Bruce. Bruce wagged his tail and stopped bristling.

"They won't be ready till eleven."

"Okay. Well, let's see your poetry anyhow."

Without a word I handed him my pages of poetry. I hadn't dared to borrow Angel's typewriter for them, but I'd copied them in my very best writing, and I didn't think he'd have any trouble reading them.

He read very slowly and carefully, reading some of them twice. It took him half an hour, because I timed him. When he finished, instead of saying anything about my poems, he said, "And you're going to Barnard next year?"

"Yes. Did you—what about my poems?"

"Why did you choose Barnard?"

"I didn't choose it, exactly. Angel thought it would be good because of the cultural advantages of New York. I've already been to the Guggenheim five times. I like the Frick better, but Angel sends me to the Guggenheim. What about my—"

"Isn't there any culture in Vermont?"

"Angel *is* culture where we live. I mean, nobody thinks anything about her cookbooks, but they all think her poetry is wonderful. She's president of the Women's Club and the Book Group and the Musicale. What about my poet—"

"But what about you?"

"I'd give my—I'd give my *glasses* if I could stay in the dormitories and Angel went back to Vermont!" I cried. I was surprised at my own vehemence and hoped he wouldn't misinterpret it.

"Well, look, Amy," he said. "I can get a contract for your mother to go to France and do a cookbook on life in a French kitchen from a Vermont farmwife's point of view."

"You *can*?" I breathed.

"And I'm sure she'd go. I don't think even Angel could resist that. I've been working on it ever since that night we went out to dinner and the theatre together."

I sat very still, letting the implications of this sink in.

"Life in the dormitories of Barnard is fairly liberal," he said. "Do you think we could have dinner and the theatre again once or twice?"

"Oh—*several* times!" I cried. "But Roscoe, what about my poetry?"

He looked at me very kindly and rather sadly. "Amy, don't stop writing poetry. Go on with it. You'll learn a lot in college."

"You mean what I gave you—it stinks?"

"No, Amy, I didn't say that at all. But it's only a beginning. You've still got a long row to hoe. Remember that nothing that's worth anything comes easily."

I felt like a balloon with the air slowly fizzing out of it. I felt that Roscoe saw himself in the grown-up world and I was just a little girl who belonged to one of his clients.

Then he looked at his watch. "Come along, Amy," he said. "It's time to go pick up your glasses."

We went to the shop in silence, because I couldn't talk, and Roscoe didn't seem to want to; he seemed to be thinking deeply about something. And Bruce doesn't talk. The glasses were ready, and the minute they were on, right there in the shop, right there in front of everybody, with me able to see him and everything, Roscoe kissed me. ME!

You know what? Being kissed with glasses on is one of the loveliest feelings in the world.

The Moment of Tenderness

The village of Mt. George in Vermont, to which Bill and
Stella Purvis had moved from New York, was a monoga-
mous one. In the three years they'd been living there they'd never
heard of anyone being divorced, and adultery was unheard of.
Once, in a neighboring and slightly more sophisticated village, in
which both separations and divorces were not unknown, a summer resident was said to have entertained men friends in a more
than casual way while her husband was overseas during the war,
and a nice, juicy scandal evolved; this rather ancient morsel was
still considered a tasty tidbit on the Mt. George party lines.

There was plenty of gossip in Mt. George, much of it un-
founded and a good bit of it malicious, and there was a raw edge
where the village was divided between the old timers who had
been there for generations and the newcomers, like Bill and Stella,
who had moved in since the war, and who now numerically
equaled the natives. Even where warm friendships were formed
between the old and the new there was still the unhealed wound

that might break open at any time: over redecorating the church, or who should head the committee for a church supper, over PTA programs or the Republican caucuses, or simply over the fact that the newcomers had installed indoor plumbing and thermostatic heating immediately and as a matter of course; one does not live without these things; whereas for the people who were born in Mt. George and whose parents and grandparents were born there before them, a privy and struggling with coal and chopping wood or an ugly kerosene heater out in the middle of the living room had been an accepted part of their upbringing, and an indoor toilet, which they called a "flush," was something for which they might have waited twenty years. Stella could easily understand an unformulated resentment over the fact that the newcomers took two bathrooms and a warm house for granted.

Not that any of them were rolling in wealth; there wasn't a swimming pool or a tennis court in the village. Bill, like most of the newcomers, was what was called a "young executive" in one of the factories in the neighboring manufacturing town of Stonebridge (So one can't escape being a commuter, one can't escape suburbia, Stella thought; it can happen even in Vermont). The Stonebridge country club was on the outskirts of Mt. George and most of the newcomers belonged to it, rather grimly enjoying golf or the Saturday night dances.

It was at one of these dances that Bill and Stella first got to know Steve and Betty Carlton. Steve and Betty were in a way a bridge between the old and new residents in Mt. George, since Betty was a native and Steve was from Stonebridge. Steve was a doctor and Stella had had him in once for one of the children and liked then his quiet manner and obviously innate kindness. On this particular evening the Purvises and the Carltons happened to be the only people from Mt. George at the country club so it seemed natural for them to have a drink together, and then Bill asked Betty Carlton to dance and after a moment Steve asked Stella.

He was not a brilliant dancer, not nearly as good as Bill was; he simply walked with an easy rhythm about the dance floor, managing not to bump into anybody else, not seeming to notice the intricate steps that Bill and Betty and some of the other couples were executing. It was rather, Stella thought, like riding one of the old stable horses that are saved for the children or for people who have never ridden before: easy, pleasant, and completely unexciting. He looked rather tired, and Stella was tired, too, her three children having been unusually rambunctious that day, so they simply moved quietly about the floor together, not talking much except to mention the weather and the unusual amount of rain, and the fact that there was nobody else at the country club from Mt. George.

When the music stopped Stella looked over at Bill and Betty, who stood, talking animatedly, waiting for it to start again, and then at Steve, the tired old stable horse standing there smiling quietly. "Let's sit down," she said. "Do you suppose there's such a thing as a glass of ice water in this place? I'm terribly thirsty."

They went back to the table where they had joined forces and Steve asked the bartender for two glasses of ice water. "You'll have to excuse me if I'm not very brilliant tonight," he said. "I was up all night. Three babies."

"I should think you'd rather have stayed home and gone to bed than come to the dance tonight," Stella said.

"Betty likes to go out or do something on Saturday nights." Steve offered Stella a cigarette but she shook her head. "Summer's almost over: there won't be many more dances."

Stella opened her mouth to say that Betty seemed much more like one of the newcomers than one of the natives, but thought perhaps it might not be tactful and took a sip of water to cover and watched Steve light his cigarette. She liked the way he moved his hands, very certain and very quiet, with a minimum of gestures. His hands were quite beautiful, she thought, both long and strong, and it was the way he used them to light his cigarette that made her decide suddenly and say to him quickly, "Look, I'm about three months pregnant, so I suppose I'd better see a doctor or something. Could I have an appointment to see you?"

He suggested that she come in to his office on Monday, and she drank some more of her ice water, feeling rather foolish and wondering if Bill would be angry with her. Most of the old Mt. George residents went to Steve for their babies as they had gone to him for everything else since the death of the old doctor, but the new people went to one of the obstetricians in Stonebridge, and all she could say to Bill was that she had decided to have their fourth child by the Mt. George general practitioner because she liked the way he moved his hands when he lit a cigarette.

Bill indeed was annoyed, and embarrassed at his reasons for being annoyed. "It doesn't look well," he said. "It's not as though we couldn't afford an obstetrician."

"Saving a little money will come in very handy, you know that perfectly well. And I never have any trouble with my babies and I'm sure Steve Carlton's perfectly competent. He delivers plenty of babies around here. Anyhow, I've spoken to him, so it's all settled."

"You can say I'd rather you went to a specialist."

"Darling, you know the money'll be a help. And I'd rather go to Steve. I have confidence in him, somehow. So let's let it go."

They saw the Carltons occasionally that winter, played some bridge, discussed golf and skiing and the possibility of organizing a kindergarten for the Mt. George pre-school children. Stella saw Steve briefly in his office once a month and he was there in the hospital while she had the baby in her usual brief and un-complicated manner. Just when it was or why it was she began to think of him almost constantly she was not sure. She was still in love with Bill, though they did not see a great deal of each other. In the evenings one of them always seemed to have a meeting, PTA or Women's Club or Young Republicans or School Board; and on weekends if the weather was even halfway decent Bill played golf (or, in the winter, went skiing), leav-ing her at home alone with the children. The children and the house and garden seemed to take up all her time; she had been an omnivorous reader; now it seemed to take her a month to get through a book. She had been in the habit of listening to a great deal of music while she did her housework, but the records seemed to disturb the baby, who cried more than the others, and so the phonograph stayed silent for days on end, and instead of listening to Bach or Bartók while she did the dishes or the mending she thought of Steve Carlton and his hands. She had taken the births of her children matter-of-factly and easily, never dwelling on them before or after, but now she found herself re-living her last delivery, Steve's absolutely steady and gentle hand resting for a moment on her belly as he felt the contractions, and the sweetness of his smile as he held the baby, slick and wet and incredibly new, out to her. She and Bill had decided that four children was more than plenty, but she almost wanted another simply to have an excuse to see Steve for five minutes once a month and for the brief moments of work intimately shared in the delivery room.

And why? Why this obsession with Steve Carlton? she asked herself one Saturday afternoon when Bill was, as usual, out playing golf, the baby on the porch asleep in his carriage, and the older three children playing noisily down by the sandbox. She sat rather wearily on the back stairs, leaning against the broom with which she had been sweeping them. Why had it started, this preoccupation with Steve? She knew that it was completely one-sided, that she probably never entered his mind unless she called him, which she did not do often, to ask about one of the children's minor ailments, or he happened to be sitting at the same bridge table with her. And then she would deliberately have to keep her eyes off his hands as he shuffled, as he dealt the cards, as he played them with a quiet sureness. It was his hands always that she remembered, going out to the kitchen with him once at a small party the Carltons were giving, and standing, watching him, while he made her a drink, taking ice out of the ice box, moving with the quiet sureness that was so different from Bill's equal sureness which somehow never, it seemed to her, avoided noise and aggressiveness.

Then there was an incident so slight that she was ashamed to remember and treasure it. It was at a church dinner and Stella and Bill were seated at one of the long tables set up in the church basement before the Carltons arrived. Stella saw them as they came in and looked up and smiled, and as they passed on their way to empty seats at the other end of the room Steve dropped his hand for a moment against her shoulder, saying, "How goes it?"

I am a fool, she thought, sitting there on the back stairs, leaning her cheek against the handle of the broom. He's not particularly attractive, or particularly intelligent or interesting. I don't think he's even a particularly brilliant doctor, so why does the thought of him make my knees buckle? Then there was a cold, rainy day when she wakened with a throbbing headache, chills, and fever. It was too wet to send the children out to play and they soon had the house a shambles. She felt too miserable to get them to tidy up or to play in one room; it was easier to trail around, picking up after them. In the afternoon she called Steve's office and he said that he would drop in on his way home. She fed the baby and put him in his play pen, and, telling the other children to amuse him, curled up in a miserable heap on the sofa. When there was a knock on the door she did not get up to answer it, but called, "Come in," and Steve came into the house, speaking to the children and coming on into the living room. The children followed him in but he sent them back out to the baby, quietly, but in an authoritative manner which they obeyed at once. Then he pulled up a chair and sat looking at her for a moment. "What's the matter, Stella?" he asked.

"I'm all aches and pains," she said. "I think it must be the flu. I'm sorry to get you over here, Steve. I've been taking aspirin but it hasn't helped." He sat there gravely looking at her while he took her temperature, put his fingers briefly against her wrist. Then he took out his stethoscope and asked her to take off her sweater and listened to her chest and back. "Your diagnosis was correct. I'm going to give you a shot of penicillin and some more to take orally and I think you'll feel a lot better tomorrow. Where's Bill? Can you get right to bed?"

"He ought to be home any minute now. I don't think he has anything on for tonight. Oh, poker. No, that's tomorrow."

Steve put the back of his hand for a moment against her cheek. "Feel pretty rotten, don't you? You get into bed and I'll tell Bill to keep the children away."

"Thanks," she said. "They'll be climbing all over me otherwise."

He went out to the kitchen and she could hear him explaining to the children the hypodermic needle that he was preparing, and telling them that they must be quiet and not disturb Mommy. Bill came in then, wanting to know what was going on, and then came and stood over the couch, saying gruffly that he was sorry she didn't feel well.

When she was in bed in the dark bedroom she felt better. She was even able to go over in her mind the gentleness of Steve's hands, the quick skill with which he had given her the penicillin so that she had hardly felt the needle. She was even able to remember what she had felt too sick to notice at its moment of occurrence, the touch of his hand against her cheek.

That was it! she thought. That was what undid her, the moment of tenderness. That was what it had been all along. And why? She was not particularly starved for affection. Bill was an enthusiastic and frequent love maker. The children were always covering her with slobbery kisses and handing her mangled loving bouquets in summer or melting snow balls in winter. So why was she undone by these impersonal glimpses of tenderness in a man who was kind and good but with whom she had in reality nothing in common?

Why did the memory of a hand on her belly during childbirth, a pressure of the shoulder at a church dinner, the polite fixing of a drink by a host for his guest, dissolve her utterly?

She fell asleep then, and in the morning when she felt, as he had assured her she would, better, she determined to put him from her mind. This unreciprocal obsession was neurotic and unfair to Bill and she must rid herself of it. And she remembered, too, with hot shame, hearing Betty talk once of the trouble doctors have with female patients falling in love and making fools of themselves. "Of course it doesn't mean anything to Steve," Betty had said, "but sometimes it can be awfully annoying."

But I am not in love with Steve, Stella thought, and it is not love I want from him, just those little moments of tenderness.

Nevertheless she determined to put him from her mind. She succeeded pretty well. They still saw the Carltons occasionally at the country club or for bridge; she called Steve in when the children had, one after another, mumps, chicken pox, and measles. But she no longer thought of him constantly; she could see him without feeling that she was going to melt.

Then one day her oldest boy fell out of a tree and gashed his head and broke his arm. Her nearest neighbor, hearing the screams, came and took the other three children and called Steve, and Stella rushed Billy down to Stonebridge to the hospital. Steve was waiting for her and in an incredibly short time Billy had five stiches in his head and his arm in a cast and Steve was telling her he thought the boy ought to stay in the hospital overnight.

Then he was looking at a place on her hand where she had burned herself badly the week before and which was not healing properly. "I've got to stop off at the office for a few minutes before I go home," he said. "Come along and let me dress that burn for you. It's really simpler to do it there than here."

She followed him to the office and then, after he had bandaged her hand, he continued to hold it for a minute, saying with a tired smile,

Mica, mica, parva stella,
Miror quaenam sis tam bella,
Splendens eminus in illo,
Alba velut gemma caelo.

"What's that?" she asked.

"'Twinkle, Twinkle, Little Star.' It was the first thing I learned in Latin and for some reason I've never forgotten it. *Mica, mica, parva stella.* You're not twinkling as much as usual, are you, Stella?"

"I'm just tired, like everybody else," she said. She did not take her hand out of his, and he did not put it down.

"Can't get off the merry-go-round, can we?" he asked. "Even if we don't really like it. What Betty wants is to have it go faster and faster. She'd like to move, you know, somewhere where people have a little more money and social prestige counts for more. I don't know why. I don't think she'd really be happy out of Mt. George, not living the kind of life we have to lead anyhow. Mt. George is in her blood, but though she pretends to resent all the new people like you and Bill and to blame you for higher taxes and the roads not being cleared soon enough in winter, she'd be miserable without you. Bridge and golf and the country club dances and coming in to Stonebridge for some function or other, all the things that nobody from Mt. George has ever cared about, are the only things that seem to matter to her."

He had never talked so much before and he did not talk quickly or excitedly now, but quietly, pausing here and there. When he had finished he sat silently holding her bandaged hand for a long time, and then he bent forward and kissed her.

When he had finished he said, "I'm sorry." But all she could do was to shake her head, not speaking.

"This is something that has never happened to me before," he said. "This is something I've never done before. Please believe me."

She nodded slowly, still unable to speak, unable to take her eyes off him.

"I apologize," he said again. "It would for some reason be very easy for me to fall in love with you, parva Stella, but it's something that should never have come out into the open."

At last she was able to speak. "Why?" she demanded passionately. "Why, Steve? We aren't going to let it make any difference. We aren't going to have an affair. You're going to stay with Betty and I'm going to stay with Bill, so why shouldn't we say it just this once? There's so little real love in the world, isn't it wrong not to acknowledge it when it happens? What you've said is going to make all the difference in the world to me, just to know that somebody sees me as a human being, as Stella, as me. And it can't hurt anybody, can it, if you know that I'm thinking about you and caring when you're up all night and tired and maybe discouraged sometimes? We're not going to say it again or let it make any difference in the way we live our lives, so how can it be anything but good to have said it just this once and to know it for always?" Then she stopped, confused and embarrassed, fearing that in her joy she had said too much, more than he'd meant.

But after a moment he said, looking at her with his steady, serious gaze, "What a wise little star you are. Yes, we'll always know, and the knowledge will be good. Now go home, Stella, otherwise I'll kiss you again and that might destroy everything you've said."

She stood up and he did not help her into her coat and she knew that at this moment she could not have endured the touch of his hands. She left his office blindly without saying goodbye and drove back to Mt. George and got the children from her neighbor.

After that, despite the ecstasy of those few minutes in Steve's office, things seemed to run along pretty much as usual. She and Bill went to meetings, had friends in for cocktails or bridge, Bill played golf and poker with the boys, and Stella took on a Sunday school class. She had Steve in once or twice for the children, but they spoke only of whatever childhood ailment was the immediate problem, and the only way she knew she hadn't dreamed Steve's words or his lips on hers was the way his hand always, as though by accident, managed to touch her before he left.

She wasn't sure just when she began to sense a new and different antagonism from the natives. One of her neighbors said once, "Bill must do very well, the way you're able to have Steve Carlton every time one of the children sneezes." She didn't think of it at the time, only remembered it later. There was no reason for the feeling, silent and unexpressed for the most part as it was. No one could know of that afternoon in the office, and she and Steve had hardly spoken or looked at each other on the few occasions when they were at parties together. Perhaps it was Betty's cruel and un-erring instinct and caustic tongue.

She only knew that one night when the baby had a temperature of 104, Bill looked at her and said, "Let's not fool around with Steve Carlton anymore. We'd better call in the pediatrician, what's his name, Hunt, from Stonebridge."

With the hot, unhappy baby in her arms, she said, "All right, Bill, you call him." She rocked the baby and sang, softly. It didn't matter. It didn't make any difference, to her or to Steve or to Bill or Betty or Mt. George. There'd be something bigger and better to talk about on the party lines soon enough, and the mo-ment had happened; it was there for her forever, the gentleness of Steve's hands and the feel of his lips and the quietness of his words.

After the pediatrician, a pleasant enough man, had left, and the baby was asleep and quiet, Stella said, "I'm going out for a few minutes, Bill."

"Why?"

"I haven't been out of the house all day and I need a breath of air."

She put on her old blue tweed coat and walked down the sleeping village street until she came to the Carltons' house. There was a light on in the front hall, and she could see that his car was not in the garage. She stood there for a few moments in the shadow of one of the elms, resting, not thinking, just lean-ing against the tree, and while she was standing there, Steve's car drove up and he put it into the garage and then went, walking slowly, as though he was tired, into the house. Over the garage where his car was she saw a star, quite small, but quietly brilliant.

She looked at it for a long time, memorizing its place in the sky, almost as she might have, in the spring, planted a flower in a special place in the garden.

She looked back at the house again. The light in the hall was out; the house was quite dark. But the star over the garage had not moved, and when she walked home she found that she was humming.

The Foreigners

Whenever anybody moves into a village the size of Mt. George, it's a big event. We all live so close together, we know each other so well, that each new family can actively affect the climate of the town.

I was one of the first to see the Brechsteins. I was at the store as usual during the noon hour, and Wilburforce Smith came in for some teat dilators for his cows and asked if I'd seen the new people who'd bought the old Taylor house. And about an hour later Mrs. Brechstein came in.

She had on tight-fitting orange slacks and a chartreuse shirt and dangly bronze earrings. Her two little boys had on shabby blue jeans and one of them had a hole in his T-shirt. It wasn't the kind of shabbiness we're used to in the village, where nobody has very much money. It was ostentatious. It was obvious she could have had them dressed any way she liked.

All right, let's be honest. I didn't like her right from the start.

There was the way she and the children were dressed and the way she asked me if our eggs were fresh.

I explained to her that we got our eggs from a neighboring farmer and that they were fresh daily. But the shells weren't white enough to suit her. I said that in the country many of us prefer the brown eggs for their flavor, and that the white eggs are usually cold-storage eggs. Of course I should have kept my mouth shut, but I'll never learn.

She went back to the meat department, and I could hear her saying that she could get a certain cut of meat cheaper at the A&P. I could see Chuck, our butcher, getting a little red in the face, but I had another customer to wait on so I didn't quite hear what was going on. After a while Mrs. Brechstein came back with filet mignon and calf's liver and sweetbreads. As I was checking her out and putting her purchases in a bag, I asked her how they were getting on, if they were getting settled all right, and if there was anything we could do to help them.

She smiled at me condescendingly and said that if she decided to pick up odds and ends at the store it might be simpler for her to have a charge account.

I didn't like the words nor the manner of delivery, so perhaps my voice wasn't very warm when I told her that she would have to speak to my husband about it.

"The name is Brechstein, you know," she drawled, "and of course we're so often confused with the Chosen People. But we don't happen to be Jewish," she said, smiling at me tolerantly, as though I hadn't been able to understand her in the first place.

"I'm so sorry," I murmured absently as I put her purchases in a bag.

As she left, Wilburforce Smith came in again, this time for cigars, and accompanied by the second selectman, Harry Nottingham. "Seen the Jews who bought the old Taylor house?" Harry asked him.

"Ayeh."

"Putting in two new bathrooms," Harry said. "Must be full of piss."

Well, you see, that was all part of it. I don't mean the Brechsteins. I mean Mt. George. When Hugh and I first took over the general store, there weren't many people around who hadn't been born within ten miles of the center. And we, like almost everybody else who moved into Mt. George shortly after the war, had a naive idea, as we filled our houses with furniture and furnaces and families, joined the church and the PTA, that after a year or so we would no longer be considered newcomers but would be accepted as belonging to the village.

Now let me tell you a story I was told when we hadn't been here a year. It's supposed to be true, and even if it isn't, it could perfectly well have been. It's the story of the young couple who moved into Mt. George with their infant son. The baby grew up and became a man and then a very old man without moving from the house his parents had brought him to. When he died he was the only one left in his family and the townspeople got together and gave him a fine funeral and burial and had an imposing tombstone erected for him. On it was inscribed, *Dearly beloved, though a stranger among us.*

So I wasn't surprised, one day, when Mrs. Brechstein came into the store and said to me accusingly, "I hear there was a Republican caucus last night."

"Yes, I believe there was," I said.

"Why weren't we told about it?"

"I don't know," I said. "I suppose for the same reason we weren't. They didn't want us to know about it."

"Well, why on earth wouldn't they want us to know?"

"Well, until after the war," I tried to explain, "things hadn't changed for a long time around Mt. George. The old residents have been running the town for a long time and they want to keep on running it."

"Do you think this is a good idea?" she demanded.

I was filling an order for another customer. "No," I said as I weighed a peck of apples. "But there isn't much we can do about it."

Wilburforce came in then to get his mail.

"Ask Wilburforce Smith," I said. "He used to be a state senator."

So Mrs. Brechstein bustled up to Wilburforce Smith.

"It was posted on the door of Town Hall," he growled.

"But who goes and looks at the door of Town Hall?"

She was so right. When people want anything spread around in Mt. George, they don't paste a minuscule sign on the door of Town Hall, hidden by the shade of the elm where no one will see it; they make three signs, one for the store, one for the garage, and one for the fire-house. I'd offered time and again to make the signs for town meetings or caucuses.

And when I wasn't asked and blustered to Hugh about the comparative cleanliness of Tammany Hall, he said, "Look at it their way. They don't want newcomers butting in and telling them how to run things. You can't blame them. Everybody hates change."

"I don't."

"Sure you do. Remember looking at the baby tonight and saying you hated having him grow up? Same difference. And around here everything had been going on peacefully for years and years and suddenly after the war a lot of people move in who promptly have quantities of small children, and suddenly everybody has to shell out a lot of money for a new school and taxes go up and naturally everybody yaps."

"I think it's un-American," Mrs. Brechstein was saying to Wilburforce Smith. "Positively un-American."

Wilburforce Smith chewed on his cigar and narrowed his eyes. I thought maybe I was going to enjoy a good fight between the two of them, but Wilburforce shrugged and went out.

"I don't understand it," Mrs. Brechstein said. "I don't understand it at all."

I was really on Mrs. Brechstein's side, though I hated to admit it. But I tried to explain. I tried to sound just like Hugh when he talked reasonably to me. "Well, you can't blame them for resenting it when people like us come along and buy up the big old houses for our families and then splash on fresh coats of white paint a lot of the old people can't afford, and put in flush toilets when they've struggled with outhouses, and buy automatic washing machines and dryers and dishwashers. And there's even the swimming pool. There was a lot of talk about that swimming pool!"

"I don't see why there should be," Mrs. Brechstein said coldly, and I could see she didn't like being included in the "us."

Anyhow, I'd tried to explain it to her and it was all quite true and I understood it, or thought I did, and it still bothered me.

It bothered me as much as it bothered Mrs. Brechstein. Because we got plenty of it in the store. We got it from both sides. We heard people say in a perfectly friendly way that everything would be all right if it weren't for the newcomers; but they hadn't forgotten we were newcomers. In a store, of course, the customer is always right, and it's my husband's displeasure I have to live with if I lose my temper there, not the person's whose remarks rankle. But it upset me because no one seemed to understand even the simplest things, like the need for a fire escape because there are now thirty pre-school children (including two of mine) in an upstairs fire-trap in an old wooden church every Sunday during Sunday school.

"Never had a fire," I heard Wilburforce Smith say when it was brought up at a church meeting. "Aren't likely to have one."

One weekend in the spring when the Brechsteins had been in Mt. George for a little over a month, we were invited out to dinner by the people with the pool. They live quite near the Brechsteins, and my hostess told me she'd invited them, too, and I thought it a commendably neighborly and hospitable thing to do.

"Aren't they just fascinating?" she asked me. "We're so lucky to have cultured people like that move into town."

Maybe I just see the wrong side of Mrs. Brechstein, I thought.

But that was the night that Mrs. Brechstein made the first of her famous remarks. We'd all been for a swim, and in spite of the warmth of the June evening, a cool night breeze had come up, and all of us women congregated in the Pools' lovely bedroom were shivering as we rubbed ourselves down and dressed. Now, we all knew each other pretty well, having moved into town at more or less the same time and having served together on innumerable church and school committees, and I don't think any of us are particularly prudish, but there was something a little too deliberate about the way Mrs. Brechstein walked around stark staring naked and then leaned her elbows on Mrs. Pool's bureau, looking at the pictures of the little Pools and of Mr. Pool, most handsome in his navy lieutenant's uniform.

"For a man who's spent most of his life selling insurance, your husband has quite an interesting mind," Mrs. Brechstein said to Mrs. Pool. But that, though not exactly the epitome of tact, was not the famous remark. I only came in for the great moment. I looked up from a conversation to see Mrs. Brechstein, still naked, sitting on Mrs. Pool's bed and pulling one silk stocking up onto one gloriously tanned leg. Her leg was not the only tanned part of her, and her body did not have the usual white areas.

"Of course, every intelligent woman," she was saying, "should have at least one affair after she's married. How else can she possibly continue to interest her husband?"

The words fell like stones in troubled waters.

"Well!" Mrs. Pool exclaimed brightly. "Let's all go downstairs and have some dinner, shall we?"

The next day almost everyone who was at the party happened to drop in at the store.

"Of course, she didn't mean it."

"Oh, yes, she did, she meant every word."

"She was drunk, then."

"No, she wasn't. She was stone-cold sober."

"She drank like a fish."

"She can certainly hold it, you have to say that for her."

"Well, I'm out of luck if that's the only way I can manage to hold on to my husband."

Oh, I got an earful!

A few days later I got a different kind of earful.

The Brechsteins, like everyone else except the Pools, took their children swimming in the pond. Sometimes the mothers swam, too, but most of the time they sat around and kept an eye on the kids and gossiped. They also tried to be friendly to the Brechsteins and their two skinny little boys. When the boys threw stones, nobody liked it, but in all honesty the Brechsteins were not the only people in Mt. George who did not believe in disciplining their kids. But permissive upbringing and allowing the tots to express themselves at all costs seemed to sit even less well on the Brechsteins than anybody else. However, what stuck most in the craw were their responses to such well-intentioned questions as:

"How are you enjoying life in the country?"

"It's much pleasanter than the city, isn't it?"

"Isn't it wonderful for children here?"

The answers ran: "No, we much prefer the city to the country. We are stuck out here only because of the littlest boy's health. No artist can create except in the city, where he is surrounded by other artists. The children have no cultural opportunities here. There are so few people one can really talk with."

Naturally, the next thing that happened was someone leaning across the counter, saying, "So-and-so is sure the Brechsteins are communists."

I suppose the same thing happens in many communities. Certainly, it has reached a peak of inanity here. The minute Wilburforce Smith and any of his friends and relatives don't like anything a new resident does, the new resident is called a communist. This kind of gratuitously vicious slander is particularly sickening, and it made me feel for the Brechsteins, though it couldn't make me like them.

Come autumn and the start of the school year, the Brechstein boys went to school, and there were quite a few sharp comments about the Brechsteins actually condescending to send their children to our public school, wouldn't have thought it'd be good enough for them. Mrs. Brechstein spoke loudly on all matters at PTA meetings and Mr. Brechstein joined the Volunteer Firemen, though he wasn't wanted, which must have been unfortunately obvious. One of the most tactless things he did was to win enormously at the regular weekly firemen's poker game.

One evening, about six thirty, as I was waiting for Hugh to come home and the children were setting the table, we heard the sickening wail of the fire siren. It was, fortunately, only a chimney fire, but the next morning it was all over Mt. George that Mr. Brechstein had been telling all the firemen how to do everything. The worst thing about it, Mr. Pool informed us, was that the man had some damned sensible ideas. The firemen had grudgingly followed some of them and hated him all the more for being right. But Wilburforce Smith leaned over the counter, talking to two of the farmers who happened to be in the store, and said, "Damn interfering fool, doesn't even know what he's talking about. I wouldn't raise a finger to help if his house burned down. Serve him right. We don't want newcomers coming in and telling us to do things we can do in our sleep."

The Brechsteins, of course, were atheists, but the little boys wanted to go to Sunday school with their friends, so the Brechsteins, after too many too public conversations on the subject, decided it wouldn't contaminate them, and let them go. The next thing we knew the Brechsteins were single-handedly going from door to door trying to raise money for a fire escape.

Now, we'd all been working in our own quiet ways on that fire escape for some time; it bothered all of us that the inadequate Sunday school facilities, particularly the kindergarten and primary rooms that were upstairs, were fire-traps, and we'd been working very hard trying to do something about it. Most New Englanders, my husband included, will not do today what can be done tomorrow, but we were beginning to make progress. It was going to be brought up again at the annual church meeting in January, and we all felt that the money for the fire escape would be appropriated and that perhaps we might even get somewhere on building a parish house with proper Sunday school facilities. When Mr. Brechstein came to our house, full of zeal and enthusiasm and talk about the safety of the kiddies' bodies as well as their souls, I wanted to tell him, *Listen, Mr. B., you've just killed all our chances of a fire escape and parish house. Don't you, with all your pretensions to intellect and psychology, know that if you want to get something like this done in New England you have to sell it to a couple of open-minded old residents here and let* them *do the canvassing?* But he was somehow so pathetically eager and he looked, with his balding head with the curly dark hair over the ears, so like a spaniel that I dug down and produced ten dollars instead.

"Fire is something you can't be too careful about," Mr. Brechstein said. "Next week we're having our whole house rewired as a precaution."

So most people forgot the fire escape and remembered Mr. Brechstein.

"I won't have that damned communist telling me what to do."

"They ought to be driven out of town."

"They better watch out."

Of course Wilburforce Smith and his gang were behind most of the talk, or at least the gentle push that was all that was needed to get it going, and if anybody had asked me whom I liked least, Mr. Brechstein or Wilburforce Smith, I'd have been hard put to it to decide.

It was pretty gruesome, and it also got very tiresome, having everybody talk about nothing but the Brechsteins. Sooner or later someone else would do something or something would happen to deflect people's tongues, but the Brechsteins were the current scapegoats.

One afternoon, Mrs. Brechstein dropped into the store for a loaf of bread and nobody else happened to be there.

"Why," she demanded, looking me straight in the eye, "doesn't anybody like us?"

I was too embarrassed to say anything.

"No, please tell me," she said. "We both know it's true. I didn't expect to find any intimate friends in a place like this, of course, but—"

"Well, maybe it's because you didn't expect to find friends," I said tentatively.

"But it's more than that," she said. "I can do without friends, with my independent mind, but I don't understand the feeling of dislike we get everywhere we go."

"Well," I said, "you know you've talked a good deal about how you bring your children up, about how you never tell them what to do, but try to unobtrusively guide their minds to the right decisions? It might be better if you treated everybody else that way, too."

"What do you mean?" she demanded.

"People around here don't like being told what to do. It isn't just the new parish house and the fire escape. It's everything else. You tell us all how we should run our lives, what we should read and what we should think of what we read, and what kind of wallpaper we should use and what colors we should wear, and even who we should go to bed with."

"What do you mean by that last remark?" she snapped. And then to my horror a great tear slipped out of one eye and trickled down her cheek. "Of course I know what you mean," she said. "I'd had too much to drink and I was scared out of my wits by all of you people who knew each other so well. And I did expect to make friends, but I didn't know how. So I said it just to bolster my self-confidence. Of course I don't go around having affairs. I just thought it would make you—make you—" and she rushed out of the store and got in her car and drove off.

I was appalled. And ashamed. Surely we should have realized. All that brashness. All that arrogance. Just a front, and one that we should have been able to see through.

Hugh and I talked it over that evening. Mr. Brechstein had come to him, too, with complaints about the unfriendliness of New Englanders, their lack of hospitality, their suspicious natures.

"I don't think I'll ever really like them," I said, "but I do feel terribly sorry for them now. They've managed to hit me so often on my vulnerable spots that I never stopped to look at it from their point of view. Pretty Brechsteiny of me, wasn't it?"

Just after we had first fallen into sleep, that deep, heavy sleep out of which it is almost impossible to rouse, the fire siren started. The wild screech going up and down the scale, up and down, over and over, shattering the peace of the night, pierced insistently through my subconscious, until at last I was aware that I was listening to something. Unwilling to be roused, I pushed down under the covers and turned my face into the pillows. But the wailing of the alarm kept on and on until at last I wakened enough to realize what it was. I lay there and started to shiver as I always do when I hear the siren. Up and down, on and on, over and over, the high, penetrating scream probing through sleep. I raised up on one elbow and looked over at Hugh, and he was still sound asleep. He's so tired, I thought, he's been working so hard lately, I can't wake him. I turned over on my side. Still the siren screamed. Suppose it was our house, I thought, and somebody else's wife said to herself, Oh, my husband's so tired, I don't want to get him up to go out in the cold. No, I can't do it, I thought, I'll have to wake him. Even if it's only a chimney fire, which it probably is on a cold, windy night like this.

I took Hugh's shoulder and shook it gently. Against the windows the wind beat and the sound of the siren rose and fell.

"Hugh. Hugh. It's the fire siren." He groaned and rolled over.

"It's the fire siren," I said again.

Suddenly and all at once he was awake, swinging his legs out of bed, going to the south windows, then the east windows, standing with his bare feet on the ice-cold floor.

"It's in the center of town and it's a big fire," he said suddenly, and started to dress.

"Please dress warmly," I begged. "I know you're rushing but please don't forget your boots. You won't be any help to anybody if you freeze." Do *all* men, if their wives don't plead with them, tend to dash out of the house in midwinter as though it were July?

I got out of bed and went to the window, and the eastern sky was lit with a great glow. I thought of all the houses in the center but the glow was so general that it was impossible to tell where the fire actually was. "It looks as though it might be the church," I said.

"If it is, thank God it's at a time when there's nobody in it." Hugh pulled a ski sweater over his head.

"And Mr. Brechstein will be right, as usual," I said, trying to make myself smile. Hugh went downstairs for his overclothes, and I said, "Please be careful," and then he'd gone out into the dark and I could hear the cold engine of the car cough as he started it. Before he was out of the garage there was the sound of another car hurrying down the road, and then another, and then Hugh was following them.

I knew that I couldn't go to bed till he got home, so I went upstairs and pulled on my bathrobe and stood again at the east window looking at the horrible red glare. It was so violent and brilliant that I could see bursts of flames thrusting up into the night. The phone rang and I ran to answer it. It couldn't be that something had happened to Hugh; he'd scarcely had time to get to the center.

It was my neighbor up the road. "Madeleine, do you know where the fire is?"

"No. It's in the center. It looks as though it might be the church. Has Howard gone?"

"Yes. Listen, if you hear where it is, call me, will you?"

"Yes, I will, and same to you, please."

All over Mt. George women would be awake and wondering where the fire was, and there was no longer the comforting thought that on a night like this it was probably a chimney fire; that ghastly red glare was visible for miles.

I was too nervous to sit down, too nervous to do anything. I went down to the kitchen and put on a kettle for tea, and then I went back up and checked the children, tucked them in, walked our littlest boy to the bathroom, tidied up some clothes that had fallen on the closet floor, picked up Raggedy Ann and tucked her back in beside my small sleeping girl, went back down, and drank a cup of tea.

The phone rang again. Someone else wanting to know if I knew where the fire was. Three more calls. We all knew it was in the center, and we all thought it might be the church. I looked in the refrigerator to see what I could make into a sandwich for Hugh when he got home. The phone again. My neighbor. "Madeleine, it's not the church, it's down the hill to the Brechsteins'."

"I wouldn't raise a finger," Wilburforce Smith had said, "if his house burned down." There had even been some wild talk about burning those communists out.

The phone again. It would waken the children. "It's the Brechsteins," I was able to say this time.

It takes more than a phone call to rouse the children. Were those little beasts the Brechstein boys all right? Little beasts or not, the thought of a child in a burning house is an unbearable one. I rushed upstairs to stand looking at our own children, lying safe and sweet in their beds. Naughty and noisy as they might be by day, at night they looked like cherubs; all children do, and I was sure the Brechstein boys were no exception.

The phone rang again. "It's the wing of the house, Paul says. Not a chance of saving it, but they might be able to save the main house."

The wing. The wing was where the boys' bedroom was.

If it weren't for our sleeping children, how many of the Mt. George women would have followed their men over to the fire! We were thinking of the Brechstein boys, we were thinking of our men recklessly trying to fight the flames; none of us, native or newcomer, could stop our nervous pacing, and the phone was our only relief from tension.

"Those boys sleep in the wing."

"Yes, I know."

"Do you suppose they're all right?"

"My Johnny gave Peter Brechstein a bloody nose in school today. The kid asked for it, too, but now—"

"They've called the Clovenford fire department, too."

"Yes, and Litchfield."

I drank another cup of tea. I checked on the children another time. I stood at the window and the glare had died down. There was no longer the bright bursting of flames, and the sky looked murky and sick, and at last I realized that part of the light was coming from dawn.

A car came up the road, and then another, and then the kitchen door opened and I ran to meet Hugh. His face was black with soot and he looked exhausted. While I fixed him something to eat and drink he began to tell me about it.

"It was the wing of the Brechsteins' house. Burned clear down. But they saved the main house. Couldn't possibly have done it if everybody hadn't got there quickly."

"But the boys, what about the boys?" I asked.

"Wilburforce Smith went in after them," Hugh told me. "Burned his hands badly, too, but the boys weren't touched."

Relief surged through me. "No one was really hurt?"

"No. Everybody's okay, Mr. Brechstein worked like a madman. Everybody did."

"You included," I said.

"A lot of them are still there. Don't dare leave while it's still smoldering."

"How did the fire start?" I asked.

"Nobody knows for sure. They think faulty wiring." He stretched and yawned.

"Try to get a nap," I begged, "before time to get up."

A nap, of course, was all it was, and then there was the usual rush getting the children ready for school, and Hugh off for the store, and then the phone started ringing, and we were all off in a mad whirl of baking pies and cakes for the men still working on the debris of what had been the long white wing of the house, and collecting clothes for the Brechsteins, and cleaning up the main house for the Brechsteins so that there was no sign of smoke or water or broken windows. For a few brief glorious days, thousands of cups of coffee were swallowed and all the tensions were miraculously eased, and the church women held a kitchen shower for the Brechsteins because the kitchen, too, had been in the wing, and Mrs. Brechstein managed not to put her foot in her mouth, and people forgot for an evening who was old and who was new and nobody called anybody else a communist. It was at least a week before somebody else came into the store and said angrily, "Did you hear what Mrs. Brechstein did *now?*"

So perhaps New Englanders are unfriendly and perhaps they are inhospitable, and perhaps I'll never understand or like either Mr. Brechstein or Wilburforce Smith, and perhaps we'll never feel like anything but newcomers in this tight little community. But where, after we have made the great decision to leave the security of childhood and move on into the vastness of maturity, does anybody ever feel completely at home?

The Fact of the Matter

Old Mrs. Campbell leaned over the counter towards me, first looking towards the back of the store to make sure we were alone, then to the door to see that no one was coming up the steps. "How she would love to be an Eskimo just for one night!" she said softly.

"An Eskimo? Who?" I asked, stupidly, for Mrs. Campbell had been on one of her long monologues and I had only been half listening.

"Alicia. My daughter-in-law."

"But why an Eskimo?" I asked.

"Eskimos put old people like me out on an ice floe to freeze to death. Of course it wouldn't bother me too much if she did try something like that. I have my connections and I'd get off." But she sounded very agitated.

Old Mrs. Campbell talked at length to me when she came into the store, and on almost any subject, but she had never before made me wonder whether her mind might be affected. I said soothingly, "Anyhow, there aren't any ice floes around here."

Mrs. Campbell looked down at the little girl who was clinging to her. "You help Granny now, Sylvie," she said. "We'll start with the Campbell's soup, of course. Wouldn't do to slight a family connection, no matter how distant. Bring Granny a tomato soup like a good girl."

When Sylvie had gone after the soup, Mrs. Campbell leaned closer to me. "You may wonder why I'm talking like this, Mrs. Franklin, but I have my reasons. Do you know how cold it was last night?"

It had been the coldest night of the autumn so far, that first shocking plummeting of the mercury, when the grass crunches beneath your feet and the stars seem made of ice. "Well, the thermometer on our north wall said fifteen degrees this morning," I said.

Mrs. Campbell nodded. "Mrs. Franklin, last night at bedtime when I was heating water for my chamomile tea, I went to let in Nyx"—she looked out the door to where her great cat brooded, waiting for her on the store porch—"and she took her good time about coming in, mincing across that frozen lawn as though it were mid-summer. And when I turned to go back into the house the door had been shut behind me. Shut and locked. And it was my daughter-in-law who did it."

"Oh, nonsense, Mrs. Campbell!" I exclaimed in a shocked voice.

"Nonsense my aunt Osiris," Mrs. Campbell retorted. "We may not have any ice floes, but if I had been left on the doorstep all night I would have died of the cold or had pneumonia at the very least."

"But you weren't left on the doorstep," I said comfortingly.

"Oh, yes, I was serious, that door was shut and locked. On purpose. But I got in. So, yes, I got in. I know a few little tricks, I do. And when she saw me she looked as though I were a ghost. She didn't expect me back in that house alive. 'Why, Granny, I thought you'd gone up to bed,' she said, 'and I locked the door. How did you get in?' Not much point in telling her, was there? I was in and that was the point. And my fool of a son sat in front of the television grinning at some program without the least idea of what was going on in his own house. Of course I've always told him he underestimates her."

"But, Mrs. Campbell," I tried. "You can't mean what you're saying! Surely Alicia wouldn't do anything like that. You said yourself she thought you were upstairs. And anyhow, you know how good she is, always thinking about other people."

For Alicia Campbell has the unusual reputation of being as saintly as she looks.

Old Mrs. Campbell shook her head. "Yes, that's what bothered me. First time I've ever known Alicia to do anything human." She leaned across the counter. "Mrs. Franklin, you believe me, don't you?"

"No, of course I don't," I said.

"Oh, yes, you do," she whispered. "You don't like Alicia, do you?"

This is not the kind of conversation the wife of the owner of a general store ought to get involved in. Fortunately, just at that moment the bells over the door jangled. Old Mrs. Campbell

cackled and whispered to me, "Speak of the devil," and cackled again, and Alicia came in. "And I don't intend to ask her
where she's been," she said, sotto voce, "because she's probably
been doing her marketing at the A&P. As for me, I would never
darken the doors of a concern that changed such a beautiful and
melodious name as the Great Atlantic and Pacific Tea Company
to anything as plebian and unpoetic as the A&P."

"Oh, there you are, Mother C.," Alicia said in her crisp, no-
nonsense voice. "You and Sylvie can ride home with me. It's
really much too cold for you to walk."

"Thank you, no, Alicia," old Mrs. Campbell said, equally
crisply. "Nyx does not like cars and Sylvie and I prefer to walk.
We like the exercise."

"It's too long a walk for Sylvie," Alicia Campbell said, rather
irritably, but she was not going to cross her mother-in-law in
public. She turned to me, angelically beautiful and devilishly ef-
ficient. "Madeleine, my scout troop is having a big resale next
Saturday to raise money for an outing. Is it all right if we use the
store? Of course if it is warm we will use the porch; otherwise we
will have to bring the things inside."

On Saturday the store is apt to be crowded; I looked out at
Alicia's car and saw the back seat loaded with groceries from the
A&P which she could've bought right here; but the scouts are not
responsible for the fact that I don't care for Alicia Campbell, so I
just said, "You'll have to check with Hugh, but I imagine it will
be all right."

"Fine. Don't you forget to come to the PTA this week. I have
a very good speaker lined up." Alicia is vice president of the PTA.
She is a trustee of our church and she teaches Sunday school and

is den mother, and no matter how much she takes on she seems capable of even more, and she always looks beautiful and she never seems tired.

"You're sure you don't want to ride home with me?" she asked old Mrs. Campbell.

"Thank you, no, Alicia."

"Sylvie, come along with me."

But Sylvie just clung to her grandmother's skirts.

"Say, 'No, thank you, Mother.'"

Sylvie hid her face.

"Really," Alicia said, her violet eyes clouding with annoyance. "Sometimes I think you aren't quite bright. I'd really think you didn't know how to talk if I didn't hear you at home with Granny." She swept out of the store; she wasn't used to being crossed, and it rankled that I had seen it. As she got into the car, the sunlight glistened on the pale gold of her beautiful hair.

"Where's my marketing bag, Sylvie?" Mrs. Campbell asked.

The marketing bag was in old Mrs. Campbell's hand and Sylvie pointed to it silently. "Ah!" Mrs. Campbell said. "Come along, Sylvie." And they trotted out the door and down the steps. Slowly Nyx, the cat, stood up on the rail, stretched lasciviously, arched its back, fluffed out its tail, drew its claws destructively along the rail, and trotted daintily down the highway.

That night I had just finished putting the children to bed and was setting the table for breakfast when the phone rang. My husband called me from the living room. "It's for you."

"Who is it?" I asked, coming in, carrying the children's three milk mugs.

"She wouldn't say."

I put the mugs down on the desk by the telephone, annoyed, eager to get upstairs and into a hot bath and our nice warm bed. "Hello?"

"Mrs. Franklin, this is Mrs. Campbell. Old Mrs. Campbell."

"Oh, yes, hello," I said.

"Mrs. Franklin, I want to see you," she said.

"I'll be at the store at the usual time tomorrow," I promised her. "Twelve to three."

"No. I want to see you tonight."

"We're just on our way to bed," I said.

"Mrs. Franklin, do you remember what I told you this afternoon?"

"Yes," I said.

"You didn't laugh at me. You contradicted me, which wasn't polite, but you didn't laugh at me. You've never laughed at me, and I've given you plenty of cause. I've got to talk to you. I have to talk to someone and there isn't anybody else. It's terribly important."

"Won't tomorrow do as well as tonight?" I asked.

"No, I have to make up my mind by midnight. As far as I'm concerned there isn't any problem. It's Sylvie I'm worried about. I don't know whether or not I have any right to make a decision like this for Sylvie. It's her whole life."

"If it's that important, I should think your son would be the one to talk to, not me."

"Him!" she cried in scorn. "He'd go right to her. And they're both so good. It's not that you're not good, of course, Mrs. Franklin. You're just not good in the same way. What I thought I'd do, if you don't mind, is walk over and have a few words with you. I won't keep you any longer than I can help. But you'll see when I get there how important it is, and that I can't take all the responsibility myself."

"Mrs. Campbell," I said swiftly, "it's much too cold for you to walk tonight."

"I'll walk fast," she said, "and I have my old sealskin. Tonight I'm prepared for it; last night I didn't even have my sweater. I'll start out on foot and if you think it's so cold that you'd feel better if you came and picked me up in your car, I'll be on the look-out for you. But not your husband, please," she said in sudden warning; could she read my mind? "Just you." And before I could answer, she had hung up. I knew that almost immediately she would be putting on that old black sealskin coat and slipping out of the house.

I turned to my husband. I had told him of the conversation at the store, and now I told him what Mrs. Campbell had said on the phone. "I'm worried about her," I said, "and in a funny sort of way I've grown fond of her. I better hop in the car and go over and see what's what."

"Don't you think you ought to call Jack and Alicia?" he asked.

"Yes," I said, "I think I ought, but I'm not going to. It would be betraying her, and I can't do it. I'm going to get in the car and meet her. Okay?"

Sometimes I think my husband is too difficult to alarm. So I was a little surprised when he said, "Take Alexander with you. And if you're not back in a reasonable length of time I'm coming after you."

"Okay," I said, and whistled for Alexander as I went out to the pantry and took my polo coat off the hook. Alexander's ancestry is unknown, but there are sizable traces of both Great Dane and St. Bernard in him. He is gentle as a lamb and has raised our three children almost as well as Nana in *Peter Pan*, but he looks quite frightening and his bark if he thinks anyone is coming too close to any one of his family will make a strong man sweat.

About half a mile before the Campbell house, I saw two small, intense green lights and two larger, duller ones, and then I realized it was the beams from the headlights of the car being caught and thrown back by Nyx's eyes and Mrs. Campbell's spectacles. Mrs. Campbell stopped and waited, and when I had drawn up beside her and opened the car door she looked in carefully, saying, "You sure your husband didn't come?"

"He's home with the children," I said reassuringly.

She looked at Alexander and her face and voice were dubious. "I'm not sure about the dog."

"Oh, Alexander wouldn't hurt a flea," I said.

"It wasn't *that* I was worried about," she said with some asperity. Before she shut the door she leaned out of the car and called to the cat, "It's all right, Nyx."

In the glare of the headlights, Nyx waved his enormous tail menacingly, turned, and disappeared into the bushes at the side of the road. Through the undergrowth I thought I could still see the two lamps of his eyes.

For quite a long time, Mrs. Campbell just sat in the seat beside me, not speaking, but I could sense that she was trembling, very slightly, but constantly. Alexander, who had been sentenced to sit in back, leaned over the front seat and nuzzled her gently. If Alexander hadn't done this I think I would have started the car, driven old Mrs. Campbell home, and delivered her into the hands of Jack and Alicia, betrayal or no. I was thoroughly scared, as I felt that I had taken too much responsibility upon myself if the old lady was spiraling into a mental breakdown. Who was I to think I could handle it alone? But Alexander has a nose for illness and abnormality. Once a placid-looking salesman came to our door; a more innocuous man was never seen, but Alexander would not let him in the house. Hugh read in the paper the next day that he'd had a complete mental crack-up, assaulted a housewife in a neighboring village, and been taken to a mental hospital. If there were anything seriously wrong with Mrs. Campbell's mind Alexander would not have nuzzled her so gently; it was one of his forms of giving the seal of approval.

Mrs. Campbell broke out of her trance, smiled at Alexander with very much the same warmth she usually reserved for Sylvie, and turned to me with a worried frown. "I don't know why your dog likes me," she said. "Dogs oughtn't to. Not under the circumstances."

But she *must* be batty!

"Turn out the lights, please, my dear. I'd rather we weren't seen. Just pull off the road a few yards and into that *dull* picnic area, will you please? Can you imagine people wanting to have picnics there in full view of every passerby?"

I had to admit that it was a wonder to me, too, as I passed on summer weekends with every table crowded, and table cloths laid on the few bare patches in between. I drove into the small half-circle driveway, and though we would be able to see any car or small animal coming down the night road, I suddenly felt very alone and isolated.

"Mrs. Franklin," Mrs. Campbell demanded, "do you remember when you joined the church?"

"Why, yes," I said.

"Was it important to you? It mattered, didn't it?"

"Yes," I said. "It's mattered very much or I wouldn't have done it."

"I knew I could trust you!" she cried triumphantly. "I've been watching you and testing you for a long time. You may not have realized it, but I have been. I knew you wouldn't be like those women who do it because everyone else is doing it, just the way they join a bridge club or try to get their husband to take out a membership in the golf club. It ought to mean more than bridge or golf, oughtn't it?"

"Yes," I said, "though I do enjoy a good game of bridge once in a while. Haven't time for golf."

"Stop trying to keep this on a light plane. I know what you're trying to do. Humor me along because you think I'm mad. But in your heart, you see, you're not quite sure, and that's why you're here with me at all. This isn't a light or laughing matter, Mrs. Franklin. It's deadly serious. Think about how you felt when you made your decision to join the church. Think how you felt when the hour approached. That is the way I feel now."

Mrs. Campbell paused, but evidently she didn't expect me to say anything, because after a moment she went on. "We were talking about Alicia this afternoon, weren't we? Mrs. Franklin, everything Alicia stands for I'm against. Now you're going to remind me that I come to church every Sunday with Alicia and Jack and the children. Yes. The church has meant a lot to me during my life. But now I go each Sunday because it's quiet and

I can sit and think what I want to think. It's always noisy in our house, and Alicia thinks it's ungrandmotherly of me if I lock my door. But you see, Mrs. Franklin, I want to join another church now, and that's what I want to talk to you about, because if I do, I've promised to take Sylvie in with me. There's my problem, you see. Sylvie's not old enough to decide for herself, and so have I the right to do it? And I have to make my decision by midnight."

"What possible church could want this of you?" I asked uneasily.

"The church of the devil."

In the back seat of the car Alexander moved uneasily, but he did not growl. The silence in the darkness pressed about us was like the silence and darkness that comes before a thunderstorm, but this was the fall of the year, and the night was clear and cold.

"I hope you don't mean that," I said finally.

"But I do. Alicia represents our church. Therefore, I am against our church. But, like most thinking human beings, I feel the need of a god to worship and to go to for comfort and succor. Therefore I'm going to the devil."

"All right," I said, "go to the devil if you must, but you're quite right, you have no right to take Sylvie with you."

"But those are his terms," she said sadly. "My soul is not enough. I'm old and almost finished. He wants Sylvie, too."

"That ought to show you he's not fit to worship."

"Oh, but he is! Make no mistake about it, Mrs. Franklin, he is! Have you read Milton's *Paradise Lost*? Milton knew. He didn't intend to make the devil the hero of his greatest work, but that's exactly what he did. Oh, he's worth worshiping! And if God approves of people like Alicia, he doesn't want *me*; and the devil does. It's nice to be wanted, Mrs. Franklin. I haven't been wanted for a long time now."

"But—"

She did not allow me to speak. "Please, I have one more favor to ask of you and then I won't bother you again."

"What is it?" I asked warily.

"We're meeting at the fairgrounds at five minutes before midnight. Please bring your car and park it just at the entrance to the fairgrounds and wait there for half an hour. If I haven't come to you with Sylvie by then, you'll know that I made my decision and what it is and you can go on home. If you care what happens to my soul—and I think you do care about people's souls, Mrs. Franklin—you'll come. Won't you?"

"Yes," I said wearily. "I'll come."

"Aaah!" She gave a great sigh of relief and leaned back. "There's my good girl!"

Had she hypnotized me? No, I can't shuffle off the responsibility like that. I did it of my own free will. I took her home, then went home and to bed quite normally, and when Hugh had gone to sleep I got up and went downstairs and dressed and got back in the car and drove over to the entrance of the fairgrounds.

I took Alexander with me. Maybe I thought this would appease Hugh a little when I told him about it later. Because I would still have to tell him.

I sat there and waited in the dark. I don't smoke, but at that time I would have given anything for cigarettes to choke over, anything to occupy my hands and my mind. I thought of turning on the car radio and decided against it. In the eastern sky behind the fairgrounds a tired and ancient-looking moon rose, turning slowly from a large red flattened-out sphere to a small, dwindling white one. From the church steeple, slow deep strokes of midnight began to toll.

And still nothing happened. I counted the bells. Twelve of them. And still nothing. Had Mrs. Campbell made her decision? Did I really believe any of the wild tales she had told me?

Silence and darkness. I was shivering. Then across the fairgrounds I saw two figures streaking, barely illuminated by the worn-out moon. It was Mrs. Campbell. Mrs. Campbell and Sylvie. They were running fast, much faster than I would have believed possible for an old lady and a small child to run. Then it seemed that there were other figures streaking after them, gaining on them. I flung open the door of the car. In the seat beside me I could see the fur rise on Alexander's back. Before I could stop him, he jumped out of the car and went flashing across the field. The two small figures were slowing down now, stumbling, exhausted.

"Hurry! Hurry!" I found myself screaming, the sound thin and frightened against the night.

Now they were covering the last few yards. The dark, almost shapeless figures behind them were almost on them. "The sign of the cross," Mrs. Campbell screamed. "Make the sign of the cross!"

Involuntarily I obeyed.

She and Sylvie flung themselves into the car as the two foremost following figures caught up with them. A great dark, hairy figure. And behind him, blond hair flowing, eyes gleaming redly, angelic face alight with satanic fire—no, it couldn't be, it couldn't possibly be—

"Angels and ministers of grace defend us!" Mrs. Campbell screamed and made the sign of the cross.

And suddenly the figures fled.

"Did you see her?" Mrs. Campbell demanded, her voice still an exhausted scream. "Did you see Alicia? It was one of her tricks all along! All the church work, all the being so good, just a trick to get our souls for him! If it had been anybody but Alicia I'd have done it, too! But now I shall go back to God, Mrs. Franklin, and to hell with the devil!"

She sank back against the seat of the car, exhausted. Sylvie climbed up into her lap and twined her arms about her grand-mother's neck. Alexander came racing across the field and jumped panting into the back and gave Mrs. Campbell an affectionate nuzzle. He was holding something in his mouth; he had evidently taken a bite out of somebody's garments. His kiss seemed to rouse the old lady and she said briskly, "Now if you'll just be kind enough to take us along home, Mrs. Franklin, I'll take Sylvie to bed. Oh dear, I'll need keys tonight, won't I?" She looked through her handbag. "I have them! No, we won't have to disturb anybody."

I took them home and saw them safely into the darkened house. I went home myself and crawled into bed beside Hugh. I told him about it when I wakened in the morning, before the children were off, when we were still lying together in bed. And he laughed.

"It isn't funny," I said tensely.

He looked at me skeptically. "You don't believe it, do you?"

"Of course."

"You're still half-asleep," he said. "Come on, wake up. Wake up!"

I got out of bed and went to my closet and plunged my hand down into the pocket of my coat. There it was, the thing I had taken from Alexander's teeth the night before, neither the skin of an animal nor the cloth from the garments of a human being, a scrap of something red and rough and repulsively hairy.

Poor Little Saturday

The witch woman lived in a deserted, boarded-up plantation house, and nobody knew about her but me. Nobody in the nosy little town in south Georgia where I lived knew that if you walked down dusty Main Street to where the post office is, and then turned left and followed that road a piece until you got to the rusty iron gates of the drive to the plantation house, you could find the goings-on would make your eyes pop out. It was just luck that I found out. Or maybe it wasn't luck at all. Maybe the witch woman wanted me to find out because of Alexandra. But now I wish I hadn't because the witch woman and Alexandra are gone forever and it's much worse than if I'd never known them.

Nobody'd lived in the plantation house since the Civil War, when Colonel Londermaine was killed and Alexandra Londermaine, his beautiful young wife, hung herself on the chandelier in the ballroom. A while before I was born, some northerners bought it, then after a few years they stopped coming and people

221

said it was because the house was haunted. Every few years a gang of boys or men would set out to explore the house but nobody ever found anything. And it was so well boarded up it was hard to force an entrance. So by and by the town lost interest in it. No one climbed the wall and wandered around the grounds except me.

I used to go there often during the summer because I had bad spells of malaria, when sometimes I couldn't bear to lie on the iron bedstead in my room with the flies buzzing around my face, or out on the hammock on the porch with the screams and laughter of the other kids as they played torturing my ears. My aching head made it impossible for me to read, and I would drag myself down the road, scuffling my bare sun-burned toes in the dust, wearing the tattered straw hat that was supposed to protect me from the heat of the sun, shivering and sweating by turns. Sometimes it would seem hours before I got to the iron gate near which the brick wall was the lowest. Often I would have to lie panting on the tall prickly grass for a minute until I gathered up my strength to scale the wall and drop down on the other side.

But once inside the grounds it seemed cooler. One funny thing about my chills was that I didn't seem to shiver nearly as much when I could keep cool as I did at home, where even the walls and floors, if you touched them, were hot. The grounds were filled with live oaks that had grown up unchecked everywhere and afforded an almost continuous green shade. The ground was covered with ferns which were soft and cool to lie on, and when I flung myself down on my back and looked up, the roof of leaves was so thick that sometimes I couldn't see the sky at all. The sun that managed to filter through had lost its bright colorless glare and came in soft yellow shafts that didn't burn you when they touched you.

One afternoon, a scorcher early in September, which is usually our hottest month (and by then you're fagged out by the heat anyhow), I set out for the plantation. The heat lay coiled and shimmering on the road. When you looked at anything through it, it was like looking through a defective pane of glass. The dirt road was so hot that it burned even through my calloused feet and as I walked clouds of dust rose in front of me and mixed with the shimmering of the heat. I thought I'd never make the plantation. Sweat was running into my eyes, but it was cold sweat, and I was shivering so that my teeth chattered as I walked. When I finally managed to fling myself down on my soft green bed of ferns inside the grounds, I was seized with one of the worst chills I'd ever had, in spite of the fact that my mother had given me an extra dose of quinine that morning and some 666 malaria medicine to boot. I shut my eyes tight and clutched the ferns with my hands and teeth to wait until the chill had passed, when I heard a soft little voice call:

"Boy."

I thought at first I was delirious, because sometimes I got delirious when my bad attacks came on; only then I remembered that when I was delirious I didn't know it—all the strange things I saw and heard seemed perfectly natural. So when the voice said, "Boy," again, as soft and clear as the mockingbird at sunrise, I opened my eyes.

Kneeling near me on the ferns was a girl. She must have been about a year younger than I. I was almost sixteen, so I guess she was fourteen or fifteen. She was dressed in a blue and white checked gingham dress; her face was very pale, but the kind of paleness that's supposed to be, not the sickly pale kind that was like mine, showing even under a tan. Her eyes were big and very blue. Her hair was dark brown, and she wore it parted in the middle in two heavy braids that were swinging in front of her shoulders as she peered into my face.

"You don't feel well, do you?" she asked. There was no trace of concern or worry in her voice. Just scientific interest.

I shook my head. "No," I whispered, almost afraid that if I talked she would vanish, because I had never seen anyone here before, and I thought that maybe I was dying because I felt so awful, and I thought maybe that gave me power to see the ghost. But the girl in blue and white checked gingham seemed as I watched her to be good flesh and blood.

"You'd better come with me," she said. "She'll make you all right."

"Who's 'she'?"

"Oh—just Her," she said.

My chill had begun to recede by now, so when she got up off her knees I scrambled up, too. When she stood up her dress showed a white ruffled petticoat underneath it, and bits of green moss had left patterns on her knees, and I didn't think that would happen to the knees of a ghost, so I followed her as she led the way towards the house. She did not go up the sagging, half-rotted steps, which led up to the verandah about whose white pillars wisteria vines climbed in wild profusion, but went around to the side of the house where there were slanting doors to a cellar. The sun and rain had long since blistered and washed off the paint, but the doors looked clean and were free of the bits of bark from the eucalyptus tree that leaned nearby and that had dropped its bits of dirty brown peel on either side; so I knew that these cellar stairs must be frequently used.

The girl opened the cellar doors. "You go down first," she said. I went down the cellar steps, which were stone and cool against my bare feet. As she followed me, she closed the cellar doors after her, and as I reached the bottom of the stairs we were in pitch darkness. I began to be very frightened until her soft voice came out of the black.

"Boy, where are you?"

"Right here."

"You'd better take my hand. You might stumble."

We reached out and found each other's hands in the darkness. Her fingers were long and cool and they closed firmly around mine. She moved with authority through the pitch blackness of the cellar as though she knew her way with the familiarity born of custom.

"Poor Sat's all in the dark," she said, "but he likes it that way. He likes to sleep for weeks at a time. Sometimes he snores awfully. Sat, darling!" she called gently. A soft bubbly blowing sound came in answer, and she laughed happily. "Oh, Sat, you are sweet!" she said, and the bubbly blowy sound came again. Then the girl pulled at my hand and we came out into a huge and dusty kitchen. Iron skillets, pots, and pans were still hanging on either side of the huge stove, and there was a rolling pin and a bowl of flour on the marble-topped table in the middle of the room. The girl took a lit candle off the shelf.

"I'm going to make cookies," she said as she saw me looking at the flour and the rolling pin. She slipped her hand out of mine. "Come along." She began to walk more rapidly. We left the kitchen, crossed the hall, and went through the dining room, its old mahogany table thick with dust, although sheets covered the pictures on the walls. Then we went into the ballroom. The mirrors lining the walls were spotted and discolored; against one wall was a single delicate gold chair, its seat cushioned with pale rose and silver woven silk; it seemed extraordinarily well preserved. From the ceiling swung the huge chandelier by which Alexandra Londermaine had hung herself, its prisms catching and breaking up into a hundred colors the flickering of the candle and the few shafts of light that managed to slide in through the boarded-up windows. As we crossed the ballroom, the girl began to dance by herself, gracefully, lightly, so that her full blue and white checked gingham skirts flew out around her. She looked at herself with pleasure in the old mirrors as she danced, the candle flaring and guttering in her right hand.

"You've stopped shaking. Now what will I tell Her?" she said as we started to climb the broad mahogany staircase. It was very dark, so she took my hand again, and before we had reached the top of the stairs, I was seized by another chill. She felt my trembling fingers with satisfaction. "Oh, you've started again. That's good." She slid open one of the huge double doors at the head of the stairs.

As I looked into what once must have been Colonel Londermaine's study I thought my eyes would pop from my head. Seated at the huge table in the center of the room was the most extraordinary woman I had ever seen. I felt that she must be very beautiful, although she would never have fulfilled any of the standards of beauty set by our town. Even though she was seated I knew that she must be immensely tall. Piled up on the table in front of her were several huge volumes, and her finger was marking the place in the open one in front of her, but she was not reading. She was leaning back in the carved chair, her head resting against a piece of blue and gold embroidered silk that was flung across the chair back, one hand gently stroking a fawn that lay sleeping in her lap. Her eyes were closed and somehow I couldn't imagine what color they would be. It wouldn't have surprised me if they had been shining amber or the deep purple of her velvet robe. She had a great quantity of hair the color of mahogany in firelight, which was cut quite short and seemed to be blown wildly about her head like flame. Under her closed eyes were deep shadows, and lines of pain about her mouth. Otherwise there were no marks of age on her face but I would not have been surprised to learn that she was a hundred—or twenty-five. Her mouth was large and mobile and she was singing something in a deep rich voice. Two cats, one black, one white, were coiled up, each on a book, and as we opened the doors a leopard stood up quietly beside her, but did not snarl or move. It simply stood there and waited, watching us.

The girl nudged me and held her finger to her lips to warn me to be quiet, but I would not have spoken—could not, anyhow, my teeth were chattering so from my chill that I had completely forgotten, so fascinated was I by this woman sitting back with her head against the embroidered silk, soft deep sounds coming out of her throat. At last these sounds resolved themselves into words, and we listened to her as she sang. The cats slept indifferently, but the leopard listened, too:

I sit high in my ivory tower,
The heavy curtains drawn.
I've many a strange and lustrous flower,
A leopard and a fawn

Together sleeping by my chair,
And strange birds softly winging,
And ever pleasant to my ear
Twelve maidens' voices singing.

Here is my magic maps' array,
My mystic circle's flame.
With symbols' art He lets me play,
The unknown my domain.

And as I sit here in my dream
I see myself awake,
Hearing a torn and bloody scream,
Feeling my castle shake . . .

Her song wasn't finished but she opened her eyes and looked at us. Now that his mistress knew we were here, the leopard seemed ready to spring and devour me in one gulp, but she put one hand on his sapphire-studded collar to restrain him.

"Well, Alexandra," she said. "Who have we here?"

The girl, who still held my hand in her long cool fingers, answered, "It's a boy."

"So I see. Where did you find him?" The voice sent shivers up and down my spine.

"In the fern bed. He was shaking. See? He's shaking now. Is he having a fit?" Alexandra's voice was filled with pleased interest.

"Come here, boy," the woman said.

As I didn't move, Alexandra gave me a push, and I advanced slowly. As I came near, the woman pulled one of the leopard's ears gently, saying, "Lie down, Thammuz." The beast obeyed, flinging itself at her feet. She held her hand out to me as I approached the table. If Alexandra's fingers felt firm and cool, hers had the strength of the ocean and the coolness of jade. She looked at me for a long time and I saw that her eyes were deep blue, much bluer than Alexandra's, and so dark as to be almost black. When she spoke again her voice was warm and tender: "You're burning up with fever. One of the malaria bugs?" I nodded. "Well, we'll fix that for you."

When she stood and put the sleeping fawn down by the leopard, she was not as tall as I had expected her to be; nevertheless she gave an impression of great height. Several of the bookshelves in one corner were emptied of books and filled with various shaped bottles and retorts. Nearby was a large skeleton. There was an acid-stained wash basin too; that whole section of the room looked like part of a chemist's or physicist's laboratory. She selected from among the bottles a small amber-colored one, and poured a drop of the liquid it contained into a glass of water. As the drop hit the water, there was a loud hiss, and clouds of dense smoke arose. When it had drifted away she handed the glass to me and said, "Drink."

My hand was trembling so that I could scarcely hold the glass. Seeing this, she took it from me and held it to my lips.

"What is it?" I asked.

"Drink it," she said, pressing the rim of the glass against my teeth. On the first swallow I started to choke and would have pushed the stuff away, but she forced the rest of the burning liquid down my throat. My whole body felt on fire. I felt flame flickering in every vein, and the room and everything in it swirled around. When I had regained equilibrium to a certain extent, I managed to gasp out again, "What is it?"

She smiled and answered:

Nine peacocks' hearts, four bats' tongues,
A pinch of stardust and a hummingbird's lungs.

Then I asked a question I would never have dared ask if it hadn't been that I was still half-drunk from the potion I had swallowed. "Are you a witch?"

She smiled again, and answered, "I make it my profession."

Since she hadn't struck me down with a flash of lightning, I went on. "Do you ride a broomstick?"

This time she laughed. "I can when I like."

"Is it—is it very hard?"

"Rather like a bucking bronco at first, but I've always been a good horsewoman, and now I can manage very nicely. I've finally progressed to sidesaddle, though I still feel safer when I ride astride—I always rode my horse astride. Still, the best witches ride sidesaddle, so ... Now run along home. Alexandra has lessons to study and I must work. Can you hold your tongue or must I make you forget?"

"I can hold my tongue."

She looked at me and her eyes burned into me like the potion she had given me to drink. "Yes, I think you can," she said. "Come back tomorrow if you like. Thammuz will show you out."

The leopard rose and led the way to the door. As I hesitated, unwilling to tear myself away, it came back and pulled gently but firmly on my trouser leg.

"Goodbye, boy," the witch woman said. "And you won't have any more chills and fever."

"Goodbye," I answered. I didn't say thank you. I didn't say goodbye to Alexandra. I followed the leopard out.

She let me come every day. I think she must have been lonely. After all, I was the only thing there with a life apart from hers. And in the long run, the only reason I have had a life of my own is because of her. I am as much a creation of the witch woman's as Thammuz the leopard was, or the two cats, Ashtaroth and Orus. (It wasn't until many years after the last day I saw the witch woman that I learned that those were the names of the fallen angels.)

She did cure my malaria, too. My parents and the townspeople thought that I had outgrown it. I grew angry when they talked about it so lightly and wanted to tell them that it was because of the witch woman, but I knew that if ever I breathed a word about her I would be eternally damned. Mama thought we should write a testimonial letter to the 666 Malarial Preparation people, and maybe they'd send us a couple of dollars.

Alexandra and I became very good friends. She was a strange, aloof creature. She liked me to watch her while she danced alone in the ballroom or played on an imaginary harp—though sometimes I fancied I could hear the music. One day she took me into the drawing room and uncovered a portrait that was hung between two of the long-boarded-up windows. Then she stepped back and held her candle high so as to throw the best light on the pictures. It might have been a picture of Alexandra herself, or Alexandra as she might be in five years.

"That's my mother," she said. "Alexandra Londermaine."

As far as I knew from the tales that went about the town, Alexandra Londermaine had given birth to only one child, and that stillborn, before she had hung herself on the chandelier in the ballroom—and anyhow, any child of hers would have been this Alexandra's mother or grandmother. But I didn't say anything, because when Alexandra got angry, she became ferocious like one of the cats and would leap on me, scratching and biting. I looked at the portrait silently.

"You see, she has on a ring like mine," Alexandra said, holding out her left hand, on the fourth finger of which was the most beautiful sapphire and diamond ring I had ever seen, or rather, that I could ever imagine, for it was a ring apart from any owned by even the most wealthy of the townsfolk. Then I knew that Alexandra had brought me in here and unveiled the portrait simply that she might show me the ring to better advantage, for she had never worn a ring before.

"Where did you get it?"

"Oh, She got it for me last night."

"Alexandra," I asked suddenly, "how long have you been here?"

"Oh, a while."

"But how long?"

"Oh, I don't remember."

"But you must remember."

"I don't. I just came—like poor Sat."

"Who's poor Sat?" I asked, thinking for the first time of whatever it was that had made the gentle bubbly noises at Alexandra the day she found me in the fern bed.

"Why, we've never shown you Sat, have we!" she exclaimed. "I'm sure it's all right, but we'd better ask Her first."

So we went to the witch woman's room and knocked. Thammuz pulled the door open with his strong teeth and the witch woman looked up from some sort of experiment she was making with test tubes and retorts. The fawn, as usual, lay sleeping near her feet. "Well?" she said.

"Is it all right if I take him to see Poor Little Saturday?" Alexandra asked her.

"Yes, I suppose so," she answered. "But no teasing." She turned her back to us and bent again over her test tubes as Thammuz nosed us out of the room.

We went down to the cellar. Alexandra lit a lamp and took me back to the corner farthest from the doors, where there was a stall. In the stall was a two-humped camel. I couldn't help laughing as I looked at him because he grinned at Alexandra so foolishly, displaying all his huge buckteeth and blowing bubbles through them.

"She said we weren't to tease him," Alexandra said severely, rubbing her cheek against the preposterous splotchy hair that seemed to be coming out, leaving bald pink spots of skin on his long nose.

"But what—" I started.

"She rides him sometimes." Alexandra held out her hand while he nuzzled against it, scratching his rubbery lips against the diamond and sapphire of her ring. "Mostly She talks to him. She says he is very wise. He goes up to Her room sometimes and they talk and talk. I can't understand a word they say. She says it's Hindustani and Arabic. Sometimes I can remember little bits of it, like: *iderow, sorcabatcha,* and *anna bibed bech.* She says I can learn to speak with them when I finish learning French and Greek."

Poor Little Saturday was rolling his eyes in delight as Alexandra scratched behind his ears. "Why is he called Poor Little Saturday?" I asked.

Alexandra spoke with a ring of pride in her voice. "I named him. She let me."

"But why did you name him that?"

"Because he came last winter on the Saturday that was the shortest day of the year, and it rained all day so it got light later and dark earlier than it would have if it had been nice, so it really didn't have as much of itself as it should and I felt so sorry for it I thought maybe it would feel better if we named him after it . . . She thought it was a nice name!" She turned on me suddenly.

"Oh, it is! It's a fine name!" I said quickly, smiling to myself as I realized how much greater was this compassion of Alexandra's for a day than any she might have for a human being. "How did She get him?" I asked.

"Oh, he just came in."

"What do you mean?"

"She wanted him so he came. From the desert."

"He *walked*?"

"Yes. And swam part of the way. She met him at the beach and flew him here on the broomstick. You should have seen him. He was still all wet and looked so funny. She gave him hot coffee with things in it."

"What things?"

"Oh, just things."

Then the witch woman's voice came from behind us. "Well, children?"

It was the first time I had seen her out of her room. Thammuz was at her right heel, the fawn at her left. The cats, Ashtaroth and Orus, had evidently stayed upstairs. "Would you like to ride Saturday?" she asked me.

Speechless, I nodded. She put her hand against the wall and a portion of it slid down into the earth so that Poor Little Saturday was free to go out. "She's sweet, isn't she?" the witch woman asked me, looking affectionately at the strange bumpy-kneed, splay-footed creature. "Her grandmother was very good to me in Egypt once. Besides, I love camel's milk."

"But Alexandra said she was a he!" I exclaimed.

"Alexandra's the kind of woman to whom all animals are 'he' except cats, and all cats are 'she.' As a matter of fact, Ashtaroth and Orus are 'she,' but it wouldn't make any difference to Alexandra if they weren't. Go on out, Saturday. Come on!"

Saturday backed out, bumping her bulging knees and ankles against her stall, and stood under a live oak tree. "Down," the witch woman said. Saturday leered at me and didn't move. "Down, *sorcabatcha!*" the witch woman commanded, and Saturday obediently got down on her knees. I clambered upon her, and before I had managed to get at all settled, up she rose with such a jerky motion that I knocked my chin against her front hump and nearly bit my tongue off. Round and around Saturday danced while I clung wildly to her front hump, and the witch woman and Alexandra rolled on the ground with laughter. I felt as though I were on a very unseaworthy vessel on the high seas, and it wasn't long before I felt violently sea-sick as Saturday pranced among the live oak trees, sneezing delicately. At last the witch woman called out, "Enough!" and Saturday stopped in her tracks, nearly throwing me, and kneeling laboriously. "It was mean to tease you," the witch woman said, pulling my nose gently. "You may come sit in my room with me for a while if you like."

There was nothing I liked better than to sit in the witch woman's room and to watch her while she studied from her books, worked out strange-looking mathematical problems, argued with the zodiac, or conducted complicated experiments with her test tubes and retorts, sometimes filling the room with sulfurous odors or flooding it with red or blue light. Only once was I afraid of her, and that was when she danced with a skeleton in the corner. She had the room flooded with a strange red glow, and I almost thought I could see the flesh covering the bones of the skeleton as they danced together like lovers. I think she had forgotten that I was sitting there, half-hidden in the wing chair, because when they had finished dancing and the skeleton stood in the corner again, his bones shining and polished, devoid of any living trappings, she stood with her forehead against one of the deep red velvet curtains that covered the boarded-up windows and tears streamed down her cheeks. Then she went back to her test tubes and worked feverishly. She never alluded to the incident and neither did I.

As winter drew on, she let me spend more and more time in her room. Once I gathered up courage enough to ask her about herself, but I got precious little satisfaction. "Well, then, are you maybe one of the northerners who bought the place?"

"Let's leave it at that, boy. We'll say that's who I am. Did you know that my skeleton was old Colonel Londermaine? Not so old, as a matter of fact; he was only thirty-seven when he was killed at the Battle of Bunker Hill—or am I getting him confused with his great-grandfather, Rudolph Londermaine? Anyhow, he was only thirty-seven, and a fine figure of a man, and Alexandra only thirty when she hung herself for love of him on the chandelier in the ballroom. Did you know that the fat man with the red mustache has been trying to cheat your father? His cow will give sour milk for seven days. Run along now and talk to Alexandra. She's lonely."

When the winter had turned to spring and the camellias and azaleas were blooming in a wild riot of color in the overgrown garden, I kissed Alexandra for the first time, very gently and shyly. The next evening when I managed to get away from the chores at home and hurry out to the plantation, she gave me her sapphire and diamond ring which she had hung for me on a narrow bit of turquoise satin.

"It will keep us both safe," she said, "if you wear it always. And then when we're older we can get married and you can give it back to me. Only you mustn't ever let anyone see it or She'd be very angry."

I was afraid to take the ring, but when I demurred, Alexandra grew furious and started kicking and biting and I had to give in.

Summer was almost over before my father discovered the ring hanging about my neck. I fought like a witch boy to keep him from pulling out the narrow ribbon and seeing the ring, and indeed the ring seemed to give me added strength, and I had grown, in any case, much stronger during the winter than I ever had been in my life. But my father was still stronger than I, and pulled it out. He looked at it in dead silence for a moment and then the storm broke. That was the famous Londermaine ring that had disappeared the night Alexandra Londermaine hung herself. That ring was worth a fortune. Where had I gotten it?

No one believed me when I said I had found it in the grounds near the house... I chose the grounds because I didn't want anybody to think I had been in the house or indeed that I was able to get in. I don't know why they didn't believe me; it still seems quite logical to me that I might have found it buried among the ferns. "But then why," they said, "didn't you tell us? Why hide it on a ribbon about your neck unless there was something strange? And where, anyhow, did the ribbon come from?"

It had been a long, dull year, and the men of the town were all bored. They took me and forced me to swallow quantities of corn whiskey until I didn't know what I was saying or doing.

When they had finished with me, I didn't even manage to reach home before I was violently sick and then I was in my mother's arms and she was weeping over me. It was morning before I was able to slip away to the plantation house. I ran pounding up the mahogany stairs to the witch woman's room and opened the heavy sliding doors without knocking. She stood in the center of the room with her purple robe, her arms around Alexandra, who was weeping bitterly. Overnight the room had completely changed. The skeleton of Colonel Londermaine was gone, and books filled the shelves in the corner of the room that had been her laboratory. Cobwebs were everywhere, and broken glass lay on the floor; dust was inches thick on her worktable. There was no sign of Thammuz, Ashtaroth, or Orus, or of the fawn, but four birds were flying about her, beating their wings against her hair.

She did not look at me or in any way acknowledge my presence. Her arm about Alexandra, she led her out of the room and to the drawing room where the portrait hung. The birds followed, flying around and around them. Alexandra had stopped weeping now. Her face was very proud and pale and if she saw me miserably trailing behind them she gave no notice. When the witch woman stood in front of the portrait, the sheet fell from it. She raised her arm; there was a great cloud of smoke; the smell of sulfur filled my nostrils and when the smoke was gone, Alexandra was gone, too. Only the portrait was there, the fourth finger of the left hand now bearing no ring. The witch woman raised her hand again, and the sheet lifted itself up and covered the portrait. Then she went, with the birds, slowly back to what had once been her room, and still I tailed after, frightened as I had never been before in my life, or have been since.

She stood without moving in the center of the room for a long time. At last she turned and spoke to me.

"Well, boy, where is the ring?"

"They have it."

"They made you drunk, didn't they?"

"Yes."

"I was afraid something like this would happen when I gave Alexandra the ring. But it doesn't matter...I'm tired..." She drew her hand wearily across her forehead.

"Did I...did I tell them everything?"

"You did."

"I—I didn't know."

239

"I know you didn't know, boy."

"Do you hate me now?"

"No, boy, I don't hate you."

"Do you have to go away?"

"Yes."

I bowed my head. "I'm so sorry...."

She smiled slightly. "The sands of time...Cities crumble and rise and will crumble again and breath dies down and blows once more..."

The birds flew madly about her head, pulling at her hair, calling into her ears. Downstairs we could hear a loud pounding, and then the crack of boards being pulled away from a window.

"Go, boy," she said to me. I stood rooted, motionless, unable to move. "Go!" she commanded, giving me a mighty push so that I stumbled out of the room. They were waiting for me by the cellar doors and caught me as I climbed out. I had to stand there and watch when they came out with her. But it wasn't the witch woman, my witch woman. It was their idea of a witch woman— someone thousands of years old, a disheveled old creature in rusty black, with long wisps of grey hair, a hooked nose, and four wiry black hairs springing out of the mole on her chin. Behind her flew the four birds and suddenly they went up, up, into the sky, directly in the path of the sun until they were lost in its burning glare.

Two of the men stood holding her tightly, although she wasn't struggling, but standing there, very quiet while the others searched the house, searched it in vain. Then as a group of them went down into the cellar I remembered, and by a flicker of the old light in her eyes I could see that she remembered, too. Poor

Little Saturday had been forgotten. Out she came, prancing absurdly up the cellar steps, her rubbery lips stretched back over her gigantic teeth, her eyes bulging with terror. When she saw the witch woman, her lord and master, held captive by two dirty, insensitive men, she let out a shriek and began to kick and lunge wildly, biting, screaming with the blood-curdling, heart-rending scream that only a camel can make. One of the men fell to the ground holding a leg in which the bone had snapped from one of Saturday's kicks. The others scattered in terror, leaving the witch woman standing on the verandah supporting herself by clinging to one of the huge wisteria vines that curled around the columns. Saturday clambered up onto the verandah and knelt while she flung herself between the two humps. Then off they ran, Saturday still screaming, her knees knocking together, the ground shaking as she pounded along. Down from the sun plummeted the four birds and flew after them.

Up and down I danced, waving my arms, shouting wildly until Saturday and the witch woman and the birds were lost in a cloud of dust, while the man with the broken leg lay moaning on the ground beside me.

That Which Is Left

Matilda's cable was phoned to me. I was in my garden, painting. Pink roses with a tinge of lavender climbed against the deeper rose of the brick wall which enclosed the garden on two sides, the L of the house making the third and fourth. Indoors the phone rang. Still holding my brushes, annoyed at the interruption, I nevertheless ran to answer it.

PLEASE MARTIN COME NOW

She did not say whether it was Mother or Father. Her Yankee blood restrained her from phoning except in case of death, but presumably something was wrong with one of our parents. And I had promised each summer, on my annual pilgrimage to the home place, that if ever she really needed me, if one of our parents became really ill (I could use the word "dying" in connection with Mother and Father but never quite mean it) all she needed to do was send for me and I would come. At any time. All the way across the Atlantic. Brother Martin's big dramatic gesture, but sincerely meant.

I went back out to my garden, past the old, beautiful pieces of Georgian furniture I had slowly collected to go with my old, beautiful house, of which only the newest wing, the long side of the L, was Georgian. In the garden the pale April sun was gentle against the daffodils, which burned almost too brilliantly in the borders. I looked at the almost-finished portrait on the easel, a middle-aged woman, Lady Elinor Broughan, greying hair, hawkish aristocratic face: How did that happen? Some strange genetic throw-back? Lady Elinor's father had been a pork butcher and Lord Evelyn Broughan had plucked her from behind the counter when she was sixteen and married her, to give their child a name, in a quixotic gesture against the establishment. So now I painted her, Lady Elinor Establishment, helpmeet to her mate, devoted and beloved daughter-in-law.

I yawned, which in me is always a sign of anxiety. There was something in my portrait of Lady Elinor which reminded me of my sister Matilda. Was it Mother or Father she had cabled about? They were both near ninety: Matilda, Helen, Billy, and I, born late in their marriage.

I took Elinor-Matilda indoors and dismantled the easel and all my painting things. I would never be as good a painter as Father, but I was far more successful, and my popularity eased any sense of bitterness I might otherwise have had. Father was long out of fashion, though he still painted. It was probably Father, possibly a stroke or a heart attack. We had always had a family joke that one day we would find Father draped over his easel, dead, a paintbrush still in his hand.

The joke had begun to wear a bit thin the past several summers. It took him months now to finish a canvas, though the results, it was my private opinion, were still extraordinary; one day Father would be rediscovered, and I think I hated him for that. I hated him far more for being silly. He lost things constantly: his fork at table, his glasses, his painting glasses, his current kitten. Sometimes he thought I was his brother instead of his son. He moved into a realm of chronology into which I could not and did not want to enter. Only Matilda, his first born, could push him out of it and into the passive present.

Or Mother. Mother had been bed-ridden now for three years, but she was—as she herself put it—catching up on her reading. During my visit the past summer—I always stayed at least two weeks—she had piled on the big table by her hospital bed Nietzsche; Heidegger; *Remembrance of Things Past*; five Margery Allingham mysteries; a history of the Wars of the Roses; a biography of Catherine the Great. It wasn't display. She knew what she was reading, despite the idiotic variety; she kept the authors and characters straight, and by the time I left the pile had changed. She was rapidly becoming physically incontinent, though Matilda kept her immaculate with disposable diapers; but, unlike Father, Mother knew where she was in time and space.

Matilda did not cable me three years ago when Mother fell and broke a hip. She wrote. Mother had gotten up to go to the bathroom during the night. Matilda heard the great thud as she tripped over something—what? A kitten? A turned-up edge of the hooked rug?—and her obese body, over two hundred pounds, went down like a felled tree, though that's too poetic an image; we used to say that Mother was four feet around in any direction.

Still, it was more likely Father.

I yawned again and phoned my travel agent. Then I cabled Matilda—I, too, saved the phone for death, though, unlike Matilda, I always wrote airmail. Matilda wrote sea mail, except for events like broken hips. I told Matilda that I would arrive the next night, catch another plane to the local airport, rent a car from there, no need to meet me, and would drive over early the following morning.

I tend to sleep late but the five-hour time difference was in Matilda's favor, eleven o'clock my time as I stood shaving, six o'clock Matilda's.

As always, when I approached the long macadam road that wound uphill to our house, I felt an ambivalent churning in my gut, a longing to be home and a feeling of terror at what new changes time had wrought. I longed for Father's ability to move in time. If I could return, during my visits, to the way things used to be, then it would bearable.

It was the first time in years that I had come before midsummer, and I had forgotten the difference between April in old England and New England. In shadowed curves of field and roadside lay tired patches of snow. The trees were still winter-bleak, the new budding barely visible against the grey sky. Stone walls scratched black lines across pastures. In my brick-walled garden, I had roses year round.

The house was at the top of the road after an interminable climb, a grey shingle house that looked as though it had been blown by sea-salt winds rather than the north wind from the hills. In the winter, more than summer, it went with the stark landscape: I had forgotten that half the year the land was not gentle. I had come expecting to see orchards in bloom, the lilac bursting, the new green trees embracing the house. From the upstairs bedrooms in the summer I always had a sense of being *in* the trees.

But the maples and oaks were still skeletons, and another of the elms was down, only the sawed-off trunk a reminder of where it had stood. The elms had somehow been part of the house itself, so that now there was a dying look to the unprotected front door. Nothing to keep out the cold, and the wind that was always alive on the crest of the hill, cool and comforting in summer, but bitter now, taxing the heater in the rented car.

I went past the front of the house, turned down a small dirt road, and drove to the old barn that served, among other things, as garage. The red paint was wintered off, grey wood showing through. Beyond the barn was another, also paint-peeling, which was my father's studio. When we were little, we all had easels in the studio, and were allowed to paint with Father for an hour every day. For the other three, it was only a comfortable memory of childhood. I still drew upon the things I had learned paint-ing beside Father. I wondered if he was already at work; he liked the early morning light, and even in his latest work, the absolute newness of the first light was what struck one most forcibly.

As I got out of the car and left the barn, planning to walk back to the studio and look in on Father, Matilda came running to me, followed by Scar, the old hound. She was pushing her arms into an old coat, a man's coat, not my father's. I did not recognize it. She flung herself into my arms and simultaneously managed to hold me. Scar jumped up and barked in greeting. Matilda said, "Down." I have never been very fond of Scar.

I pushed Matilda away to look at her; she smelled of fatigue, an odd odor for Matilda the Immaculate, always recognizable by her personal scent, the Madame Rochas with which I provided her and which I took in through contact with her flesh. "What is it, Tilly? Why did you send for me? Is it Father?"

She shook her head in negation at the same time that she said, "Yes." Then, "It's everybody. Father. Mother. Me. Bless you for coming, Marty, though you're earlier than I expected and the house—oh, Martin, it's just all got"—she held out her arms in a strange gesture of helplessness—"too much." Helplessness was not a characteristic of my elder sister, who always stood tall and austere over every situation.

I said, "The barn needs painting."

"Yes. And the house. Oh, Marty, I'm sorry about the house. Lily couldn't come yesterday and I haven't had time to get things tidied..."

"We better have the house and barns painted this summer."

"We can't afford it, Marty."

"Why? What's happened to their money?"

We were walking towards the house, arms around each other. I could not now see the gauntness of her face where the skin stretched thinly over the bones so that she had reminded me of Father. It was Helen and Billy who had inherited Mother's tubbiness—Helen was always on a new diet. Matilda and I were long and lean. She said, "Money doesn't go as far as it used to. I sell one of Father's paintings occasionally and that helps, but we have more expenses now."

"What?"

"I can take care of Mother, except for lifting her, I need help with that. But Father—"

"Is he ill?"

"Not—physically."

"What, then?"

"His mind. You saw yourself last summer that it was going."

"It's worse, then?"

She did not answer.

"Is he painting?" I gestured towards the barn.

Again she did not answer.

I said, "As long as he paints, he'll—"

Leaving Scar to whine outside, we went into the house by the low east door, which led us through a stone pantry to the kitchen. The front door was used only in summer when all doors and windows were flung open so that the house could drink in the blue and gold and green.

Today all doors were closed, and windows, and, as Matilda opened the door to the kitchen, I could feel the atmosphere of the house take me unaware and slap me across the face. Always when I crossed the threshold I thought of Mother's bread baking in the oven; I smelled comfort and Queen Anne's lace and the north-west breeze.

It was as though I had entered a strange place. The kitchen floor needed washing. There was a pile of soiled sheets sending up the stink of urine on the floor by the washing machine. This mixed with an equally strong stink from the cat's box, which needed changing. There were dirty dishes in the sink, something unprecedented. Then I saw the chair by the hearth, but turned away from the fire so that the occupant could look out the window, across the cold fields and scars of stone walls, out across the bare valley to the hills. Our old cat crouched on the high back of the chair, staring unblinking, unwelcoming.

"Father."

"When the days begin to lengthen, the cold begins to strengthen. Who's that? Is that you, Billy?"

Billy was dead, dead in a war as stupid as every other war. Sharper, more self-protective than Billy, I'd managed to duck out of the war, sent cables after Matilda's brief, dry phone call, cried hot tears with Mother and Father the following summer, and asked if I could have Billy's magnificent captain's desk shipped to England. It was perfect in my study, but I always felt a shock when I went into his room, as though seeing someone with their front teeth pulled out. It was right that I should have Billy's desk—everybody said so. But I also want it to be in his room, too: simultaneously.

"Go away, man," Father said, "we don't know you."

It was like looking into Billy's room and expecting to see the desk: something was gone, something was not there that should have been there. It was not simply the appalling changes that less than a year had made in him physically: the silver hair was limp and lifeless; the contours of his face seemed to have fallen in; all his bones, indeed, seemed to have crumbled, so that the once erect old man was a huddle of bones held loosely by the wrinkled skin. The hands on the arms of his chair trembled.

"Father, it's Martin. It's Martin, Father. I've come home."

"I'll put green paint on your nose," the old man said. "That may possibly improve it." Tremulously, he started to rise.

249

From the shadows of the hearth behind his chair a girl emerged, a stocky creature, probably in her late teens, with lank brown hair straggling about her coarse features. Calmly and firmly she pushed the old man back into the chair. "It's all right, Gramps," she said in a loud, cheerful voice, as though she were speaking to a not very bright child. Then, to Matilda, "Lily called just now. She'll be over this afternoon to clean things up. I'll get the washing machine going in the meantime. Don't you fret, Miss Tilly, I'll get the dishes out of the way in a few minutes now that I've got Gramps settled."

Matilda put her hand over Father's to pet it. "Marty, you remember Daphne. She takes care of Father in the mornings."

I murmured something that I hoped sounded affirmative.

"Daphne is Harriet Cooley's youngest. The Cooleys have the big garage down in the valley. You remember."

"Oh, yes, yes of course."

"I don't know how I'd manage without Daphne. Do you want to see Mother now, Marty?"

Want. Yes, but not now, not today. Then. Yore. Ten years ago, when Mother waddled happily between her rows of flowers and vegetables wearing one of those loose shifts of subtle blues or rusts or greens, exotic patterns she had created and dyed herself and which strangely suited her comfortable bulk. Her white hair was braided and coroneted, and her face, devoid of makeup, was alert, questioning, welcoming. She would sit down on the rich soft ground between a row of zinnias and a row of brussels sprouts and talk: about my latest portrait—she was inordinately proud of my success; about Billy's brilliant PhD thesis—Macmillan was publishing it; about Helen and her husband and the children living in

California, and how Helen never wrote but always came once a year with the children; about how spartanly Matilda was bearing the death of her husband and children in an automobile accident—we never said that Malcolm had probably been drunk, only how terrible for Matilda, the waste of four lives and the death of her world. Then we would turn from the subject, the wanton reasonlessness of life and death, and talk about Father's painting, about mine, and finally Mother would say, when reason returned, "You'll have to help pull me up, Marty. There are disadvantages to being shaped like a cannon ball and I don't want to roll into the vegetables."

In the house now, in April, a log crumbled. The smell of burning applewood covered the smells of the unclean house. I was grateful that it was only because Lily, whoever she was, hadn't come. In his chair, my father leaned forward, and I saw spittle dribble down the corner of his mouth and hang off the point of his chin. He had been shaved, and I wondered whether Matilda or Daphne had shaved him. "Why don't you change the cat's papers?" I said sharply.

"Marty." Matilda's voice was quiet, hurt. "Do you want to see Mother?"

No.

I followed her to the ground floor room that had been made into a bedroom for Mother when she broke her hip. It had once been a formal Victorian parlor. Now there was only a hospital bed, a chair for visitors, and shelves for Mother's books. The back of the bed was slightly raised, and Mother lay there inertly, her soft bulk covered by a throw, another of those exotic, subtle pieces of material she had designed and executed. There was one book on her table, and an enormous magnifying glass.

"Marty's here, Mother."

She opened her eyes. "Marty, where are you?"

"I'm here, Mother, right here."

Her rheumatic hands groped towards me. "Marty—where—"

Matilda gave a shove. "Go to her, Marty. She can't see you un-less you're close."

"But..."

"Her eyes are going, rapidly."

"Can't anybody—"

"No. Marty—"

I went to the bed, and I took Mother's hands in mine. They were as always, dry and warm. Her grip was firm. She spoke, and suddenly it was her own voice, familiar, reassuring. "Matilda, I'd like some coffee, and I wouldn't be surprised if Martin would join me in a cup." Then she gave her inimitable giggle. "Though we'd both look rather foolish, both trying to sit in the same cup."

I laughed, too. "I'd love a cup of coffee, Tilly."

As Matilda's steps retreated, Mother said, "How does she look?"

"Tilly?"

"Who did you think I meant? The kitten?" And I noticed the inevitable kitten curled between Mother and the wall. There's a new kitten every summer. When they grew up they stayed in the barn—behind the garage section we kept a milk cow—and in Father's studio.

Mother spoke with an unwonted edge of impatience. "How does she look? Damn it, Martin, I can't see for myself. I can only *feel* how she looks, and l don't like the feeling."

"She looks tired," I said.

"And well she might be. What else?"

"There's a good deal more grey in her hair."

"And—?"

"She's not standing as straight."

"Go on."

"Mother, I've only been here a few minutes."

"You're a portrait painter."

"She doesn't look like one of my portraits anymore. She used to. Now—maybe Grant Wood. She's thinner. Everything about her is tight. That—oh, sort of grace and fluidity—is gone."

"What about her eyes?"

"They're veiled."

"Tilly was never one for letting anyone in. Generous to a fault about everyone else, but too proud ever to let us be generous in return." Then Mother's nostrils twitched, very slightly. I was glad she could not see my face. She said, "Malcolm, please ask Tilly to come change me. I am soiled."

Her voice was calm, matter-of-fact, and perhaps I only imagined the humiliation behind this horrendous reversal of roles.

Tilly, the eldest, could probably remember me, and even Billy and Helen, being bathed and powdered and diapered by Mother. Although it seemed to me that I remembered lying on Mother's and Father's big bed, on a towel soft from age, while Mother's firm hand rubbed cornstarch over my bottom, pinned on the clean nappie, and set me, fresh and powdery, in my crib.

I said, "Where's Mrs. Matson?"

Mother said, "She died a month ago. We haven't had anybody to take her place. Tilly's looking. We have three girls to help take care of Father: Daphne, Lily, and Grace." Again her irrepressible giggle. Then, "We're very lucky, because they're all kind and patient with him. Please, Martin, I am quite uncomfortable. Call Tilly, and then leave the room."

Mrs. Matson wasn't—had not been—much older than Tilly. It did not make sense for her to be dead and Mother alive. I went out to the kitchen and Tilly was at the stove, cooking something—for lunch, I suppose. It smelled like a kind of stew— Tilly was always a good cook—and this homey odor was a relief.

"Mother wants you, Matilda."

From his chair, Father said, "Matilda is brutal to your mother, Billy, brutal. How any child of mine can be so cruel—"

Daphne, pushing a strand of oily brown hair out of her eyes, stopped him cheerfully. "Oh, come now, Gramps, you know that's not so."

"She's cruel, Marty, she won't let me paint, she hides my brushes—"

Matilda, walking to Mother's room, was suddenly more erect, so I knew his words had hit her.

Daphne's warm smile belied the forced heartiness with which she called Father "Gramps." "It's a sickness in his arteries, you know. He doesn't really mean it."

Father raised his voice. "Don't talk about me as though I'm not here. She bullies me. I'm not a child. Take her away."

"Take who away, Father?"

Daphne said, "Gramps, do you need to go to the bathroom?"

"No. I can mess if I want to, like you-know-who."

I said, "I'm going to my room." I went upstairs. Past Billy's open-doored room with the hole where his desk had been, the color of the wallpaper less faded. Past Mother's and Father's room, the great bed unused now, or did Father still sleep in it? Past my own room to the nursery, where Matilda's children in summer had wakened the entire household at a proper seven or seven thirty in the morning (Mother would already be in the garden, Father in his studio), and where now Helen's brats disturbed me during their visits by screaming for water at least three times a night and no one was allowed to sleep after five a.m. On to Matilda's room, the smallest and always the coziest, reminding me of Emily Brontë's room. Mother had made the curtains and the bedspread for the small bed that Matilda had moved into after Malcolm's death. Mother had done the stencils on the walls, too, all in soft shades of brick rose, so that the room reminded me of my garden. I was relieved that the room was unchanged until I saw the picture—if one can call it a picture—over the bed. Matilda seldom bothered to show up at any church, casually calling herself a Unitarian. What in God's name was my Unitarian sister doing with a cheap, gaudy, bleeding heart framed and hung over her bed? It destroyed the room. I backed out, did not go to Helen's predictable room, but returned to my own, which was always a paradoxical blow to me, clean, impersonal, pleasant, but hardly mine anymore since I had virtually stripped it for my house.

I sat on my bed. How long does she want me to stay? Why did she send for me? Does she need more money? If I accept just a few more commissions, it won't be a hardship for me to send more money.

I heard steps on the stairs. Heavy steps. Like Mother's. Mother would come clumping up the stairs at bedtime and squeeze into the big wooden rocker. She might be four feet in all directions,

255

but she managed to have a mammoth lap, big enough for several babies simultaneously, and an unending repertory of seventeenth-century songs, some of them extremely bawdy.

Mother: singing to me: to my nephews and nieces: simultaneously.

Matilda came into my room. "Marty. There's a tray of coffee in Mother's room, and some hot muffins."

"Tilly, what the hell is that bleeding heart doing over your bed? Have you gone to Rome?"

Tilly's laugh was often reminiscent of Mother's joyous chiming. Now she sounded like Father. "Hardly. It's simply a reminder that life is a bloody farce."

"You need to be reminded?"

"Sentences need periods at the end of them. It's also a slim hope that somebody who once shared in the comedy may also be laughing at it."

"You still believe in God?"

"On occasion. That's why I use a bleeding heart for punctuation. Mother's waiting for you."

"Her eyes—"

"Part of the farce."

"The magnifying glass—"

"She can still read for a few minutes at a time."

"Why did you send for me? Is she dying?"

"Nature is not that kind."

"Then—"

"Martin—I tried to tell you. Sometimes one needs—support."

We went downstairs. Tilly buttered a muffin. "Mother, Grace made these muffins for you."

Mother said, "Grace comes at night. You remember Grace. Grace Butler."

I didn't, but I let it go. "To help Tilly with you?"

"Father," Tilly said. "The girls often bring their friends, too. I really have lots of help."

"What about Mother, now that Mrs. Matson's—gone?"

"Jamie Hooper comes to help me after he's finished with chores. It really takes a man. And Ted comes in at least twice a week."

"Ted?"

"Ted Orthos. The doctor."

"Miss Tilly!" Daphne called from the kitchen.

When Matilda was out of earshot, Mother fumbled for her coffee cup, almost overturning it with groping fingers. "Ted Orthos's coat is the only comfort Tilly has."

I had noticed the man's coat over Tilly's shoulders—when? Only an hour ago, maybe less than an hour.

Mother sipped her coffee, slowly, as though she was thinking: then, "Tilly needs someone to love."

"Who doesn't?"

"Those who can't love without devouring are better off without. Ted needs loving."

"Why don't they marry?"

"Ted has a wife. I wouldn't mind her looking like a codfish if she didn't feel like a codfish as well. Ted's coat is cold comfort, but it's something. It's a promise."

"Of what?"

"That there is love in the universe. Please eat my muffin, Martin."

"I'm not hungry."

"Then dispose of it. Tilly will fuss."

Matilda had come in silently, deliberately silently, I thought, so that Mother, who couldn't see her, would neither hear. She said, "Yes, indeed, Tilly will fuss. You don't have any right to starve yourself, Mother."

"Why not? It's all I have left. The right to choose not to eat."

"That's suicide."

"There's a great deal of blubber left for my body to feed on. I wish I could think of a quicker way."

"It's taking life," Matilda said, "into your own hands."

"I wish I knew what life is. Then I might understand the yes and no of taking it."

Matilda picked up a coffee cup and held it for a moment to steady her trembling lips. "We don't know what life is, Mother. We don't. So we have no right to take it."

"Why don't you sell the dining room set?" Mother suggested. "It's back in style and we won't use it again. You could get some more help in with the money, Tilly. You need to get away. I made Tilly cable you, Martin. Helen's no help. You were always fond of Tilly. Can't you see what this is doing to her?"

"It's all right, Mother," Tilly said. "I don't mind."

She didn't mind. I really believe she didn't. I did. I went back to the kitchen. The smell. Where the hell was Lily to clean things up? A cat was squatting in the ancient box. Daphne had my father's trousers down and was cleaning him with a wet cloth. Her warm smile came again. "We'd do anything for Miss Tilly, Grace and Lily and me. Sometimes when Gramps and Granny are asleep, we have such good talks. In spite of everything she has on her mind, she always listens to us. The other kids, too. They like to drop in of an evening. There aren't many older people who remember what it was like to be our age. Miss Tilly says it's what she has left that nobody can take away from her— remembering. She's told us lots about Gramps and Granny, the way they used to be. Not so much lately, since they've been so much worse. She needs a vacation, Miss Tilly does." Daphne had tidied Father up and he was back in his chair, snoring lightly. So the good memories were being taken away from Tilly. That as well as everything else.

And from me. I had always thought that when people kept on working they didn't become senile. Stokowski. Stravinski. Scarlatti. Maybe only people who begin with an *S* and end with an *i*.

Mother, no longer able to read her way through everything. Father, within a year no longer Father . . .

Daphne continued, "But it's more than that with Miss Tilly anyhow. She makes us feel she really cares."

"She does care," I said automatically.

The bleeding heart. Because some mythical god came and cared?

"Tell Tilly—" I started, yawned, then finished, "I'll be back"— I went into the pantry—"this summer"—and out of doors— "maybe." Scar greeted me eagerly, great tongue lolling, jumping up at me for petting. I pushed him down, let him into the pantry, and shut the door on him. Then I went to the barn and drove to the airport.

If I stayed unwillingly, ungraciously, even a few days, even a few more hours, I would kill the only thing of the old things left, the still warm fragment of Tilly's love.

I waited for the moment when the stewardess would ask if I wanted a cocktail after take-off. When I closed my eyes I could see the vulgar bleeding heart over Tilly's bed, red and distasteful.

After the first martini I was able to see the roses on my rose brick wall.

A Sign for a Sparrow

Sunday was a clear, brilliant day, the air suddenly sharp and clean after almost three weeks of fog, fog so thick that if you held your hand out you could feel the droplets of moisture, and anyone walking even a few blocks was almost as wet as though it were actually raining. But on Sunday it was hard to believe that the fog had ever been, and spirits that had been weighted down by the heavy, humid atmosphere suddenly soared again.

Just as Robert Stephens was ready to leave the house to go to the hospital to see his wife and infant daughter, there was a knock on the door. He knew what it would be. And he knew that Ginnie, waking in the hospital to a clear shining dawn instead of the oppressive fog, would be expecting it, too. At least the fog had given them the extra weeks so that he would be with her to take her to the hospital when her pains started, could hold his new-born child, could show Ginnie his love and his pride.

He opened the door to the uniformed messenger, and thanked him.

Yes. Tomorrow. Tomorrow at dawn.

Then he walked the three miles to the hospital, leaving his little bug of a car in the garage. It was no surprise, the pale blue envelope. His call might have come any time during the past six weeks, and if it hadn't been for the fog it would certainly have come sooner. Nevertheless, now that it had actually arrived he felt extraordinarily as though someone had kicked him in the belly, hard.

At the hospital he went first to the nursery. There were about twenty babies there, an unusually large number for any one time. His was in a crib close to the big double glass window, and he could stand there and look down at her as she lay sleeping. It was her unutterable perfection that brought a catch to his throat. In spite of the fact that the doctor had reassured them time and again that there was nothing to fear, and had given them double sets of genetic and radiological tests, they had feared. In the early months of Ginnie's pregnancy, her older sister had given birth to an imperfect baby, small and shrunken of body, huge and bloated of head. But when the baby had died after a few days and Rob had remarked that it was a blessing the infant would not have to join the swelling hopeless ranks in the state nurseries, Ginnie had burst into sobs so vehement and uncontrollable that it had taken him over an hour to calm her down. But now—now she had a baby of her own, lying there in the white crib in the hospital nursery, tiny fists clenched close to her face, a small scratch on her nose which she had given herself, swiping at her face with those incredibly small pink fingers. The hair that lay damply against her head was in soft ringlets, and there was a distinct touch of red to it. She had Rob's hair, and it was much better hair for a girl than a boy. He kept his hair in a butch, but even so, about three days after he'd been to the barber it would begin to curl. However, on a girl, instead of being a pain in the neck—or rather on the head—it would be highly satisfactory. Everything would be highly satisfactory if, as usual, he hadn't gotten his timing all wrong. Or had he? For the past months, how often had he and Ginnie said that if only the baby came and was all right, then *everything* would be all right?

He moved on down the corridor to Ginnie's room. As he pushed open the door he could hear a voice reading, and he knew that Matt MacDonald, their closest friend, was there before him. Matt was spending a good deal of time with Ginnie now, trying to help, the way sometimes someone on the outside can help better than two people who are too close to each other.

Rob stood just inside the door for a moment, listening and looking. Ginnie's bed was cranked up and she sat there, listening to Matt, her eyes closed. Her gentle, intelligent face was almost devoid of expression, and this composure, Rob knew, was deliberate, a resignation to the inevitable which they both knew would come with the change in the weather.

Matt was reading from a small green book, his head bent over the words, a tuft of fair hair sticking up from the crown of his head, so that suddenly to Rob he looked as vulnerable as little Ginnie. Matt, who always seemed a tower of strength, was short and robust with enormous strength of arm and leg, and with his mop of tawny hair and beard he usually reminded Rob of a young lion, so that this glimpse of almost childish innocence came as a shock.

"'I have bene accompanyed with many sorrows, with labour,

hunger, heat, sickenes, and peril.'" Matt read, looked up, and saw Rob. He grinned and said, "Listen to this, Rob: 'It was impossible either to ford the river or to swim it, both by reason of the swiftnesse and also for that the borders were so pestred with fast woods as neither boat nor man could find place, either to land or to imbarke: for such is the fury of the current, and there are so many trees and woods overflowne, as if any boat but touch upon any tree or stake, it is impossible to save any person therein. Besides our vessels were no other than whirries, one little barge, a small cockboat, and a bad Galiota, which we framed in hast for the purpose at Trinidad. I have consumed much time, and many crownes, and I had no other respect or desire then to serve her Majestie and my country thereby.'" He looked up and grinned again. "That was Sir Walter Raleigh. Rather a favorite of mine, by the way. Voyages of discovery were pretty tremendous in his day, too."

"Matt," Ginnie said, "if you think you're going to make me happier by belittling what Rob has to do, you're mistaken."

Matt looked at her in shocked surprise. "I'm not belittling Rob or anything about him, Ginnie! I'm just sort of pointing out that he's in company, and good company, too. And think of some of the things Walter Raleigh had to fight that Rob won't: Many of Raleigh's men believed that the world was flat like a tray. They were quite literally terrified that their flimsy little ships might fall off the edge. And they believed, too, in the most horrendous kinds of sea monsters, huge enough to swallow a whole fleet of ships in one gulp."

Ginnie's lips quivered ever so slightly. "Rob's ship seems very flimsy to me for where it's going, Matt. I'm afraid of its falling off the edge, too, and I believe in monsters who can swallow it in one gulp." She smiled a watery smile.

"But this is the age of reason," Matt said, an unusual edge of bitterness in his voice. "Everything can be explained in a scientific manner."

"If I fall off the edge it won't be an imaginary edge, at any rate," Rob said. "It will be a real, comprehensible, and scientific one. Somebody will be able to tell you exactly *why* the ship fell and what the edge is and where it drops to. This isn't the Age of Reason. That was back in the eighteenth century, wasn't it, Matt? This is the Age of Reasons. Two different things."

"Very comforting, both of you," Ginnie said.

"Darling, I didn't mean to sound off," Rob said quickly. "I'm not going to fall off any edge. It's going to be a tremendous adventure, the most tremendous adventure anybody's ever had, and I'll be back to tell you all about it. Just hold the good thought."

Matt was leafing through his book again. "Hey, Rob, there was a fellow in your field on one of Sir Robert Dudley's expeditions. Here's a whole list of words he made in Trinidad. 'Guttemock': a man. 'Tabairo': the hair of one's head. 'Dessine': the forehead. Here's a good one: 'Cattie': the moon. Maybe they were contemplating space travel even back in those days. Once you've climbed a mountain or crossed a river nothing seems impossible." He sighed then, and an expression of pain and sadness momentarily flickered across his face, to be replaced almost immediately with his usual confident, serene smile. But Ginnie had seen, and asked, "Matt, you aren't yourself today. What's wrong? Has something happened?"

For a moment he looked down at the book. Then he said, "I

hadn't meant to tell you. You have enough problems of your own right now without my burdening you with mine."

"Matt, you know your problems are ours just as ours have always been yours. Out with it."

Matt did not look up from the book. "My church is being closed," he said. "As a matter of fact it's going to be turned into a state nursery. Heaven knows nurseries are needed, but so are churches. Only nobody realizes it. The government can issue reasons why nurseries are needed, but not churches. They won't go so far as actually to outlaw churches, but it is being done subtly, nevertheless. God is not reasonable. Nurseries are. Faith is not reasonable. Radioactive wastelands are. As far as closing my church goes they had reasons if not reason. There were three people in it last Sunday." His voice was bitter. "It's a funny thing, kids. After the war the scientists and the men of God got it alike. The scientists were to blame for the war and because three-fifths of the surface of the Earth won't be habitable for at least another hundred years. And the men of God were to blame because they—and their God—hadn't done anything to stop it. But the scientists are back in grace because without them we'd be back in the caves, and the men of God are still in disgrace because only a handful of people realize that to all intents and purposes we *are* back in the caves."

"Will you get another church, Matt?" Ginnie asked gently.

"Maybe. I don't know. All I do know is that no matter how often I fail I have to keep on trying. If it weren't for a handful of people like you two, to give me hope ... and your baby. I have to keep on trying for the kind of world I would want your baby to grow up in. Well," he said, looking down at the little book again, changing the subject, "Here's something Lawrence Keymis said, around 1596, about his 'beleefe we need no farther assurances, then we already haue to perswade our selues that it hath pleased our God of his infinit goodnesse, in his will and purpose to appoint and reserue this Empire for vs.' So there's a nice prejudiced and on-our-side God for you. Tell me in all honesty, Rob, how about this little jaunt of yours? Is there absolutely no idea of conquest, of the possibility of resettling some of our population? Aren't we kind of hoping, in spite of all our noble talk of the cosmic rays suddenly falling into a pattern, indicating that there may be a highly civilized race there signaling us, aren't we still kind of hoping that if there's any population at all it will be a backwards one and we can move in, just as the English did back in the sixteenth century?"

Rob shrugged. "All that kind of thing is top top secret."

"But you've been working on those patterns of rays?"

"Yes. And getting nowhere. It may be a pattern, but so far it seems to be a meaningless one. It might be caused by the rotation of the planet's moons. After all, the pattern only became apparent with the new instruments, so it could quite easily indicate nothing at all."

"In other words," Ginnie said, "Matt's right, and it's nothing but an excuse." Suddenly she began to cry, and both Matt and Rob looked stricken, realizing that they had forgotten, in the easiness of their relationship, that nothing was easy at this point for Ginnie. "And Rob has to be caught up in it, and why, Rob? There are plenty of other cryptologists."

Rob tried to grin, to make a joke of it. "Because I'm a little runt," he said.

"You're not!" She defended him quickly, automatically. "What's that got to do with it?"

"It has a lot to do with it," he said. "I'm small boned and wiry and strong and I don't take up much room or add much weight. That has a lot to do with it. There are plenty of other cryptographers."

"Not as good as you are."

"Two that I can think of off-hand who are better. But one is six foot seven and plays basketball as well as he decodes, and the other weighs three hundred-odd pounds. No matter what their other qualifications, their physical size eliminated them before they even started. And they both applied. They told me they're green with envy."

"And I bet," Ginnie said, "their wives are getting down on their knees every night to thank God. If they believe in him."

"Ginnie, do you believe in him?" Matt asked.

"You know I do," she said.

"Then live your faith. I know you're worried about Rob. I suppose Sir Walter Raleigh's wife was pretty upset about some of *his* trips. Excuse me if I keep harping on him, but he was quite a guy, and his faith saw him through some pretty dark spots. How he would have loved to be along with Rob! A brand-new world to explore, and how many worlds opening up. And if there's any-one to communicate with, Rob will be the one to make the communication."

"If I could just go partway with him," she said. "If I could just go with him to the moon and see him take off."

"To the moon," Matt said. "See how easily you said that. The moon was a lot further away to our grandparents than the planets are to us."

"Matt," Ginnie broke in desperately, "faith in the infinite by the finite is such a precarious thing. Maybe if we went back to idols the way some people have, if we had something tangible to worship, to believe in—"

"Go ahead," Matt said gently. "If you can believe in one of the idols, if it will give you any comfort."

"You know it won't. It's just that sometimes trust in a God we know we're too puny ever to begin to comprehend seems a pretty tall order. Pray with us, Matt, will you please?" She bowed her head, clasped her hands, and after a moment Matt and Rob followed suit. They sat in silence until the tenseness began to leave the room. When at last Matt spoke it was not words of his own devising, but words that were familiar to them all:

O Lord our Lord, how excellent is thy name in all the earth!, who hast set thy glory above the heavens.

When I consider thy heavens, the work of thy fingers, the moon and the stars, which thou hast ordained;

What is man, that thou art mindful of him? And the son of man, that thou visitest him?

For thou hast made him a little lower than angels, and hast crowned him with glory and honour.

He stopped and much of the pain seemed to have eased from his own eyes. Rob stood up and went slowly to the window, the jerkiness gone from his movements. Evening was falling and lights were beginning to come on in various wings of the hospital. Across the lawn came two nurses in white uniforms and dark capes. At the horizon the sky was suffused with rose, and against the rose began the greenish night flickering of the radioactive wastelands. They were used to it, they took it for granted, but familiarity did not make it cease to be sinister, and it contradicted the comforting colors of the sunset and the words of the psalms. Rob turned from the window, and as he did, Ginnie said, "Your orders came today, didn't they?"

Ginnie did not cry when he left the hospital. He felt that he himself was the nearer to tears, so determined was she to be brave and not make it harder for him. He paused for a moment at the nursery, looking down at his baby. Then he set out for home, again taking the long walk. He would be exhausted by morning, but perhaps that was just as well. There would not be a great deal for anyone to do on the trip out; certainly many of the old shipboard mutinies came from the boredom of the voyage and the uncertainty of the sailors to their eventual arrival, and the monotony of this trip through the uncharted seas of space would not be dissimilar to that of the old ships alone in the unknown enormity of ocean.

After the fog, the air had turned cold as well as clear and he walked briskly. He passed by Matt's church, small and dark, and he knew what the loss of it meant. Officially the state did not believe in God, but it permitted the various religions that had been springing up, in much the same way that, a century and a half before, the Soviet state had winked at the onion-domed churches to which the people continued to flock on Sundays. And there was the same infinite variety of religious belief—no, even greater variety—than there had been back in the mid-war days. Only two blocks after Matt's austere white building was the imposing stone structure of the Sacred Heart. This was tied up, Matt had explained, with the old pre-war Christianity, but had not much to do with the Jesus who was one of Matt's favorite teachers. Once a year, though this was definitely frowned on, there was an actual sacrifice in front of the altar, with the bleeding heart extracted from the still warm and twitching victim. Then there was the flourishing sect of the Golden Lamb, and the Society of Warlocks, all colorful, subtly (and sometimes not so subtly) sadistic organizations. Matt's group, searching, groping, never presuming, called contemptuously the Godders by the more wealthy and highly organized groups, was the only one which had wakened a response in Rob and Ginnie. It was certainly the least successful of the religious groups, perhaps because it demanded the most of its members. No one going to Matt's church could throw his responsibilities onto the shoulders of bishop or priest; no one was given easy answers, or told that truth was tangible and God immanent and comprehensible. It was not an easy religion, but nothing worth anything, Rob thought, was easy, and wanting religion to be all cozy and comfortable was like trying to get back in the womb again.

Rob stopped suddenly on the quiet night street. The sky that had been sullen with fog now stretched to infinity. If he looked directly upwards he could no longer see the green flickering, only the dark chasm of sky and the pulses of stars and the steady glow of planets. O God, if you are, he begged silently, care for us, be great enough to comprehend the small, do not forget thy sparrows.

★

Then there was the journey, cramped in the small dark cabins of the ship, and at least Raleigh's sailors had had the open deck to walk upon, the sight of ocean stretching out to the horizon on all sides, the stars at night. Was it more fearful to be allowed to see infinity than to have it shut out by cabin walls? Two of the men on the crew panicked to such an extent that they had to be heavily sedated by the ship's doctor. This was a dark-skinned man, Bill Hayes, who became Rob's only close friend on the voyage out. He and Rob played chess, read, talked, helped separate two young lieutenants who got into a fistfight and had a hard time with the artificial gravity. One struck his head against the ceiling and got a mild concussion and had to be put to bed in the tiny sick bay. Bill in a way reminded Rob of Matt, in spite of the fact that physically and intellectually they seemed to be diametrically opposite. It was Bill's quiet way with the men when they were in trouble, the unassuming strength and compassion, Rob finally decided, that made him feel a similarity. Bill had no illusion about the reasons for the voyage. "Of course we're looking for a place where we can expand and settle, and we want to do it before anyone else does. You Godders are always so hopeful that people are doing things for the right reasons. If you'd only accept the fact that people *always* do things for the wrong reasons, everything'd be much simpler for you."

"We don't need to colonize yet," Rob argued. "With only one woman in ten able to conceive, with two-fifths of the babies having to be put in state nurseries for their few sad little years, the population isn't growing rapidly enough to make us feel any desperate need for expansion."

"But it will," Bill said. They had switched from chess to cribbage and he put his cards down. At the other end of the mess table a poker game was in progress. "The eastern nations who've always spawned more rapidly than we have are already beginning to feel the pinch. That's why we've got to get in first, before anybody else does. Maybe we know enough to share. They don't."

"And suppose the patterns do mean something? Suppose there's a race more cultured and advanced than our own who have no idea of being exploited and colonized?"

"That's a risk we have to take, isn't it?"

"I suppose so."

"And tell me honestly, Rob, have you found any meaning to the patterns? Has anybody?"

"Not that I know of."

"And in spite of popular superstition," Bill continued, "official opinion is that it's a meaningless accident, isn't it?"

"I guess." Rob picked up the peg board and studied it as though there he might find the answers.

"So why the hell do you think we're sitting in this—this artificial womb, waiting to be spawned on an unknown planet? Expansion and colonization. And why not? What's so wrong with it? Why shouldn't we get there first? What's so selfish about it? After this, the possibilities are unlimited. If we make it, of course."

The captain, who had seemed to be immersed in poker, raised his head. "We'll make it."

"Captain," another officer asked, "aren't we running behind according to calculations?"

The captain nodded imperturbably. "Right. So did Columbus, I believe. The ocean was larger than he'd anticipated, and he didn't get to where he expected, but as far as history's concerned, where he did get to was much more important." There was a twinkle in his eye. "So let's just take the historical point of view, men."

"My wife prefers her history in the form of fiction," one of the men said.

But the captain turned back to the cards. "My deal, I believe."

When the ship was three weeks overdue, the men began to get restless. They had seen all the movies twice, they were bored with poker, with sleeping, with playing tricks with the artificial gravity. Although at this stage of the journey, moving through the dark wastes of space, they were using practically no fuel, the captain eyed the fuel gauges speculatively. All through the small, pressurized cabins of the great ship there were murmurs. Bill Hayes tried to get a laugh by calling the captain "Chris." The laugh was feeble, but the name stuck.

"Sir. Captain Columbus, sir."

"Yes. What is it?"

"I have a petition, sir, signed by all the men of the crew, sir. We want to turn back."

"We don't have enough fuel to get back," the captain said. "Bear with me, men. To turn back means death to us all. Our only hope is to push on."

Irrationally, the men still wanted to turn back. If they were to die, they wanted to die heading towards home instead of the unknown. Bill spent a great deal of time with the crew, giving a kind word and a joke wherever possible, medication when necessary. One morning he arrived in the crew's quarters to find a table made into a crude altar and one of the men stretched out on it. The knife had already cut into his skin when Bill, suddenly and for the first time on the voyage losing his temper, punched his way through the men and knocked down the sailor who was acting as priest. Then he overturned the table and turned, white with rage, to face the men.

The sailor who was acting as priest said, "Don't be so angry, Doc. You know how the men are. Just a little ceremony to propitiate the gods; the man was perfectly willing to be offered up as a sacrifice."

Bill still shook with anger as he took the man to sick bay to dress his wound, and met Rob waiting for him.

"You goddamn Godders," he said. "What kind of a God is this of yours?"

"My God?" Rob asked. "Ever hear of Moses, Bill?"

"Yeah."

"Remember the golden lamb? This isn't my God or anybody's God. It's an idol."

"So? What's the difference?"

There was no assurance or calmness in Rob as he looked at Bill, his usually rather florid face still mottled with rage.

"Okay, tell me," he demanded, not wanting to know, wanting only in his fury to hurt Rob. And all Rob could do was to try not to let his own confusions show as he spoke fumblingly, trying to think what Matt might have said.

"Idolatry is turning away from God, turning inwards instead of outwards. Most people say that we Godders have no faith because we don't try to make God understandable, but we have to make the biggest leap of faith of all."

"Can't be a very satisfactory sort of god, can it?" came a voice from behind him, and he turned to see the captain.

"Oh. Good morning, sir."

"At this point I'm inclined to sympathize with the men and their sacrificial offering. How can this incomprehensible God of yours give you any comfort?"

"My friend Matt believes that there are signs along the way."

"We could do with a sign right now," the captain said bitterly. "Frankly, boys, if I believed in God I'd be saying my prayers."

"Well, sir," Rob said, "Bill and his idol-smashing reminded me of Moses and the golden lamb, and after Moses had demolished the lamb and been furious at his men, he asked God for a sign."

"So did God give him one?"

"Well, Moses was on a journey, remember, just about as impossible as ours, and he said to God, 'Show me now thy way, that I may know thee, that I may find grace in thy sight...For wherein shall it be known here that I and thy people have found grace in thy sight? Is it not in that thou goest with us?'"

The captain smiled. "So what did God say?"

"God said, 'My presence shall go with thee, and I will give thee rest.' But Moses, like most of us, wasn't satisfied. He said, 'I beseech thee, show me thy glory!' And God said, 'I will make all my goodness pass before thee, and I will proclaim the name of the Lord before thee...But thou canst not see my face: for no man shall see me, and live.'" Rob looked at the captain apologetically. "My wife thought idols would be easier, too, but if I have to make my faith comprehensible I'd rather go along with the state and worship science."

"Want to make a bet, Rob?" Bill asked suddenly.

"What?"

"When we reach our promised land, if we find that the patterns have after all been sent, if there is a rational race there, I'll bet that you'll give up your God. Let's put it this way: If there is a God he'll send you—or us—a sign. No sign, and you give him up."

"Okay," said Rob rather grimly. "At this point I'm willing to bet on that."

"Let me know who wins," the captain said. "By the way, I want to see all the officers in the mess in ten minutes. We're going to have a full-size mutiny on our hands if we don't do something, and do it quickly."

The men had just gathered around the mess table when there was a shout from the crew member at the instrument board. "Captain Columbus, there's a blip! There's a blip!"

With a sudden loss of discipline by mutual consent, everyone crowded to the door of the instrument room. The captain pushed his way in, looked at the screen, and turned triumphantly to the men. "Every man to his post. We are nearing our destination."

Now at last through the screen there was more than darkness and distant stars. The planet approached rapidly, became the size of Earth's moon. It became the size of the sun. Now the murmuring and games of poker and petitions stopped. There was silence throughout the ship. The planet grew. It was suddenly enormous, hurling itself at them. They felt the tremendous impact of atmosphere and deceleration. They were there. They had not fallen over the edge.

It was dawn and they had landed on a desert not unlike the one from which they had taken off, though the instruments showed them that the temperature was some fifty degrees lower. And here there was no green glow on the horizon, visible even in the daytime as a faint miasma. The atmosphere here was thin and the visibility tremendous. Taking turns at the screen, they felt as though they had all been given new spectacles which enabled them to see better than they had ever seen in their lives, as though a long-term myopia had been suddenly and dramatically corrected. The captain, out for a brief reconnoiter, reported that the atmosphere was just over the border of being too light, but was otherwise pure. They would need helmets, but could probably breathe for a brief period without them in an emergency. He had seen no sign of life, but they would send out their signals at once. Rob, in charge of this, went to his board and pressed the buttons and pulled the switches that would send out signals both visual and audible, signals that could be caught by ear, eye, instrument, or nervous system attuned to any kind of vibration. He felt unaccountably nervous, like an actor making his first appearance and afraid that his audience may not hear or understand him, or that he might get the words wrong. And any misunderstanding at this point could have far more drastic potentialities than any of them could understand.

They all sat watching the instrument board for a while, but when there was no response of any kind, the captain chose a small party to go back out with him. Rob looked after them longingly. His job was by the message center but his every instinct was to don a space suit and follow the others out, the first men ever to step on an alien planet. He sat in the instrument chamber restlessly, moving from the complicated wall of the message center to the viewer and back. The men in their cumbersome space suits seemed to move easily in the thin clear air, and he looked at them eagerly. From the viewer he could see great stretches of sand, and in the distance trees of an extraordinarily clear and shimmering green, some of which had rosy blossoms. There was nothing tropical about their look, however; the green was the pale green, touched with yellow, of early spring, and the flowers, in spite of their hue, had nothing lush about them. They were exquisite, but cool.

Rob finally in lonely desperation sent a message to Bill Hayes: "If you see anything unusual, for heaven's sake tell me. I'm going bats here all alone. Please tune in to me."

There was a click from Bill's set, and he relayed back, "Okay," and after that, from time to time he made comments in his laconic manner: "Insect life; a rather large grasshopperlike thing, but all pale yellow. Beautiful. Wonder if it's destructive. Ah. Have him in my jar for Benson. Hey, a kind of praying mantis bug. Wonder who he's praying to on *this* planet. Maybe he's just thumbing his nose at us. Don't forget your bet, old boy. Small yellow flowers. Sticky. Yellow seems to be the predominant color here. Wonder if it always is or if this is spring. Everything seems tender and young. Tracks. Small rodent-like animal, I'd guess. Ah. Nest. Could be bird, could be rodent. Definitely animal life as well as plant. Good Lord, bird tracks, enormous. My God, Rob, those birds must be man-size. Hope they aren't predatory. Could easily swoop up a man, even in a heavy space suit, in those claws. Better let the captain in on this. Signing off for now."

Rob waited impatiently at the silence. Then a message, urgent: OPEN THE HATCHES! QUICK! A garble of too many voices coming to him at once, Bill's loud and angry: "Don't shout, you fool!"

The sound of machinery groaning as the doors to the outer chamber opened, shut, then the doors to the inner chamber. A scramble of men into the ship. The call for a general meeting in the mess, men and crew.

And suddenly Rob's instrument board was alive, lights flashing on and off, dit–dits sounding. Two minutes of it. Then complete silence.

"You're excused from the meeting," the captain told Rob. "Stay and work on your decoding. And quick."

"What's up, Captain?"

"The last we saw of Bill Hayes he was being flown off in the claws of an enormous bird," the captain said grimly. "One of the men lost his head and fired after them. The idiot. Fortunately he missed his mark. A fine way to start a friendly relationship all round. Get at your decoding, man. It may mean Bill's life."

In fifteen minutes the captain was back. "What do you make of it?"

Rob shook his head. "Nothing. Not as far as understanding what it means. I do think, though, it seems to bear some kind of relationship to the patterns in the cosmic rays. There's a pattern, all right, but I can't make head or tail of it."

"Send return messages in every medium at your disposal, explaining that we have received their messages but we cannot decode them."

"Right, sir."

The captain stood by him, waiting. When Rob had finished, he said, "Okay. We'll wait half an hour for a return of some kind of response. If we receive none I'm going out again with two volunteers."

"Count me in, sir," Rob said quickly.

The captain shook his head. "No, Rob. If we establish any kind of communication it has to be through you. We can't risk your going."

"But why not, sir? If one of the same birds comes after me that flew off with Bill maybe I can manage to figure out a way we can talk. They may not be unfriendly, sir."

"Hold it," the captain said, and looked at the board.

A message began to sound out, very slowly, in a code so old Rob didn't recognize it at first. Then he realized that it was Morse.

"Can you understand me? Can you understand me?"

"Fire ahead," Rob tapped back.

"Learned this as a gag when I was a kid. Never realized it would come in so handy."

"Who are you?" Rob tapped, puzzled.

"Bill, you idiot."

Suddenly the code began to come quickly, professionally. "We have mastered your code," it said rapidly. "Welcome to our planet. Your representative has given us a brief picture of your culture and assures us that you are not unfriendly. We will be glad to entertain you and show you anything that you wish to see. Your representative mentioned your need for expansion. You would find our planet completely unsuited to your purposes. However, we may be able to help you in finding other areas for colonization provided we have some assurance that you will not misuse them. You will be called upon in two hours by three of our representatives, who will escort you to our president's house, where you will be quartered—housed, that is, of course, not drawn and quartered—and where we will try to answer your questions. We are in the meanwhile returning your representative."

"Can you decode this one?" the captain asked Rob.

"Yes, sir. It's an old code and an easy one. Bill evidently learned it as a scout or something and those birds—those birds is right— picked it up from him in no time flat, including our language, even to being able to pun in it. This is no backwards civilization, Captain!" He handed the captain the decoded message.

"Six of us will go," the captain said. "And six stay with the ship." He smiled at Rob. "Count yourself in."

The ingress bell rang and the captain bent quickly to the screen. "It's Bill," he said. He and Rob ran quickly to the inner hatch and were standing there when Bill emerged, red in the face and rather ruffled. He grinned at them and tried to look nonchalant.

"I think you've lost your bet," he said to Rob. "Captain Chris, sir, they picked my mind. They communicate by a kind of telepathy that's in shorthand. What takes us half an hour to think takes them half a minute. I'll bet you the reason we couldn't decode any of their messages is that their shorthand's too damned short for us." He spoke breathlessly, as though he had been running. "They made me think faster than I've ever thought in my life," he explained. "My mind is reeling. I suspect I might catch on to it eventually, not thinking as fast as they do, but thinking a lot faster than I'm used to. You know how fast you can run if something's after you and your life depends on your speed? Much faster than you can under any normal circumstances. That's what my mind was doing. May I have some water, sir? There is water on the planet and it's pure, or at any rate they said they could purify it for us so we could replenish our tanks, so if it's all right, sir, I'd like a pitcher."

"Calm down, Bill. Come along, let's sit down. I'll order the water."

"Sir, I don't mean to be difficult, but could it be just with you and young Rob here for a few minutes? I seem to be rather exhausted."

"Would you like to rest?"

"No, sir, I'd like to talk. But at this point I don't know what's going to spill out or how, and until I get my mind organized again, I'd rather keep it semi-private at any rate."

They went to the tiny hole that was the captain's cabin. Bill thirstily drank glass after glass of water, offering it to the captain and Rob, then drinking it himself. "They're about two billion years beyond us," he said. "They've evolved in the form of birds, rather like enormous sparrows, but they have highly developed hands as well as wings. No houses. Just strange, indescribable things, very beautiful, with sort of perches. Of course birds, even civilized ones, wouldn't be comfortable in chairs or beds, would they? A great interest in the mind. My God, with minds like that I should think they would, but they explained that their minds evolving to such a point has only been in the last million years. Wonderful schools they have, and libraries, and theatres and concert halls. Their libraries seem to be the things they're proudest of, though. A complete recording of everything that's been written for the past two billion years. Two billion, sir. The library I saw was tremendous, and yet almost everything is in this terrific shorthand. Some of the earlier books aren't. Their earliest books, they said, are in a language that moved at about the speed of ours. No churches, Rob. I asked them. They didn't seem to understand what a church was."

There was a knock and a young lieutenant said, "There's a message coming in at the communications center, sir."

"Go get it, Rob," the captain ordered.

The message was again in Morse code. "Perhaps it would be of interest to you to see if you can decode some of our earlier languages which are more in tempo with yours. We still have one book in current use today—it is, in fact, our most used book—which dates back to the older languages and which, therefore, you may be able to decode. If you will have your representative wait outside your ship, we will send a messenger with a copy. In this book are many of the precepts by which we live and it may aid you in an understanding of our culture. It is very tiring to us to go back to archaic forms of communication, so a small amount of pre-knowledge on your part may prove helpful to us all."

It was a large book that Bill brought him, carrying it gingerly, and in a kind of hieroglyphic-like bird trackings that at first made absolutely no sense to him. Finally he began to find a pattern in the strange markings, and with a sense of excitement realized that it was written in a language that, while it was completely unknown, was no more alien to his own than Chinese or Russian.

Bill came in and leaned over his shoulder.

"Go away," Rob muttered. "I'm getting it."

"You're sweating," Bill said. "Take a five-minute breather. That's doctor's orders."

Rob raised his head and realized that he was indeed sweating and that his hands were shaking. "Something about this language," he said. "It seems to make my mind work faster. Or maybe that's just because you put it into my head that I'm getting it, Bill. I'm getting letters and words."

"What's it mean?"

"Give me time, man! Give me time!"

Bill looked at the strange markings. "A book they've been using for billions of years. Quite a thing. By the way, Rob, sorry about your bet."

"I haven't lost it yet," Rob said stubbornly.

"No? A race as highly developed as theirs and no churches and you're still a Godder. Where's your sign, Rob? You were supposed to receive a sign."

"Five minutes is up," Rob said. "Let me get back to work."

"Five minutes is not up. But go ahead. Like a cup of tea?"

"Yes, I would. Good and strong. I work better on tea than coffee." He bent over the pages again. He was chewing his pencil, making occasional excited markings, when Bill himself came in with the cup of tea. Not even saying thank you, Rob drank half of it, then began to write rapidly. Suddenly he let out a shout.

"Got it?" Bill asked eagerly.

And Rob read, "'In the beginning was the Word, and the Word was with God, and the Word was God. The same was in the beginning with God. All things were made by him; and without him was not anything made that was made. In him was life; and the life was the light of men. And the light shineth in darkness; and the darkness comprehended it not.'"

About the Author

MADELEINE L'ENGLE wrote more than sixty books, including the classic *A Wrinkle in Time*. Born in New York City in 1918, L'Engle was educated in Switzerland, South Carolina, and Massachusetts. She moved back to New York City hoping to become a playwright, but her career as a bestselling novelist took off after an editor read a short story of hers—"Summer Camp"—in a magazine and asked if she was working on a novel. L'Engle wrote fiction and nonfiction for adults, as well as poetry. She died in 2007.